Think You Know Me

Think You Know Me

Book three of the Being Me series

by Tricia Copeland

True Bird Publishing LLC

Think You Know Me?

Book three of the *Being Me* series
by Tricia Copeland

Copyright © 2016 True Bird Publishing LLC
All rights reserved

ISBN-13: 978-0692670101
ISBN-10: 0692670106

Edited by Tia Silverthorne Bach
Interior Formatting by Jo Michaels
all of Indie Books Gone Wild

Cover by Daryl A. McCool of d.a.m. Cool Graphics
Published by True Bird Publishing LLC, Superior, CO

acknowledgements

To Tia who cheered me on from the beginning and helped me see this project through. Thank you for the awesome editing and feedback!

To Sara who continues to be one of my biggest fans. Thank you for being there!

To Jo who is always on the other end of my email, text, or phone call. Thank you for the amazing formatting!

To Daryl, for my perfect cover and wonderful graphics!

To my beta readers Jaci and Danielle, thank you!

To my proofreader Cheryl, much appreciation!

To Jaci, thank you for all your great docs, promos, graphics!

To my readers, friends, family, husband Jim, and my kids! Thank you for all the support!

Chapter 1

March 20

The familiar nightmare woke me, and I sat straight up, sucking in a breath. I reached for my phone and swiped my finger along the screen. The display read 5:50 a.m. Finding my journal under the covers, I opened it to the first blank page. Northie lifted his head and yawned. I stroked his fur, staring at the page.

Holding a pen above the paper, I wavered. *I miss Doug.* "I'm not writing this again." I flung the pen on the table and shut the book. "Let's go." I patted the bed beside the puppy. He sat up and jumped off the bed. Already in leggings, I opened my door and crossed the living room to open the blinds. Northie trotted behind, sprawling on the floor to expose his belly when I stopped.

❯ I ❮

"I know, boy. It's raining again." I pulled on my rain boots, slid into a jacket, and grabbed his leash. "You ready?"

He sat in front of me, nose in the air, and I snapped the leash on his collar. As I opened the door, a gust spattered raindrops against my face, and I tugged my hood down almost to my eyes. "Only a short walk today, Northie."

We walked along the sidewalk to the grassy area. I waited while he did his doggie business and then scooped it up with a bag and tossed it in the trash. "Come on." He followed me towards the trail. It was a short loop, but it would have to do. The cold had already penetrated through my layers, and I shivered in the wind. I took him around the perimeter of the grounds and back to my apartment.

Inside, I shed my boots and jacket and toweled him off. I blew warm air into my balled fists. "Gloves, Northie. I need gloves next time." *I'm talking to a dog.*

I shook off the thought and looked at my watch. It was about ten in the evening Tokyo time, so I dialed Doug's number. Tucking Northie under my arm, I plopped down on the couch.

Doug answered immediately. "Twelve days."

I smiled. "Twelve days."

"Why aren't we videoconferencing?"

"I just got up and went for a walk in the rain. I have a cold and look miserable."

"I doubt you look that bad, and I wouldn't care anyway."

"Let's just talk," I told him, not wanting to repeat our same fight.

"Okay, well it's cold here too."

He told me about the market outlook, and I reiterated my disdain for my classes. "Only one more quarter of chemistry left, right?"

"I guess." It seemed like we had the same conversation every day. I had to get out of my rut, or he was going to tire of me for sure. Spring break would change everything though. We would be together for seven days. I planned to pick a school and then move in the summer. I'd definitely have the money by August.

A knock caught my attention. Northie ran to it, and I followed, scooping him up and opening the door. My forever perky friend Kate smiled and waved as I let her in. "Good morning." She edged into the room shedding her shoes and pack.

"Hi." I shook the phone in the air.

"That Doug?"

I nodded, and she leaned towards my phone. "Hi, Doug."

I held a finger to my lips and pointed towards Lila's room. "She's still sleeping."

"Sorry," Kate whispered.

I put the phone back to my ear. "Looks like that's it for us."

"I'll talk to you in the morning. Sleep well. I love you."

I ended the call, and Kate plopped down on the bar stool. "What's the countdown?"

"Twelve days."

"You're so lucky."

I retrieved a blender from the cabinet. "I can't wait to be done with this quarter and have a whole week there."

"It's not going to be warm."

I opened the fridge to get yogurt and fruit. "I know, but I don't care." I turned back to her. "Hey, it's test day, you want avocados?"

"Definitely."

I set the items on the counter and grabbed a knife.

Kate rested her elbows on the bar. "Hey, are you feeling okay?"

"Sure, why?"

"You look tired and pale."

"What, paler than normal?" I laughed and shrugged, adding the ingredients to the blender. "I had a cold last weekend, and I just got back in from walking Northie."

I lied to her as I had to Doug. I'd been feeling low on energy for a month, but it would all be worth it when I saw Doug. Starting the blender, I retrieved two glasses from the cabinet. Pouring our smoothies, I passed one to Kate. She was the only friend to embrace my smoothie addiction, and it had become our morning ritual.

Taking a seat beside her, I held up my glass. "To the last week of classes?"

"I'll drink to that." She lifted her glass and took a sip. "I'm worried about you. Seems like you got sick a lot this winter."

"I know. I think running outdoors is hard on me. I should probably add kale to this thing." I took a sip of the smoothie.

"That's going too far."

"I can't stomach it either." My alarm beeped on my phone, and I picked it up. "Are you ready for this test?"

"Yep. I'll be happy to be done with physics labs."

We finished our drinks, grabbed our bags and coats, and headed out to my car.

"Thanks for driving," Kate said as we got in.

"You don't have to thank me every time. We're going the same way."

"I know, but taking the bus isn't fun, so I appreciate it."

"You know you can get a ride whenever."

"I at least owe you for the smoothies."

It was a five-minute drive to campus, and we found a parking spot easily. Last year I'd done everything I could to avoid being up by eight, much less sitting in class by then. Wanting to be up to talk to Doug, and the desire to find a good parking spot, led me to adopt an early morning schedule.

We sat through the physics lecture and then walked to the lab building. The test seemed easy, and Kate and I finished about the same time.

"What did you think?" Kate asked as we took the stairs to the bottom floor.

"Easy peasy." I held my hand in the air, and she pressed hers to mine.

"What are you doing now?"

Outside, I looked around. It was still cold and gray. "Going to the library."

"Okay, I'll hang with you. I need to study too."

We walked to the second floor and found a table, studying in silence. We both got up to stretch a couple of times, but otherwise we were in our own worlds for the better part of two hours.

Her phone dinged, and Kate set down her book to look at her screen. "Hey, I'm going to get lunch. Want to come?"

"No, I'm meeting Lila." I stood and slung my pack onto one shoulder. "Do you want a ride home this afternoon? You could meet me at my car after four."

"Sure, that's great. Thanks." She waved as we exited the building.

I sent Lila a text letting her know I was getting lunch at the coffee cart.

She messaged back right away. AT THE FRAT HOUSE. TOO DREARY TO GO OUT. YAY YOU FOR BRAVING THE COFFEE CART.

I hated the food truck. Only the smokers went there in the winter. Cigarette smoke, or really any smoke, still bothered me.

I messaged her from the line. ONLY TWELVE DAYS TILL SPRING BREAK.

I KNOW. I AM SO EXCITED ABOUT MEXICO. AND YOU GET TO GO SEE DOUG.

Smoke from the guy in front of me wafted back, and I tugged my sleeve over my hand and covered my nose.

YOU'LL BE OKAY, she texted me.

HOW DID YOU KNOW?

HAD A FEELING.

The guy in front of me continued puffing away. I tried to focus on Lila and her conversation, but the odor distracted me. I pressed my thumb into my sternum, trying to slow my breathing and stop the arrhythmia.

"Yes," the worker behind the counter called out.

I looked up at the aproned girl who stood hand to hip and stepped up to the cart. "I'll have a coffee, one cream." I passed my credit card to her. I told myself that I needed a good lunch to fuel up for a long run later, but after standing behind smoker guy for five minutes, my stomach was doing cartwheels.

I walked along the sidewalk, trying to escape the smell of cigarettes.

My phone dinged, signaling the receipt of another message. YOU GET LUNCH? Lila asked.

YES, I lied.

MY MOM IS FLIPPING OUT ABOUT ME GOING TO MEXICO.

PEOPLE GET ABDUCTED THERE ALL THE TIME.

PEOPLE GET ABDUCTED HERE. WHATEVER! DID YOU TELL YOUR PARENTS ABOUT VISITING THE COLLEGES IN JAPAN?

I downed a big gulp of my coffee. It was so cold I couldn't stop shivering, but I needed a break from the library. NO, ARE YOU CRAZY? ON TOP OF ME VISITING DOUG FOR A WEEK, THEY WOULD FREAK.

WE'RE PRETTY MUCH BOTH ON THE OUTS WITH PARENTS.

BE CAREFUL. I CAN'T LOSE MY BEST FRIEND AND ROOMMATE.

MORBID. HEY, WHAT'S YOUR SCHEDULE LIKE THE REST OF THE DAY?

CLASSES, STUDYING, MAY TRY TO EXERCISE.

YOU SHOULD TAKE IT EASY. GIVE YOUR BODY ANOTHER DAY AFTER THE COLD.

PROBABLY. I'LL SEE YOU BACK AT THE APARTMENT TONIGHT.

YEP, LOVE YOU!

Love you too!

Walking towards class, I wrapped one hand around my cup to warm it and checked my messages with the other.

Mom's read: Good morning. Hope you are well. Are you coming home for Easter? Would like the whole family to be together.

Dad's read: Last week of classes, Study hard. FBI, CIA, Navy, here you come. Ooh-rah!

Marissa's read: Are you coming home over spring break? Let me know if you can make it one day. Mom is going nuts about u not coming on vacation with us.

If responding honestly, I would type back: I wish I didn't have to go home, no to the FBI, CIA, and Navy. Then, I'd send an apology to my baby sister for leaving her with Mom and Tia all week. Our older sister could be such a pain.

Instead I typed to Marissa: I have one night home before I fly to Tokyo and one night when I come back. Dad got me a deal on my airline flight from Champaign. Then I responded with a simple thank you to Dad, and let Mom know I was waiting to find out Doug's plans for Easter.

Finding my seat in the lecture hall, I thought about how packed my next few weeks were going to be. I hoped Mom and Dad wouldn't feel the need for a lecture on my relationship when I got home. A break from school and over-zealous parenting was much needed.

After the two afternoon classes, I found Kate waiting at the car.

"Hey, yo," she called.

"Hi." I smiled at her and unlocked the car.

We climbed in, and I started the car and turned on the heat.

She rubbed her hands together in front of the vent. "Isn't it supposed to be getting warmer? Hey, you're shivering, how far did you walk?"

"My legs were stiff from sitting, so I went around the long way." I fastened my seat belt and looked behind me, backing out into the aisle.

"Hey, do you want to hang at my apartment to study organic chemistry? We could get take out and have a study session."

"Maybe later, I have my call with Doug in a few minutes, and then I want to exercise."

"Seriously? Didn't you say you were recovering from a cold?"

"Yeah, but you know, it helps clear my head." We rode the rest of the trip in silence.

At the apartment complex, she split off towards her unit, and I took the few steps and walk to mine. Inside, I entered my bedroom and found Northie wagging his tail and stretching in his crate.

"Hi there. Miss me?" I unlatched the door. He bounded out, and I squatted to pet him. I grabbed his leash and snapped it to his collar. Finding gloves and a hat, I walked him out to the grassy area behind our building. My phone rang and I answered it.

"Hi there." Doug's voice came through the speaker.

"Hi. I'm walking Northie. Can we just talk?"

"Sure."

We chatted while I walked Northie around the complex. The sun was low, and it was already getting dark. The temperature seemed to drop as we walked, and I jogged to keep warm. Back in the apartment, I dried Northie's paws and shed my outer layers. He followed me to the pantry, where I filled his food bowl and then refreshed his water.

I loved this hour of my day, when Doug and I talked. Sitting crossed legged on the floor, I played tug with Northie.

"Hey, are you back in your apartment? If so, we should video chat," Doug said.

"My battery is dead from a day on campus."

"I want to see you."

"I'll try to have it charged for next time." We talked about his work, my classes, finals, and our upcoming visit.

"What are you up to the rest of the day?" he asked as we were wrapping up our call.

"Lila said she would be back around dinner time. Kate mentioned an organic chemistry study session."

"Okay, good. Please take it easy and rest up. You sound tired. Zack said you looked thin last time he saw you. I worry about you."

Ugh! We were back to the same thing. I was sick of being worried about. Couldn't everyone leave me alone? "I've been really focusing on my courses. Tests are next week. I should probably get to my studies. I love you. Have a good day."

"Okay, have a good night."

There was no I love you? Three months was too long to be apart. We wouldn't make that mistake again.

I ended the call and stroked Northie's head as he snuggled in beside my leg. Standing, I leaned down and extended my fingers to the floor, stretching out my back and legs. A long run would do me good. Thinking I needed a little fuel and hydration, I went to the fridge. Surveying my choices, my hand wavered between the regular and zero calorie drinks. Frustrated, I snatched the zero calorie one from the shelf. Crossing through the apartment to my room, I found my warmest running gear and stretched out, sipping the drink as I went. Finishing the contents of the bottle, I went to the pantry to toss it in the recycling bin. It landed on a newspaper, and the image on the page caught my eye.

A picture of Peter's face spanned half the folded sheet. His thin lips almost formed a straight line but tilted up on one side. Snatching the pages from the basket, I leaned against the wall and slid down to the floor. Clutching my chest with my free hand, I tried to focus on the words. PETER SCALINI, THE EIGHTEEN-YEAR-OLD FOUND GUILTY OF, the story started. How was it possible? Tears streamed down my face. It wasn't fair.

Northie sniffed at the paper, trying to squeeze between my legs. I stood. What was I supposed to do with the information, my swirling thoughts, and the rage and guilt that ate at me from the inside? I stuffed the pages back in the bin, wondering if Lila had stashed it there on purpose. I crossed to my room and found my journal. Dr. Milner said it was good to write. I snatched the book from the table and plopped down on my futon.

This isn't fair! I close my eyes and see his face. His mother's words echo in my dreams. Now he is plastered on the front page? How do I

move past the rage and guilt when he won't go away? I need him gone.
He doesn't get to win like this. I won't let him.

I abandoned the page and stood. Northie padded behind as I
found my shoes, hat, and gloves. "Sorry, boy, you can't come this
time." I led him to his crate and zipped my keys and mace into
my jacket pocket. Outside, I wound through the middle of the
complex in the opposite direction from Kate's apartment. Crossing to the back of the grounds and exiting at the far entrance, I
prayed Zack hadn't planned a run that afternoon.

I knew the route to Peter's apartment, exactly two point one
miles from mine. I hadn't been near there in six months. In the
beginning, I would forget and turn up the street, only to realize
where I was headed and turn around. Then I'd formed habits of
finding businesses in other parts of the city. I wasn't completely
sure why I needed to see his building, but my anger needed an
outlet. I needed closure.

I started with a careful slow jog, but as soon as I was on the
main road, my anger kicked in. Anger? I asked myself. Or something else? Grief? Rage? I wanted him gone. I patted my pocket
with the mace and pocket knife that hung from my keychain.

It'd gotten dark, and the air felt like icicles piercing my lungs.
The orange of the streetlights reflected off the wet sidewalks
and streets. Sets of headlights roared by one after the other.
The repetition of my feet hitting the concrete did nothing to
calm me.

It was a straight shot to his apartment, and before long I
found myself directly in front of the building. I was not a victim anymore. He didn't get to win. I looked up at the numbers
on the door and then turned back the way I came. Did I even

remember getting there? I walked back to the sidewalk trying to control my breathing. And then it happened, my heart skipped. I put my fist to my sternum and counted: one, two, three, and four. This wasn't like the other arrhythmias. I felt another beat and waited again. One, two, three, and another beat. It was slow, too slow. Sugar, calories, caffeine, something—my mind reeled. Still gripping my chest, I scanned the area.

I spotted a coffee place across the street and waited for the walk signal. Then my heart rate sped, racing too fast. Once on the other side, I entered the shop and went to the counter.

"Regular mocha," I said to the clerk.

"Whip cream?" she asked, holding a cup in one hand, a marker in the other.

I nodded and pulled my credit card from my pocket and handed it to her. Waiting at the end of the bar, I felt queasy and light-headed and sat at a table a few feet away.

"Are you okay?" I looked up to see an aproned guy holding a paper cup. "Is this yours?"

"Regular mocha?"

He held the cup out towards me. "This is you then."

"Thanks." I took the cup.

I wrapped both hands around the cylinder, realizing they were shaking. As I sipped the coffee, the liquid warmed me, but my body still shivered. I put my fingers on my wrist and felt for my heartbeat. Better, it was better. I sat breathing in the warm air and tried to relax.

I finished the drink and scanned the café, trying to remember where I was and why I was there. I sensed someone beside me and jumped, nearly falling out of my seat.

"Miss." It was the guy who'd handed me my drink. "I need to ask you to leave."

How long had I been there? I realized I was rocking. "What?" I looked around. All eyes were fixed on me.

He took a step back and jutted his hands out towards me. "I need you to leave."

"Why?" I lifted my hands and realized one held my mace and the other my pocket knife.

He took another step back. "The police are on their way."

"What?"

A girl behind him, the one who'd taken my drink order, held up her phone. "You're scaring everyone. You can't talk about killing people like that."

I focused on her. "He's dead."

She rolled her eyes. "That's what you said, and we all heard it." Her eyes cut around the room.

The only two other people in the café stood near the opposite wall, their eyes as big as saucers. Did they really think I was a threat? I wasn't sure I had the energy to walk to the other side of the room.

Flashing lights outside caught my attention, and I slid my mace and keychain into my pockets and zipped them closed. Turning, I picked up my cup from the table.

"I'm sorry." I meant to walk towards the door, but my feet were lead bricks. I looked down at them and the arrhythmia returned. Reaching out to the table to balance myself, I sat down in the chair. My lungs ached as I tried to draw in slow breaths. My hands shook as I placed them in front of my face. What had I done?

I heard the bell of the door and footsteps. A shadow appeared on the table. "Miss, do you have any weapons?" I put the mace and my keychain on the table, and he picked them up. "Phone? Credit cards?" Taking my phone, credit card, and driver's license from my other pocket, I slid them towards him. He scooped those up and stepped back. "You'll need to come with us." He motioned towards the door.

I used every bit of energy to push myself to a standing position. He and a second officer formed a chain to the door, and I inched past him. The second one walked in front of me, exiting the coffee shop and holding the door open for me. I followed him to their car. He opened the back door, and I slid onto the vinyl seat.

The interior was dark and vast and smelled of sweat and cleaner. I tugged my sleeves over my hands and cupped one on my nose. At least the car was running and the heat was on. Huddling near the door, I tried to even out my breathing. *Think, Amanda.*

One officer stood outside my window while the other stayed inside speaking with people in the coffee shop. Older than the one beside the car, the man inside wore a short graying beard. He wrote on a small notebook as the employees and customers talked to him, pointing at me and towards Peter's apartment. My torso involuntarily started to rock back and forth. Peter was dead. What had I done?

After a few minutes the officer inside closed his notebook and placed it in his pocket. He said something into his Walkie Talkie, and the officer outside my window confirmed with a simple "all clear" into his. He tipped his hat and walked towards me. The two officers spoke for a moment and then got in the car. The younger one sat in front of me, typing on a laptop. After a minute he turned the screen to the older gentleman who turned to look at me.

"I am Officer Drumheller. This is Officer Cialini." He held up my driver's license. "You are Amanda Avery?"

"Yes."

"Are you under the influence of drugs or alcohol? Have you taken any illegal substances within the past twenty-four hours?"

I doubted the shot of vodka I'd had last night to help me sleep was still in my system. "No, sir."

He shook his head and looked at Officer Cialini.

"Do you know why we're here?"

"They said I talked about killing someone."

"Can you tell us that person's name?"

"I don't know."

He looked at the younger officer who started typing on the keyboard again and then turned to me. "And you killed him?"

Tears pooled in my eyes. "He's dead. It's my fault."

Officer Cialini spun the laptop towards the older gentleman. He looked at the screen and then at me. His face still displayed no emotion, no trace of judgment.

Officer Drumheller craned his neck around to face me again. "We're taking you into the station."

I opened my mouth, but no words came out. He turned back, and after checking for cars, pulled into traffic. At least they didn't have the sirens going. I couldn't be in that much trouble if the sirens weren't blaring, right? I rested my head back on the seat. How had I gotten there? What had I done?

It wasn't a long drive to the municipal complex. Orange street-lights illuminated the building, and we circled around to the back. They pulled into a garage lit by the same orange lights. I hated those lights. Parking beside an ambulance, Officer Cialini got out and opened the door for me. I stepped out and waited for him to direct me. We had to pass behind the ambulance, and I looked the other way, scared of what I might see inside the open doors. He led me through double doors into a hallway.

The flood of bright blue fluorescent lights left me temporarily blinded. The younger officer motioned for me to sit on a bench and stood beside me. Officer Drumheller walked to the counter and set all my belongings there. He spoke to the clerk at the desk who tapped on a keyboard in response. They paused to look in my direction, and I looked down at my lap.

"Detective Gardner's not in the building right now," I heard the clerk say.

"Okay, well we'll have to wing it a bit then."

She dropped my mace and keys, phone, license, and credit card into a plastic bag. Officer Drumheller nodded towards me and pointed down the hall. "This way."

My leg began to bounce uncontrollably, but I stood. What had I done? What was happening? Had I lost time again? I was pretty sure I was crazy. My family, Doug, my friends, would I lose them all?

A female officer came out from behind the counter and followed us down the long gray hall. I counted off the fluorescent lights as we passed under them, wondering why I wasn't freaking out. It felt as if I were floating through the scene. It wasn't really happening, right? I would wake up, and it would all be a bad dream. He opened a door and led me into what looked like an exam room. A woman, dressed in a white lab coat, sat at a desk.

"We need blood samples." He handed her the papers and bag of my belongings and walked out the door. The female officer approached me, holding out her arms parallel with the ground. I copied her, spreading my legs apart. She patted me down from head to toe.

"There isn't anything to you. You might blow away if you're not careful."

"It's the drugs, see it all the time." The nurse held up her syringe.

I started to disagree but then realized it was pointless.

"I wish they'd make a legal version of that."

"Me too. I like food way too much."

Food and hunger were at least two things I was not a slave to. I placed the thought in the plus column of my mental tab.

The officer pointed at me. "She's clean." She took a chair from beside the desk, positioned it beside the door, and sat down.

The nurse asked me to get up on the exam table. She took my blood pressure, my pulse, and my temperature. She had me sign a consent form, and then she took four vials of blood from my arm. Dizzy from the sight of my blood being drawn, I lay down on the bench. She pricked my finger, squeezed the drop onto a plastic strip, and inserted the strip into a monitor.

"Your blood sugar is low. I'll order you a meal. They usually don't give meals if you come in after five, so you should eat it. Breakfast isn't until eight."

Breakfast? I would be there overnight? The light above her head flooded my vision, and tears started to pool in my eyes. *Keep it together*, I told myself. *You made your bed, now lie in it.*

The female officer stood and took the paperwork and plastic bag from the nurse. "Come with me."

I followed her back towards the entrance and past the counter. She led me down a long hall and through two sets of double doors. At a counter, she tossed the paperwork into a bin and pointed towards a bench on the opposite wall. I sat down, and she stood beside me. After a few minutes another female officer approached the counter and picked up my paperwork. She typed on a keyboard and retrieved a page from a printer. She looked at me. "This way." She swung her arm in the direction she started in. I crossed to follow her, entering a small room lined with wire shelving piled with bagged linens.

She tossed two bags to me. "Change into these. No zippers or buttons. You can keep your socks but no shoes." The two officers started to chat about their days.

A bench lined one wall, and I sat on it, removing my shoes and slipping the khaki scrubs over my leggings. Unzipping my jacket, I slid the top on. "No long sleeves or pants. You're on suicide watch." *I didn't want to die. Did I? Did I want this part of my life to be over, wiped away magically? Yes. Did I want to be dead? No. Right?*

Wondering again why I wasn't freaking out, I removed the under layers and replaced them with the scrubs. It occurred to me I'd left my apartment with my gloves and hat. Where were they?

She held a large plastic bag open for me, and I dropped my shoes and clothes inside. "Jewelry?" She waved a finger in my direction. I unlatched my watch and placed it in the bag and slipped my earrings off. "Necklaces, girlie." She put up a finger again. My hand went to my neck. The three necklaces Doug had given me lay on my clavicle, and the ring he'd given me hung on a chain just below. Taking them off one by one, I reconnected the ends and then zipped them in the pockets of my jacket and handed it to her. I thought about the ring and wondered if I would have a boyfriend after the day's events.

She dropped the bag with my phone and license in it into the larger one. She peeled a sticker from one of the sheets she held and attached it to the outside. The first officer left and the ward officer guided me down to a hall in another wing. With gray walls and floor, the section looked much like the other, but the doors were made of Plexiglas and huge windows gave you a view of each room. We walked nearly to the end of a hall, and she stopped in front of a door marked 103.

She unlocked the door, held it open for me to walk in, and then held up the paperwork in front of her face. "It says they'll bring you dinner. Don't usually see that. A hot meal always makes things better though." She closed the door and locked it behind her.

I scanned the room. There was only one window to the outside, and it was high up near the ceiling. It was dark out, so it didn't really matter. All I could see was the orange glow of the streetlights reflecting off the clouds. Dang, I hated those lights. A surveillance camera was mounted above the door. A sink and toilet were positioned in one corner and a cot took up the other. *Nothing is going to make this better.* And why hadn't they told me what I was being charged with? Or had they? Had I missed something at the beginning?

I crossed to the bench, sitting down and bringing my knees into my chest. It was completely silent, and I wondered if the rooms were soundproof. Goosebumps covered my body, and my skin felt like there were millions of tiny needles pricking its surface. I couldn't stop shivering, and I pulled my arms inside my top. Finally, I settled into a slow rock. The motion soothed me, helping my body relax. *Think, Amanda, you have to remember!*

My mind switched on, and I started to panic. No one knew where I was. Didn't I get to call someone? Who would I call? My parents? I had to call Doug. What if I only got one call? I could call Doug's dad. He was a lawyer. If anyone could help, he could, or at least he would know someone who would. Lila or Kate would be worried, right? Would the police call my parents?

I had no idea how long I'd been rocking back and forth, but the sound of the lock brought me out of the circling thoughts. A woman, a different one than before, brought in a hot tray and set it beside me. She moved back towards the door but didn't leave. Instead, she stood, her hands behind her back, leaning against the wall opposite me, silent. Why she stayed I could only guess. Probably the same reason I wasn't allowed shoes with laces or long sleeves or why there were no blankets.

Her voice startled me. "I can only stand here twenty minutes. You should eat. It's hot at least." Her words had some effect, and I uncurled and picked up the tray, setting it on my lap. There was a combination spoon-fork, wrapped in a napkin fitted with a paper ring. I removed it and started to stab the meat item.

"Most people end up picking it up," the guard said.

Figuring I could use some brain energy, I started with the potatoes. They were warm and creamy as was the spinach in cheese sauce. I ate the wheat roll and left the meat.

"You should eat the rest. It's a long time till breakfast." The idea of being there all night, alone, with no blanket, turned a switch. Fear welled up inside me. I forced myself to eat two bites of the protein, but it was all I could stomach. I set the tray beside me and slid it to the edge of the mattress. The woman looked at her watch but didn't move.

I retrieved the cup, swishing my mouth out the best I could, thinking I wouldn't be able to brush my teeth. I didn't dare ask about that. After a few minutes an alarm on the guard's watch sounded, and she walked towards me to retrieve the tray from my cot.

"Don't I get to call someone?"

"The detectives should get to you soon. It's not very busy tonight." She backed out the door, locking it behind her.

Somehow I was colder than before, and I rocked back and forth again, bringing my legs to my chest and rubbing my arms. I heard the sound of a key in the lock, and I stopped my motion. Yet a different female guard waited at the door, hands on her hips.

"You need to come with me."

I shot up, energized at the thought of figuring out what was going to happen.

In the hall, another guard followed us. They led me to a different wing of the building and into an empty room. "A detective will be here in a minute." They locked the door behind me. As in my cell, a camera was positioned above the door. There were no exterior windows in this room, only a large mirror on one wall. I avoided looking at my drawn face, choosing a seat facing the opposite way. Within minutes, Officer Drumheller and a suited gentleman entered the room.

They pulled out the chairs and sat across from me. "Ms. Avery, this is Detective Smith." Officer Drumheller cocked his head towards the other man. "Detective Gardner will join us in a minute."

I nodded. "Do I need a lawyer?"

Det. Smith opened a file he'd set on the table. "You haven't been charged with anything Ms. Avery. You are just here for questioning. The complaints against you are disorderly conduct and threat with a deadly weapon. Witnesses at the scene say you talked about killing a person, so I would say attempted murder and/or murder are on the table. Your drug and alcohol screens came back negative. Do you have an explanation for your behavior, or can you shed some light on why you talked about a murder and who that person is?"

"Should I have a lawyer?"

"If you are innocent, you don't need one."

Tears started to form, and I brushed them away with my hands. "I don't know. I don't remember what happened before I went to the coffee shop."

"We see you were the victim of an—" The door opened and a woman in a slim skirt and tailored jacket stepped in. Peter's face flashed before my eyes. I put my hands to my temple and squeezed my fingers into my skull, but the image wouldn't go away.

"Sorry, I was detained." She took the chair beside me. "I thought you were waiting."

"We can't wait forever."

I slid as far away from her as possible, clasping my hands together and resting them in my lap. Studying them, anger flooded my senses. If only I could get Peter's face out of my memory. I swiped tears from my cheeks.

"Ms. Avery." She reached out to me. A thud reverberated inside my chest, and a sharp pain shot through my left shoulder. Clutching my arm, I gasped for my breath.

Det. Gardner grabbed my shoulder. "Are you okay?"

I looked at her wide eyed. "My arm." I tried to breathe, and then I heard it again. *Boom*, my heart issued a single beat. I waited—one, two, three seconds, and again, *boom*.

She put her fingers to my wrist. "Get a nurse." She stood, pointing towards the door. "Call an ambulance." Det. Smith shot out the door.

My breathing was labored, and I put my forehead to the table. "It's okay. I have this arrhythmia."

She sat beside me placing her fingers around my wrist again. "Your left arm hurts. You barely have a pulse. You're not okay. You're having a heart attack."

Boom, boom, boom, my heartbeat echoed in my ears. The beats were too fast. Sweat formed on my face, and I shivered. The detective took off her jacket and put it around me. I rested my head on the back of the chair. The nurse who'd taken my blood entered the room and, using a stethoscope, listened to my heart.

She put her fingers to my wrist and turned her arm to look at her watch. Dropping my arm, she stepped back. "Her heart rate is all over the place. There's nothing I can do. I see this all the time."

"Her drug and alcohol tests were negative," Det. Gardner said.

"They called an ambulance."

Two medics wheeled a stretcher through the door. I shook my head and waved my hands in the air. "I don't need to go to the ER. I'll be okay in a bit." That's what I said, but I knew it was a lie. This was different.

Det. Gardner grabbed one of my hands with both of hers. "Let them help you."

I nodded, and one of the medics guided me towards the stretcher. I lay down, and then they buckled the straps over me. They raised the stretcher and rolled me down the hall, out the double doors, where we'd come in, and down a ramp to a waiting ambulance. They hoisted me into the back. One of the medics sat beside me, and then Det. Gardner climbed in.

"Detective," Officer Drumheller called, "we can have a female officer—"

She held up a hand. "I'll go. My shift's almost done."

The driver shut the back doors. Tears poured out of my eyes, and wishing I could stop them, I wiped my cheeks. I couldn't die! Why had I let things get out of control? If I did live, what was my life going to look like? Surely Doug wouldn't want a crazy girlfriend, especially after his last one. My parents and friends would be so disappointed. I looked at the ceiling, listening to the siren.

The beep of my monitor sped up and then stopped as my heart issued another thud. I sucked in a breath and squeezed the detective's hand. "Can't you give her some saline, something?"

"Might make it worse." The medic shook his head and patted my arm. "We're not far."

As my heart rate evened out and my chest muscles relaxed, I removed the oxygen mask. "What about the charges?"

"Let's make sure you're okay, and then we'll deal with it."

I vacillated between a conscious and unconscious state. My stretcher stopped under a bright light and a face appeared in my field of vision. "You did this to yourself. There's not much we can do for you."

Chapter 2

September 20 – six months earlier

Bright lights flooded my eyes and then nothing.

"I gotta go," I yell in Lila's ear, trying to be heard above the band.

"No." She catches my wrist as I pull away. Wrapping an arm around my neck, she screams into my ear. "Please stay."

Her body is hot and sticky, and I lift her arm and back away. I cup my hands around my mouth. "I have to work tomorrow."

She bounces from foot to foot in front of me and takes my hand. "I know but stay until the end of the set."

I look at my phone. The display reads eleven fifteen. "Okay." I squeeze her hand, and she turns and pulls me through the crowd to the edge of the stage. Why I do this I'm not sure. I'll definitely pay for it tomorrow. But she's my best friend, and I like making her happy.

The set ends and she encircles me in her arms, holding me against her soaked shirt. I peel one arm away and meander through the crowd toward our friends.

Ross, Mark, and Bill stand around a table sipping their beers, looking cool as cucumbers. Lila almost falls into the table, her hands slapping down on the surface. "It's so hot. I need something to drink."

Ross slides a glass of ice water towards her. She picks it up and swallows half of it in one gulp. Mark hands me a glass and I drink, letting the water tame my parched throat. When the liquid is gone, I suck a piece of ice into my mouth and put down the glass.

"I have to go."

Lila bumps her hip to mine. "One more song?"

I crunch the ice in my mouth. "No. I stayed till the end of the set."

Her arms wind around me again, and she kisses me on the cheek. "I love you. I'll see you tomorrow."

I kiss her cheek. "Yes, I'll see you tomorrow." I pry her hand from my waist.

"Where are you parked? Should I walk you out?" Mark asks.

"No, I'm good. I'm in the front row."

"Okay." He pulls me in for a hug. "Be safe. I'll see you tomorrow."

I step back and point to Bill and Ross. "See you tomorrow." They wave at me.

Outside, the cool air feels refreshing, and I take in a deep breath. It's quiet, but the noise from the band still vibrates in my ears. I walk down the stairs and step onto the asphalt.

"Amanda."

I look left then right and catch sight of an approaching form. I turn to face him. An incoming freshman I met at the fraternity house walks towards me. He's dressed the same as he has been all week, dark jeans, white t-shirt, black leather jacket. His hair is slicked back, and a metal chain ropes from his belt to his pocket.

"Amanda, hey, what are you up to?" He stops a few feet from me and stuffs his hands in his pockets.

"Hi, Peter. Just heading home." I wave my keys and spin around, backing towards the row of cars behind me.

He shakes his hand in the air. The bracelets on his wrist clink together. He steps closer. "You remember my name?"

I step back. "Course, we talked almost every day this week."

He looks back to the building and then at me. "Where are your friends? Why you leaving so early?"

"I have to work early tomorrow."

"Ha." He tilts his chin up and slides a hand through his hair. "My dad threatened to make me get a job one time. I told him fuck you." He bobs his head to the rhythm of the words and takes a step towards me. "I have to study and everything, you know, man."

"It sucks sometimes." I slip my phone out from my back pocket, sliding my finger onto the call button. "Everyone's still inside if you want to join them." I point towards the club doors.

"I saw you guys come in." He looks towards the sky and sniffs and then looks back at me. "I'm not sure I'm their type, ya know, all

fuckin' social and everything." He cocks his head back towards the end of the building. *"These guys are kinda more my group."* I look in the direction he points. Two guys lean against the wall beyond the reach of the door light. Like him, they wear dark jeans and leather jackets. One sucks in a long draw on a short cigarette bud, throws it down, and grinds it into the pavement.

"You mean like the Socs and the Greasers?" My quick wit got the best of me, and I instantly regret my words.

"Ha." He points towards me, closing the distance between us. *"What are you? Like a fucking English major or something?"*

I release my breath. *"Everyone's read* The Outsiders, *right?"* I glance back and see my car only a couple of feet away. I turn the keys in my hand, trying to find the panic button.

He holds his palms out. *"Whatcha doing? We're having a conversation, just like yesterday."*

I curse Lila for talking me into coming to this club. Why did she have to see this band? There's not a soul around except the two guys standing against the wall. *"It's late, and I have to get up early."*

I back away, but he takes another step towards me. *"Can't smoke in there. What the fuck's up with that? I mean shit."* He hits his leg with his palm. *"We're all gonna die, right?"* His head sweeps from one direction to the other. *"I can walk you to your car."*

"I'm right here." I hold up my keys and press the unlock button. The car's lights blink. I back towards the driver's side, wondering if it's a safe move. He's not a big guy but probably stronger than me. He could wrestle me into the vehicle.

I stop at the driver's door, and he stops a few feet from me. He rests one hand on the roof. *"You're not in a sorority, are you? You seem different from those other guys."*

Yeah, like freaky different, *I think. Like with parents who make you weigh in and see a psychologist different.*

It is hard to look at him, listen to him, and talk to him. A thick silver bar pierces through two points on one eyebrow, and he curses in at least every other sentence. He only talks about himself and his photographic memory. His dad is an alumnus and donates a huge sum to the Fraternity chapter every year. The most recent check came in an envelope that included a letter of recommendation, written by his Parish Priest. I know the other guys at the house did try to hang out with him. I'd see them rock on their heels, stretch, eyes darting around the room.

He runs his finger up the side of the car to the roof and takes another step towards me. In one hand I hold my keys, finger to the alarm button. In the other I hold my phone, thumb hovering on the center of the screen. I make sure my feet are planted shoulder-width apart and fight the nervous movements that might give me away.

"There are lots of different types in all organizations."

He takes another half step toward me and leans his shoulder on the roof. "So that guy, the Frat president or whoever, I saw a picture of you guys at the fraternity house. Is he like your boyfriend?"

I back away. "I'm sorry, I really need to go. But there are tons of people in there." *I point towards the door of the club again.*

"Where is he exactly?"

"Japan."

His thin lips form a smile for the first time. He looks at the ground and then back at me and rubs his chin. "No shit. Must get lonely."

"I guess. Not a big deal." *I hold up a key and shake the set.* "Sorry, but it's late and I really have to be up early for work, so..." *I point towards my car with my phone.*

"Oh." He puts his hand on the car door and pushes himself off. "Of course."

Something tickled my nose and I rubbed the tip.

I look up and see the red, yellow, and orange leaves on the trees, the wind tugging them from the branches. I lift my hands into the air, letting the breeze surround me. Crossing the street, I squint in the sunlight. The sun is low, almost to the horizon. I think to hurry. I was supposed to be at the fraternity house a half hour ago. I take out my phone when it dings, read the message, and replace it in my back pocket. The temperature is perfect, and I dread another night of mingling with the same guys.

As I approach the house, I take in a deep breath. There, in the main hall, are at least fifty freshman potentials, mingling with the brothers. One more night.

Taking the path between the houses, I mean to enter through the back so I can drop my bags off in Mark's room, like I always do. The leaves are deep on the narrow walk and cover my boots. I remember afternoons raking leaves with Dad, trudging through leaf piles that rose to my waist. I kick at the leaves like I did when I was a child.

"Well, hi." I look up. He stands about ten feet in front of me, one hand in the pocket of his black leather jacket, motionless except for a slight cock of the head. His thin lips almost form a smile—no, a sneer. "You don't have your dog with you. What's his name?"

I stop a good five feet from him. "Hi, it's Northie. He was tired from a walk."

"Right, Northie, like Northwestern?" He cocks his head again and stuffs his other hand in the other pocket of his jacket. It seems warm for leather, but he's worn the same jacket every night.

"Right." I nod and look towards the house and then back at him. He has fair skin and dark hair that's lighter at the tips. Whether the highlights are from sun or a color job is hard to tell. He's from LA but has no tan. He has a medium build, and some girls may find his slightly muscled tough guy look attractive.

"It was cool to see you last night. You hanging out at the house tonight?" He points to the building.

"Yes, are you heading in?"

"I had some dinner in there. Thought you might not come tonight. It's good to see you, princess." His mouth turns up on one side into a half-smile, and he stands there as I take a few steps towards him.

"Princess?" I try to keep my voice light, my eyes relaxed. I look up at the trees overhead, to the six-foot-high fence on my right. To my left are bushes and the brick wall of the house.

"Amanda, princess of the fraternity." The word princess sounds more like a hiss as it slides off his lips. His hand moves up and down in his pockets as if he's shaking coins. He looks at the house and back to me and shakes his head. "Do you like me, Amanda?"

I stop. "Why would you ask that?"

He walks towards me, stopping barely two feet from me. "You are, aren't you, their princess? I can't tell if you like me or not. Maybe you're scared of me or scared of wanting me."

I take my phone from my pocket, hoping a contact is accessible. I lift my shoulders and arch my back, trying to stand as tall as I can. I am scared to look away. "You said yourself you don't like being social."

He lifts his hand and puts his finger to my jaw and slides it down to my chin. I take a step back. He motions towards me. "I'm not gonna hurt you." *He shoves his hands in his pockets and bounces on his heels.* "I bet if you like me, they will, right?"

Deep breaths, *I tell myself,* no nervous movements. *My phone is in one hand, but my keys and mace are in my bag on the opposite hip. I can't get to my keys without unzipping the bag, and I can't throw the bag without lifting it over my head. Too slow, I couldn't do it fast enough.*

"Greek organizations aren't for everyone. I'm not in a sorority." *I take another step back. I'm halfway from either end of the building now.*

He nods his head, and his lips stretch into a smile. "You didn't answer my question. Do you like me?"

I tap the screen on my phone, hoping to message Lila since that was the last screen I had up. "You seem like a good guy, definitely smart."

My phone dings, and I lift it to look at the screen. He touches my other arm with a single finger, raking it down to my wrist. "Come on now, we're having a conversation. That's rude. I'm just smart? Is that the best you can do? I think I'm a pretty handsome guy." *His hand moves to his chest and rests where his heart would be. For a split second his face looks like a skull glowing in the light from my phone.*

I lower my phone but keep a good grip on it. I try to keep my voice even, and I tuck my hair behind my ear with my other hand. "Sorry, that was Lila. She's waiting for me."

"Oh, the brunette with the beefy boyfriend. She looks like trouble."

I tuck my hair behind my ear, realizing I just made that motion. Don't show fear, I remind myself. I paste my hand to my thigh. "She's a good friend."

"I like your hair down like that. It was up last night."

My hand moves to my hair, and I curse myself for the nervous motion. I suck in a breath and put my hand to my hip again. I hold up my phone. *"Sorry, I really want to get to the party. I haven't had dinner yet."*

He swings his hips to the left, then right, and back again. *"Come on, I thought we were getting to know each other better."* He steps closer.

I step back. *"Why don't we go inside?"*

He sniffs and wipes his nose. Glancing from side to side, he leans into me. *"There's no way in hell I'm getting an invite to pledge here."*

I pull back a little. *"Rush isn't until winter quarter. There are a lot of fraternities."*

"My dad wants me to pledge this fraternity. How am I supposed to do that?" He moves closer, looming over me. I feel his hot breath on my forehead. The smell of sweat, smoke, and leather combine to form a bittersweet musty odor. Beads of sweat litter his forehead, and he wipes them off. His hands form fists at his side.

I take a slow half step back. He smiles and matches my step. *"I know you have some pull in there. You know, being the ex-president's girl and everything."* In one quick movement he catches my arms and spins me so my back faces the bushes and the building beyond. *"Right?"*

I yank my arm out of his grip and reach behind my back to unzip my bag. With the other hand, I press my phone screen repeatedly.

He shoves into me, backing me into the bushes. *"As I was saying, I was thinking that maybe if you like me—"* he lifts a strand of my hair from my shoulder, I inch back, but he doesn't let go *"—well, I could get into this fraternity. I mean, I'm trying to be nice here. I'm not even cussing much."* He flips the strand of hair into the air.

I put my left foot out and start to move around him, but he blocks me with his arm. I jump the other way, and he stops me again. Duck, run, and scream, I think. I open my mouth, but his hand clamps down on it. His other arm winds around my back, forcing me into him. On my tip toes, he is only half a head taller, and we are nearly face to face.

"Why are you running away? I just wanted to kiss you so you can see if you like me."

He slides his hand off my mouth and presses his lips into mine, forcing them open with his tongue. On my toes it's hard to get much momentum, but I ram my knee into his crotch and scream as loud as I can. He barrels into me, forcing me back to the wall. Gripping my shoulders, he slams me into the bricks.

He holds me there with the full weight of his body. I tap as many spots on my phone screen as I can. "I wouldn't try that again. You like it rough? With a friend like that brunette, there has to be more to you than this." He brushes my hair from my face.

"Stop—" His hand on my mouth ends my scream. Then I hear voices in the distance, and my phone rings, signaling an incoming call.

He grabs my jaw, his thumb on one side and fingers on the other. "Who's that" He rakes his hand down my arm and jerks my phone away. Hand tight on my jaw, he drops it to the ground and thrusts his heel into the screen.

I try to shake my head back and forth. "I don't know."

He leans in so his mouth touches my ear. "Bitch, you better hope you don't remember who did this." Then he lifts his knee and slams it into my ribs. The air whooshes out of my lungs, and I fold forward. He tugs my head back, using a handful of hair. "And if you do remember, you better not tell anyone. If you do, I'll find you, and it'll be way worse than this." He drives a finger into my cheek and then looks towards the sky. He grips the back of my head. "For you and your friend Lila." His knee comes up to meet my face and then he throws me back towards the wall. I see his face, his lips formed into a thin smile for a half second, and then nothing.

"Amanda."

Feeling something wind around my ankles, I shot up, pushing back with my feet until my spine knocked against a barrier. A burning sensation ripped through my right arm and something scraped against my cheek. Finding a tube, I flung it to the ground. I could only see shadows, and I tried to scream. "Stop!" My jaw and chest seared in response, and the command came out more like a croak.

"Amanda." *He's going to drag me away.* Huddling against the hard surface behind me, I hugged my legs to my chest, blinking to clear my vision. After a few seconds I could see light and color, and the print of a hospital gown came into focus. The white sheet and blanket at my feet become clear. Zack stood a few feet from the bed, one hand stretched towards me, the other holding a phone.

"Amanda, you're safe." He put the phone to his ear. "Doug, I'll have to call you back."

He sat down at the foot of the bed. I spun back into the headboard so that one side of my body was mashed up against it. I pulled the sheet up. "Don't—" my voice cracked and I swallowed to moisten my throat "—touch me."

"Beep, beep, beep." I looked around for the source of the sound, and it felt like the left side of my face weighed a ton. I put my hand to my cheek and craned my neck to see the monitor recording my heart rate. The blips on the screen came faster and faster. I took several slow breaths and scanned the room. A man in a police uniform and a man in a suit stood near the door.

Zack stood and held up his palms towards me. "You're safe."

The chemical smell of the room hit me, and I covered my nose with the sheet. It smelled musty, and I threw it off. My breathing became labored, and as I gasped for air, another pain shot through my chest.

"Where's Lila? He said he'd get her too."

Palms still up, Zack inched towards me. When he was within a few feet, his stench, the smell of sweat that emanated from his body, conjured an image of thin lips, tilted up on one side. I cupped my hand over my nose.

Keeping his distance, Zack squatted down until we were eye level. "Lila is fine. She's at the house. They're all there, on lock down, being questioned by the police."

The suited man stepped forward and stood beside Zack. "I'm Detective Sanchez. You said 'he'd get her too'. Who is he? The person who did this to you?"

I nodded. "Peter, Peter Scalini, from the house." I looked at Zack. "He was a potential from LA."

The suited man turned to the officer. "Call the University, get an address, phone number, find a roommate, and get a picture. Anything they can give you. Get an APB out."

"Yes, sir." The officer left the room.

I looked at Zack and then down at my chest and arm. Blood stained my arm where the IV had been ripped out, and the bandages on my chest were soaked in red. "I think I need a nurse."

"I'll get one," Detective Sanchez said and then walked out.

Zack sat down on the edge of the bed and tossed my jacket towards me. "I brought this for you."

I picked it up and brought it to my face, filling my nose with the smell of my detergent and fabric softener. "Sorry, he reeked of sweat and body odor."

"The guy who attacked you? Peter?" He shook his head. "Sorry, I was working out when Lila called." He pushed himself up with his hands.

"No, it's okay. Sit with me, please." I patted the blanket in front of me but didn't relax my position.

"Doug is catching a flight. His mom, brother Michael, and Tia, went down to get food as soon as we saw you'd gotten out of surgery okay. Your parents are on their way. Doug's dad is outside with the University officials."

"Mr. Taylor, Doug's dad, is here? Doug's mom and brother too?" I rocked back and forth. "What time is it? I don't want to see anyone. Doug can't come. He'll lose his position. Tell him to stay."

"He's already on the plane. Mr. Taylor just got in from New York. Michael drove Tia down from Milwaukee."

A nurse came through the doorway, crossing to my bedside. She checked the monitor and then turned to me. She followed the IV line down to where it lay on the bed and lifted my arm. "Well, you did quite a number on that didn't you?" She raised my left arm and looked down my gown. "And on that too." She backed away. "I'll have to go get another IV kit and supplies for that incision."

As she left Ryan and Sam, Dr. Carpentar I guessed I should call him, walked into the room. It was sad that I was on a first name basis with the ICU staff. They were followed by Doug's father and a suited gentleman. I hugged my knees to my chest again, even though the stitches pulled my skin, and a searing sensation grazed my ribs.

As Ryan approached, I pointed towards the men. "I want them to leave. Everything smells, and I need a shower."

He held up his palms, and Dr. Carpentar approached the bed. "Easy there, light eyes, you're just waking up from the anesthesia. We need to make sure you're stable."

"I'm not in ICU?"

"No, didn't make the cut this time. Technically you should be in recovery, but we have you here for more space."

Remembering my head slamming against the brick wall, I felt the back of my head.

"Your head is fine, no hair loss. You have a couple of stitches and a minor concussion. You had a pretty good bump there, so you'll have a headache for a few days. They operated on your ribs, pinning one and removing the splintered end of another."

I looked down at my chest. The bandages and my gown were soaked through with blood.

Doug's dad approached, his face etched with empathy. "Amanda, I'm here with the Dean of Students to make sure you're okay. I'll help you give your statement later, okay? The detective is waiting outside. It's best to give your statement as soon as possible."

The ever prominent creases in his forehead and wrinkles around his eyes were absent, and for once, the sight of his steel blue eyes was comforting. I realized they were Doug's eyes. Doug had his father's eyes.

"Okay, thank you, Mr. Taylor." I nodded to him and then the Dean. They turned and left the room.

"Give us half an hour." Dr. Carpentar closed the door behind them.

Ryan stepped towards me, and again I couldn't stop my impulse to back away. He held up the IV kit and bandages he'd taken from the cabinets. "Do you want another nurse?"

Remembering he was the best of any nurse I'd had with needles, I shook my head.

Zack patted the bed. "I'll be outside."

I reached out to him. "No." I had no idea where the emotion had come from, but I wanted him there. I needed him to stay.

He peaked his eyebrows. "Okay, I'll be back here." He pointed towards the wall behind him.

I relaxed my position, uncurling my legs and easing my torso back onto the pillows Ryan stacked for me. He and Dr. Carpentar examined the damage I'd done to the incision in my side and decided it didn't need to be re-stitched. Ryan cleaned the wound and re-taped it. He cleaned up my right arm and fixed the IV in the left.

"Good as new." He straightened the sheet and blanket.

I rested my head back on the pillows and looked at the ceiling. Was he crazy?

Dr. Carpenter fitted an extra blanket on top of the first. "They would like to ask you some questions pretty soon, get an idea of what happened, so they know what they're up against. Can you talk to them?"

I nodded and looked up at Zack. "I'll get them." He opened the door and waved them in. The detective, the uniformed officer, Mr. Taylor, and the dean filed in as Doug's mom, Tia, and Michael appeared in the doorway. Tia inched around the men to me. Sitting down on the bed, she took my hand. "Can I hug you?"

I nodded and sat forward. She wrapped her arms around me, patting my back. When she pulled away, a tear ran down her cheek, and she wiped it away. "We were so worried about you."

"I'm okay." I clenched my jaw and squeezed her hand.

Paula, Doug's mom, sat on the end of the bed and patted my leg. Tia stood and made space for her to lean in and kiss my cheek. "*Mi nina hermosa.*" She spoke in her native tongue, water pooling in her eyes.

"I'm okay. I told Zack to tell Doug not to come. Will you call him too?"

"I will, but I think he's already on the plane."

"Okay, I'll call him after I talk to the police." I looked past her to the men gathered there.

She squeezed my hand and wiped the tears from her cheeks.

I looked her right in the eyes. "I'm okay." I wasn't going to be able to hold it together if everyone around me was crying.

She nodded and backed away. "We'll be outside."

As they left, Zack approached. "I'm going to go take a shower and then come back."

Again the irrational panic surfaced, and my heart thumped in my chest. I scanned the faces and thought about Tia and Paula on the other side of the door. "Will you stay, please?"

"In here, now?"

I scanned the men's faces and nodded.

"Course." He tapped his hand on my blanket.

"Okay." I let out the breath I realized I'd been holding.

I looked at the men gathered there, wondering what Doug's dad was thinking. Talk about a high-maintenance girlfriend. "Amanda, the detective needs the best account you can give him of what happened and everything you know about Peter Scalini."

The detective stepped forward but kept a foot between him and me. He held out his phone. "It would be good if I could record your statement."

"Okay."

He tapped on the screen and held the phone between us. "Whenever you're ready, Ms. Avery."

I started with the last incident, relating how he was upset about getting into the fraternity, how he seemed agitated, how he smelled, what he'd done, and what he'd said about me remembering and hurting Lila. By the end of the story, I found myself, knees curled to my chest, rocking back and forth again. Ryan sat next to me, holding my left arm out straight to keep the IV tubing from crimping.

I told them about how Peter had approached me the previous night, and how I'd been scared he was going to attack me then.

I described the conversations we'd had and everything I could remember about him.

When I finished, the detective asked me to repeat the story. After I'd repeated it, he asked me question after question, having me go back through the entire event. Doug's dad paced and the dean stood there stoic, almost as if he were comatose, sweat glistening on his brow. I didn't look at Zack. I couldn't look at him. Dr. Carpentar stood beside me, arms folded on his chest, and Ryan continued to hold my arm. He didn't smell like chemicals, or mildew, or smoke, or sweat. He smelled like soap. When the detective's questioning circled back around for the fourth time, Doug's dad stopped in his tracks.

"She's told the same story three times—that's enough."

The dean wiped his brow with the back of his arm. Dr. Carpenter put his hand to my shoulder. "I think she could use some rest."

The detective cleared his throat. "I have one more question, if I may." He panned his head around the room, and Mr. Taylor and Dr. Carpentar nodded.

"Were you sexually assaulted other than the kiss, Ms. Avery?"

"No."

"Are you sure? You were unconscious. There was no evidence at the scene but we need to confirm."

"No, that's all." Not caring that my side burned like someone was holding a hot iron to it, I curled up into a ball with my head resting on my knees, and my eyes sealed shut. Anything to block out the reality of what happened to me.

"I think you've gotten everything," Mr. Taylor said.

"Thank you, Ms. Avery. We will find Mr. Scalini," the detective said.

I looked up at him, my vision blurred through my tears. "Did you find my phone?"

"No, he probably took it. But it was good you got a connection with Ms. Phillips."

"Lila?"

"Yes, her voicemail recorded part of the incident. That's why they went looking for you."

"And you'll make sure Lila is safe."

"Yes, ma'am, thank you again."

I nodded and then tucked my head back between my chest and knees. I heard footsteps and then Mr. Taylor's voice. "Amanda, I'm sorry, but we'll get this guy?" I didn't reply. "Doug will be here in a few hours."

I raised my head. "Can you tell him to go back, please?"

"He won't listen."

"Gentlemen." Dr. Carpentar held the door open for them and then approached the bed.

"What else do you need? We can have someone come talk to you about the incident."

I shook my head. "I'm tired. I'd like some rest." Ryan pulled his hand from my back, and I reclined back on the pillows, stretching out my legs.

"Let us know when you need more pain meds. We can give you something to help you sleep."

The last thing I wanted were drugs to make me sleep more. I'd been out of it for too long as it was.

Zack followed behind Ryan. "Should I stay?"

"Yes." I closed my eyes.

"Where do you want me?" He scooted a chair towards the bed.

"That's fine."

"I don't smell too much from here?"

Closing my eyes, I tilted my head back and forth smiling. It hurt my face, and I grimaced. "No." I lay there trying to let it all go, clear my mind of all the swirling thoughts. It was wrong to want him there, but at six four he was the biggest guy I knew. He wouldn't let anything happen to me. I was safe with him there. Thinking of Zack, my mind jumped to thoughts of Doug. I lifted my hand in front of my face.

"Do you know where my ring is?"

He put his hands on the arms of the chair and pushed himself up. "I can find out."

"No—" I pointed behind my head "—call Ryan."

I closed my eyes. I heard voices, and then a few minutes later someone tapped my arm.

"Here." Zack held the ring above me.

I took it and slid it on my finger. "Thank you." Hugging my jacket to my chest, I rolled towards the opposite wall. I let the tears come and come, until they didn't come any more.

Chapter 3

I woke to a dark room lined with chairs that held all those closest to me. Zack was still in the same spot, and Lila was curled in Ross's lap in the next seat. Seeing Lila reminded me of Peter's threat, and his image danced in front of my eyes. I wondered if I would ever forget those small dark eyes or his pencil thin lips taut on his face. I was safe. Lila was safe. *He can't get us here*, I told myself.

Mark, Paula, and Marissa sat in various positions, asleep. I slipped on my jacket, and as quietly as I could, I swung my legs to the floor. Wheeling my IV pole to the door, I inched it open and checked the hall. Michael, Mr. Taylor, a police officer, a lady in a suit, Dad, and Mom stood beside the nurse's station. Mom noticed me approaching and crossed to me, gathering me in a loose hug.

"How are you?"

"I'm okay, Mom." The last thing I wanted to do was talk about it again.

"Sugar." Dad wrapped and arm around my shoulder.

"Hi, Dad, fancy meeting you here."

"They got him." He pointed to the police officer. "They picked him up on the south side of Chicago, trying to get on a bus to Kansas."

I looked at the officer. "Really?"

"Yes, they just booked him at the station."

I was safe. He couldn't hurt me or anyone else.

Mr. Taylor approached us. "Good thing you're up, we've got some logistics to discuss."

I sucked in a deep breath, stopping myself before I fully expanded my lungs to spare my ribcage. Logistics? I had no clue what he was talking about, and I couldn't imagine how horrible I looked.

"I need to use the restroom first." I looked between him and Ryan.

Ryan pointed down the hall, and Mom followed me. "Mom, I'm okay."

"Okay, sweetie." She took a step back and leaned against the wall.

Washing my hands, I couldn't avoid my reflection. Red marks, from his fingers digging into my face, flanked my mouth. My left cheekbone and eye socket were already purple from the impact with his knee. I splashed cold water on my face and patted it with a paper towel, wondering where I'd put the oversized sunglasses Marissa had gotten me last year.

Mom took my IV pole as I met her in the hall. At the nurse's station, Ryan was typing on a computer.

"Can I go home?"

"Yes, I'm printing out your discharge papers. As soon as Dr. Carpentar does rounds, you can leave."

Mom rubbed my back. "Are you sure? You can take as much time as you need."

"Yes, I'm sure."

Michael, Dad, the lady in the suit, and Mr. Taylor approached us. I looked at Doug's dad. "Thanks for staying. I didn't realize you were still here. They're working on my discharge papers."

"Why don't we find a place to talk?" He looked at Ryan. "Is there a private spot we could use?"

"Sure." Ryan got up and showed us to an empty room.

Inside, Mom, Dad, and I sat on the bed, Michael sat in the chair, and Mr. Taylor and the woman stood in front of me.

Doug's dad paced the floor and pointed between me and the woman. "Ms. Avery, Ms. Johnson from the University is here to help you any way she can."

I looked at her. "Thanks."

She smiled. "Glad to help."

Mr. Taylor squatted down in front of me. "Here's the story. Your parents and family experienced it as they came into the hospital, but I don't believe you are aware of the media circus that's waiting outside. There were helicopters circling campus last night."

I stared at the floor, trying to conjure a memory of chopper blades.

"Amanda?"

"Yes, sorry."

"Several news crews were there when they loaded you into the ambulance."

I scanned the room, thinking I should have some recollection of being transported.

Mr. Taylor squatted in front of me. "The only shots of you are from a distance. Long, dark hair is all they have. The press has the fraternity house and hospital exit surrounded, waiting for any information they can get. They know there was an assault. Very soon, they'll have Peter's picture, name, and a redacted copy of the police report. If you want to keep your identity private, we need to be vigilant."

My knee bounced harder and tears pooled in my eyes. I swiped the water away before it spilled over my lids. "They know I'm here, and they're waiting for me to come out?"

"Or for a leak from hospital staff, or the police station, or anyone who was at the party last night."

"Everyone knows it was me?"

"No, the police were careful about asking questions. We can't know who will leak something, but we can do everything possible to keep you from being seen or associated with the incident until you're ready."

"What if I'm never ready?"

"Well, that will be your decision."

"I didn't realize I needed a lawyer."

"Well, you do for things like knowing how to get you home and how to get you to the station to sign your statement and identify Mr. Scalini. There will be a bail hearing soon."

"They would let him out?" My chest tightened and I hugged my torso. "Do you know someone?"

Dad cleared his throat. "You can use my lawyer from Champaign or Tia could help."

"Tia isn't a criminal attorney. Is your attorney?"

"No."

I looked at Mr. Taylor. "Can you suggest someone?"

"Well, me or Chris, but if you're not comfortable with us, then I can give you some other names."

Dad stood. "How much will this cost?"

Mr. Taylor ignored Dad. "I think of you as family, and I want to help."

I swiped tears from my cheeks. "You don't have other work you need to be doing?"

He shook his head. "This is what lawyers do. We put out fires."

"Thank you."

"Of course."

Dad hiked his waistband up. "We can go to your apartment, get you packed up, go down to the station, and then head home from there. The dean said you could scan back the medical leave papers." He had kicked into drill sergeant mode.

I looked from Mr. Taylor to him. "I'm not going back to Champaign. The quarter starts next week. I'm staying here."

"Well—"

"This is not open for discussion." I looked to Mom. "Did anyone bring me something to wear?"

"Marissa brought a bag for you."

"Thanks." I turned to Mr. Taylor. "Can you get me to my apartment?"

He smiled. "We sure can. Give me half an hour and I'll have everything arranged."

As we came into the hall, Ross and Lila emerged from my room. She crossed the hall and wrapped her arms around me, squeezing me till my side ached, but I didn't care. I cried into her hair, and she rubbed my back. "I'm glad you're okay. Zack told us everything."

I was glad everyone knew the story, repeating it for my friends and family was not an experience I wanted to have.

Mr. Taylor corralled us back to my room. "This is what I'm talking about. You have to keep out of public view."

After a few minutes in Lila's arms, Ross peeled me away and hugged me. "You have to stop doing this."

I wiped the tears from my face. Ryan came into the room and checked my vitals and removed my IV. Zack, Mark, Tia, Paula, and Marissa woke up one by one. Marissa captured me in a vice-like hug.

"Whoa, thanks for coming."

"Are you kidding? Oh my God, I was so scared."

Mr. Taylor clapped his hands together. "Okay, everyone, it's still early. We should move as soon as possible before there is more press out there." His eyes scanned the room. "Most of you are blonde. Lila can you put your hair up?"

She held up a band and secured it to her hair. Mr. Taylor had them leave a couple at a time spaced about ten minutes apart. Dad, Mom, and Tia left first, followed by Lila, Ross, and Mark. Paula and Zack were next. Marissa helped me change into leggings and a t-shirt and put my hair up. Michael had a ball cap and Marquette sweatshirt for me to wear. The hat grazed my stitches but felt okay once my ponytail was looped through the opening in the back.

Dr. Carpentar made his rounds at six, reviewing the post-surgery instructions and signing my release papers. Michael and Marissa left through the front entrance, and Ryan led us through the hospital, down through the emergency room, and out the ambulance bay.

The faint light from the rising sun, the cool air, and the glow of the orange lights of the lot reminded me of the previous night. My pulse quickened, and I turned my head, scanning the lot. Mr. Taylor touched my arm.

"Easy, like a Sunday afternoon. They're twenty feet away, but they're trained to spot anxiety." I followed his gaze to a news van on the other side of the parking area.

"Okay." I forced a big smile, a short laugh, slung my bag onto my shoulder, and followed him to the car like we'd rehearsed. It felt strange, and I replayed his words in my head—alternate persona. I skipped the last step to the Mercedes and stood, one hand to my hip, waiting for him to unlock the door. He squeezed the remote, releasing the door, and I slid into my seat.

"Nice, like a walk in the park," he said as he started the engine. The car had tinted windows hiding us from outside viewers. I distracted myself, investigating the options on the display of the dash as we snaked through town and past campus. Turning into my apartment complex, I was grateful we'd chosen the more expensive gated location.

Outside, I ignored the tightening of my chest as I surveyed my surroundings. He was not there. I was safe. At my unit, I found the keys and opened the door. The television in the living room displayed a news report with an image of the Northwestern campus, but the screen turned black the second my eyes landed on it. The short glimpse of the fraternity house flanked by the tall trees—their red, yellow, and orange leaves blowing in the wind—made my stomach turn, and I clenched my jaw. Northie bounded up to me, his whole body contorting as his tail wagged back and forth. Tears pooled in my lids as I realized I'd forgotten about him.

Bending down to pick him up, I remembered I couldn't lift him. Lila put a hand on my back. "I gave Bill a key. He checked on Northie." I sank down on the couch, letting him climb up in my lap and lick my face. Poor Bill, I thought, stuck at the house surrounded by news reporters, dealing with the aftermath of the previous night. The chapter had seen more than its fair share of drama thanks to me. *No*, I told myself, *this is not my fault*. In the span of five minutes, Peter had turned all our lives upside down.

A memory of his form standing before me ran through my mind. How did a person bully, threaten, and beat a girl to get into a fraternity? What had his Dad done to make Peter so desperate to win favor or so scared to displease?

"Okay, everybody good here?" Mr. Taylor's voice brought me back. He folded his hands together and scanned the faces. My gaze followed his, seeing Mom, Dad, Tia, Marissa, and Michael gathered around our table.

Dad approached me. "I could use some sleep. We could come back in a couple of hours to take you to the station."

Mr. Taylor looked at his watch. "A break for a nap and a shower is a good idea. But we need someone else to go to the station with her."

Dad hoisted his pants and cleared his throat. "And why is that?"

"You have in-state plates, you're an alum, and they can have you identified in five minutes."

Dad pointed at him. "You're an alum."

"I'm an attorney, with a rental car, and a legal practice in New York. I'm registered in Illinois, so there won't be as much suspicion of a relationship between me and a potential victim. I've already talked with the precinct. We can park in the back and get her in through the transport bays. It's not completely hidden, so it won't be good for a whole army to walk in there. Amanda can wear a hoodie and look like anyone from fifty feet away." He motioned towards me. "It's up to you, Amanda. You can choose how you want to do this."

I didn't really want Dad or my family there, hearing the details of the attack. I looked at Mr. Taylor. "I'd like to go with you."

Dad stuffed his hands in his pockets and rocked on his heels.

Mr. Taylor clapped his hands together. "Okay, I'll be back at twelve thirty to pick you up."

Peeling off Michael's sweatshirt and hat, I avoided eye contact with Dad.

Michael and his dad left, leaving Lila and me alone with my family.

"This is ridiculous." Dad flung his arms in the air as soon as they were out the door. He pointed a finger at me. "All this is totally unnecessary. This is a family matter."

With one last pat for Northie, I stood up.

"Actually Dad—" I turned towards Tia's voice "—this is pretty standard. This is how we handled cases in my criminal internship. It's easier for victims."

Surprised Tia had actually sided with me, I steeled my expression and faced Dad. He raked his hands through his hair and lifted them towards the ceiling. "I guess you guys are the experts. I'm trying to help my daughter." His lips pursed as he stuffed his hands back in his pockets.

"Dad, you are helping by being here." I looked at my family. "I'd really like to get a shower and a nap so I'm not a zombie at the station or to pick up Doug. Tia, Marissa, you guys can grab a couch if you want. Mom, Dad, do you have a room? Kate or Zack might have some space for you to take a nap if not."

My mom put a hand on each of my shoulders. "Oh, honey, you don't need to go to the airport. We'll stay and take care of everything for you."

The thought of them in our apartment, invading my space, caused a thump inside my chest. I held my breath, waiting for the next beat, eyes trained on Mom. It wouldn't help to have them clued into an arrhythmia, if that was what it was. They would only hover more. The next beat came, and I exhaled. "I really need a good shower and a nap. Do you have a room?"

Dad flipped his keys in his hand. "There are two rooms waiting for us. We'll give you your space if that's what you want."

I slumped my shoulders and covered my eyes, wincing when I touched my cheek. "Dad, I feel gross and tired. I'd like to get a shower."

He rubbed his hands on my arms. "You've got more to deal with than gross and tired. But for now, we'll be at the hotel getting some sleep. Call us when you wake up."

"Thank you." I hugged them goodbye and closed and locked the door. Leaning into the wood, I wondered how long I could entertain them. There were too many conflicting thoughts racing through my brain without their audible concerns. Heading towards my room, Lila intercepted me. She wrapped her arms around me and held me. I leaned my head on her shoulder and let myself rest against her. After a few minutes she relaxed her grip and backed away. She lifted a strand of my hair.

"I can help you comb your hair out after your shower."

"That'd be great."

I shed my shoes and carried them to my room, with Northie trailing every step. In the bathroom, I opened my medicine cabinet to avoid looking in the mirror. My side ached and my head throbbed, and I wondered why I hadn't noticed before. But, I refused to take the opioid pain killers they suggested, opting for ibuprofen. I needed my mind as clear as possible.

I scrubbed every inch of my body and then repeated the motion as if the act could erase the event. I shaved all the way to the top of my thigh, lathered my hair, and rinsed it twice, till the steam from the water filled the room. When the temperature started to cool, I stopped the flow. Wrapping in a towel, I brushed my teeth and flossed. I slathered lotion on my face and then the rest of my body.

When I came out of the bathroom, Lila was sitting on my futon holding my comb. "Do you feel better?"

I shrugged. "I guess. I smell better, for sure." I held my hair up to my nose.

She patted the futon cushion. "This thing isn't that comfortable, is it?"

I sat down beside her. "It was the right price."

"You should have offered to let your parents sleep here. You might have gotten a new bed out of it." She combed out my hair and blew it dry until the noise was too much for my head. Afterwards, we lay down beside each other, snuggled together like we'd done at sleepovers as kids. It felt safe. Northie tried to wriggle in between us, but I settled him at our feet.

Lila rubbed her hand down the length of my hair. "I'm so relieved that you're okay."

"I'm just glad they got him."

"And you get to see Doug."

"He shouldn't be coming."

"He wants to be here for you, know that you're okay. That's all I kept thinking about when they were holding us at the house. Seeing you lying there motionless again..." Her eyes filled with tears, and she wiped them away. "All I wanted was to be at the hospital, to see that you were okay."

"Don't cry." I wiped a drop from her cheek. "I won't sleep if I start thinking about it."

"Sorry, I should be consoling you, listening to you." She got a tissue from my table.

"I can't think about it yet."

"Your parents were talking about you going back to Champaign. Are you going home with them?"

I shook my head. "No, that would be letting him win. He doesn't get to win."

"I'm glad. I would miss you."

"I can't live with my parents again."

"Good, I need my roomie."

She laid an arm around my back. I sucked in a breath filled with the floral scent of my shampoo. They'd gotten him. I was safe. Refusing to entertain his image, I stared at the ceiling, listening to Lila and Northie breathing in and out.

🐦 🐦 🐦

I woke to the sound of Lila's alarm echoing through my head. Finding her device, I silenced it. Her eyes fluttered beneath her eyelids. In full REM sleep, she was nowhere near waking. I set her alarm for thirty minutes and left it beside her. I got up and Northie jumped to the floor. He stretched and yawned, and I hustled him out of the room before he made too much noise.

Locating the oversized sunglasses Marissa had gotten me, I slipped on Michael's sweatshirt, pulling the hood up. I put on my shoes and latched Northie's leash to his chain. Poking my head out the door, I looked both ways. Seeing no one, I made my way out into the sunlight. It was nearly noon, and there wasn't a cloud in the sky. The perfect day taunted me, as if to say, "I'm beautiful, you should be happy."

I walked slowly, letting Northie sniff his normal bushes and take care of his doggie business. Scooping up the result in a bag, I threw it in the trashcan as I made my way back to our apartment. I passed a couple of kids I'd met the day before but kept my head low, and they didn't engage me.

Happy with my disguise, I decided I might never give Michael back his hoodie. I refilled Northie's bowl and got a glass of water for myself. Sitting at the table, I looked outside at the bright day. Nearly a day of my life had evaporated as if it had never existed. My heart thumped, and I pressed my thumb to my sternum. I clenched my jaw. I couldn't dwell on what was gone. I went to my room and, being as quiet as possible, found a pair of pants. In the bathroom, I changed, brushed my teeth, and put on makeup.

As I was applying some eye concealer, Lila's alarm sounded. She sat up like she'd been jabbed with a hot poker. She slammed her hand to her phone. "Damn alarm. Stop. Stop. Stop." She hit the phone again and again.

I ran into my room. "Lila, it's okay." I took the phone and silenced the alarm.

"I'm sorry. It sounded like the monitors from the hospital. What if they hadn't found you in time?"

I rested my hand on hers. "But you did. The phone call and hearing people coming out of the house scared him away. You saved my life."

Her hands shook, and she began to rock. I wrapped my arms around her and hugged her to me. "I'm sorry."

She stiffened. "Right now you have to go to the station and nail that evil boy."

I stood up as straight as I could, squaring my shoulders. "Yes, I do." The motion reverberated through my body, jostling my ribs. Flinching, I grabbed my side.

Lila got up and started going through the list of people I needed to contact. Before she could dial, her phone rang. "It's Doug's dad." She handed me the phone.

When I finished the call, I sent a text to my parents. I really didn't want them in our apartment but knew they would feel left out. I returned to the bathroom to finish my makeup. What would I be doing on a regular day? Then my brain kicked in. Clients, I had tutoring clients I'd already missed sessions for. Hurrying to my computer, I found three new messages. All were nearly the same. They'd tried to call when I didn't show, but there was no answer. *No*, I thought, *my phone was probably at the bottom of a river*. I sent texts from Lila's phone and email responses. Next, I canceled my appointments for the rest of the weekend.

Within a half hour, everyone descended on our apartment again. Mr. Taylor took another sweatshirt from his bag as we left for the station. "You need something different. If you wear the same thing every time, they're going to notice," he told me, closing the door behind us.

On the sidewalk, Kate approached from the other direction. In my incognito outfit of black pants, canvas sneakers, sweatshirt, and shades, I hoped she wouldn't recognize me. It felt mean, but I hadn't rehearsed what I would say to people and wasn't ready to talk to anyone. But, a few feet from me, she closed the distance and wrapped me in a hug.

"Amanda? I almost didn't recognize you. Were you guys at the house? Do you know the girl who got attacked?"

I cringed as she squashed my injured ribs. "Oh, sorry, I know you're not a hugger." She backed up. "I am so upset. Is Lila okay? I called but didn't get a reply."

"Yes, sorry, we're okay. Everything's a little crazy after last night." I motioned to Doug's dad. "Kate, this is Mr. Taylor, Doug's father."

She held out her hand to him. "Nice to meet you. It's too bad Doug is so far away."

Mr. Taylor shook her hand. "We're actually headed to the airport to pick him up."

Her eyebrows arched as she looked at me. "A surprise visit? That's great."

"Yeah. We'll catch you later, okay?"

Mr. Taylor put his hand on the small of my back as we continued along the path. "Is she a good friend?"

"Yes. I didn't know what to say."

"Once we finish at the station, you should take some time to think about how you want to respond. You will feel more comfortable if you get to control the message."

"Okay, thanks," I said, wondering how many cases like this he'd handled. He opened the car door for me. "This is what you do all the time?"

He walked around and sat in the driver's seat. "Not all the time. I defend and handle plaintiff's cases, and sometimes handle contracts."

Doug's dad had always seemed so distant. I was seeing a different side of him, a good change from his stoic persona. The traffic around the University was almost at a standstill. With students moving into the dorms and the news vans trying to get as close to the scene as possible, it was stop and go. Mr. Taylor wasn't patient with the traffic and snaked through the neighborhoods in an effort to avoid the gridlock. I was grateful we didn't have to drive past the campus.

At the precinct, he slapped a parking permit on the dash as we entered the back lot. The officer manning the gate waved us past. Even with Lila's pep talk and my earlier confidence about identifying Peter, being at the station made me nervous. My heart missed a beat again as we got out of the car. I put my hand to my sternum.

"You okay?" Mr. Taylor asked.

I nodded and followed him up the ramp and into the building. The stench of body odor and cleaner assaulted my senses, and I covered my nose with strands of hair, breathing in the fragrance of my shampoo.

Mr. Taylor approached the desk and showed a clerk his identification. After a few minutes the detective who'd been at the hospital approached us. He showed us to a room, where he checked my ID. Another detective was seated at the table, and we sat down opposite the officers. I held my hair across my face, trying to take slow long breaths.

The detective passed a document to me. "This is your statement we took before. Read through it, make sure it's correct. If you've thought of anything else to add, then we can add it in."

I closed my eyes and took a deep breath, and my heart thumped in my chest again. I waited until the next beat to open my eyes. As I started to read through the document, the room around me disappeared. He voice, his sneer, his odor permeated my thoughts as I relived the event. When I put the papers down, I realized my hands were shaking. I mashed my palms to the cold metal surface. Peter Scalini did not get to win.

"Is the statement accurate? Do you have anything else to add?"

I shook my head. "It's correct. I don't have anything else."

The detective handed me a pin. "You can always make additional statements if you remember anything else." He pointed to where I should sign, and Mr. Taylor put his signature under my name as a witness, as did the officer and the detective.

The detective gathered the papers and slid them into a file folder. "Okay, now is the easy part or hard part depending on how you're feeling. With the physical evidence and your testimony, we have grounds to charge Mr. Scalini with aggravated assault and sexual battery. After you confirm his identity, he will have a bail trial. In a case like this, I would expect it later this afternoon."

I looked at Mr. Taylor, and he straightened his suit. "I will be there. You have my contact information, and I'm of record in this case."

The detective explained the process for identifying Peter. I knew it wouldn't be hard, as his image was etched in my brain. I didn't really want to see him again, ever, but I wouldn't be scared into inactivity. They showed us to a room with a large window that was a one-way mirror. Speakers gave us audio from the other side, and an officer led a line of men past the window. Peter was the third to enter the room. His curly hair, small dark eyes, and thin lips were unmistakable. I gripped the arm of my chair and bounced my leg. I'd been instructed to study all of the men in the lineup before identifying him. Wanting to follow all the correct procedures, I waited. All the men were of similar coloring, height, and build. They all wore the same issued clothing, but not one of them looked like number three, Peter Scalini.

They faced left, right, and away from me. They stepped forward and each said the same phrase. "Let's get pizza tonight."

As he spoke, I didn't hear the phrase but his threat from the previous night. *You better not remember.* Watching his mouth move, I remembered his lips pressed hard on mine. I covered my mouth, to keep from gagging. Mr. Taylor put his arm around me. My pulse raced and every sense seemed heightened. Even with his cologne flooding my nose, the blinding lights, and the heat of the room, I forced myself to keep my eyes forward.

When the others finished their oration, the detective asked me if I needed more time or one of the men to step forward and speak again. I shook my head.

He pressed a button on a wall and spoke into the microphone. "That will be all."

I bounced my leg until the men filed out. "Number three. Peter Scalini is number three."

"Okay, we'll get the time for the bail hearing. The arraignment trial will probably be the beginning of next week," the detective said as he held the door open for me.

"Thank you, gentlemen." Mr. Taylor shook their hands, and I followed suit.

"Glad to see you're okay, Miss Avery. We have several options for victim support." Det. Sanchez reached in his file and pulled out some pamphlets and a business card. "Please take advantage of our groups and counselors."

"Sure, thanks." I took the pamphlets and stashed them in my bag. I stood and steadied my legs before stepping toward the door.

Mr. Taylor led me down the hall to the exit. At the doors, he stopped and peeked out the window. Then he put his head out and looked both ways. "No change, you ready?"

I pulled up my hood and put on my sunglasses. There were several news vans beyond the fenced area, at least fifty feet away. I wondered if they kept filming, hoping to get something to use later. We walked down the ramp into the sunlight. It felt like it should be dark, like we'd been inside for hours, although it was only four.

He held the door for me and walked around the car. As he pressed the ignition button, he looked at me. "You did good."

"Thank you."

He stretched out his fingers on each hand and slowly wound them back around the steering wheel as he pulled out of the lot. "So, you have some options. You can go back to your apartment or come with me to pick up Doug."

"I'd like to go meet Doug, if you don't mind the company?"

"Fine with me. I thought you'd make that choice."

It was an hour's drive to the airport. The car ride was smooth. Normally, I would've fallen asleep sitting in the warm sun, lulled by the motion of the vehicle. My leg bounced, and I bit my fingernail. I pulled my thumb from my mouth. I never bit my nails. I crossed my hands in my lap, wishing I had something more flattering on.

Mr. Taylor looked at me and then back at traffic. "I wouldn't be surprised if he's released on bail. They'll set it high, but the other side will argue that he has no record."

I turned to face him. "He basically told me he'd done it before and threatened the girls not to remember."

"Why didn't you bring it up before?"

"He didn't specifically say it. It was a feeling I got from his threat."

"He had no record. He's eighteen, anything before would have been stricken. We'll petition that he has to stay in the county, wear an ankle band, and reside at least two miles away from you and the campus. He's been suspended from school until the charges are resolved."

"Okay." I put my thumb to my mouth again.

"There will probably be a jury trial. With a jury, perpetrators have a better chance of getting off."

I gnawed on my nail. "Okay."

"You'll need to testify. They'll try to discredit you and ruin your reputation."

My leg bounced faster. "Okay." None of that mattered, he didn't get to win. "But there is a lot of physical evidence?"

"Yes, and that's good. He won't walk, at least not on my watch. You're lucky it became such a big media circus. If the campus police had handled it, he might have gotten away with a slap on the wrist and a quarter's suspension."

I looked out the window. "Good."

As we neared the terminal, I stuffed my hands in my pockets and tried to relax. I checked the mirror. I'd taken a long time with my makeup, and it still looked nice. With the sunglasses, the bruising and swelling weren't obvious.

We waited outside the international terminal for only twenty minutes before I saw Doug approaching. He must've been headed to work when he got the call, as he wore his formal slacks, shirt, and jacket. When he reached us, he dropped his bags and wrapped his arms around me. I buried my head in his chest, letting his smell seep into my skin. After a minute he loosened his grip and stepped back. Putting his lips to my cheek, he kissed me, and pulled me back to him.

I winced as he squeezed me, and he let go. "Sorry, I was so worried."

"You didn't have to come."

He reached down and picked up his bag and slung it onto his shoulder. "Like that was going to happen."

He dropped my hand and hugged his dad. I'd only seen him hug his dad one other time. "Thanks for being here."

"No problem."

We walked to the garage, my hand in Doug's. I hadn't been sure I wanted to see him, for him to see me bruised up, but I was glad he was there. I looked down at my ring and back up at him, smiling.

His dad pointed at me. "That's the first time she's smiled."

Doug kissed my temple as he set his bag down beside the car. "See, it's a good thing I'm here."

"If you lose your job, I'm going to be really mad."

"I've got it covered."

Mr. Taylor held his keys out to Doug. "Here, you drive. I have to make some calls." Mr. Taylor opened the door and sat in the back seat, and we slipped in the front.

"Wow, nice car. See what you get when you hang with my dad."

After finishing a call, Doug's dad sat forward in his seat. "We should get something to eat. Have you eaten today?"

I shook my head, and Doug dropped my hand. "Not at all?"

I tucked my hair behind my ear. "They gave me water at the station."

"Good thing you didn't have the coffee. It was horrible. Do you want sushi? No." He rubbed his chin. "Steak? I know a good place. I'll text it to your number, Doug. We've got just enough time before the bail hearing."

I read the name of the restaurant to Doug from his phone.

"Dad, I don't have a tie and Amanda—"

"They'll give you a tie, and she can wear the shades and pretend she's some stuck up star. I spend a lot of money there. It'll be fine."

He called and made a reservation, and I typed the address in the map. Doug held my hand as he weaved through traffic and I watched the cars pass by. We parked in a deck and walked a short block to the restaurant. The host was not amused with my sweatshirt, high tops, and shades. He motioned for Mr. Taylor to step closer. "Sir, if I may, I have a tie for the gentleman, but we have a reputation to uphold." The host's eyes trained from my feet to my head.

Mr. Taylor stepped back. "This happens to be a very important client, and she'd like to get a good meal while she's in this city. Do I need to speak to a manager?"

The receptionist looked between us, his gaze landing on Mr. Taylor. "No Sir. Of course, sir, this way."

He picked up our menus and walked between the tables towards the back of the room. I could see heads turn in our direction and hoped they assumed I was someone famous. I tried to remember the name of the actress Marissa had talked about all summer, the one in the popular vampire movies. She always wore jeans and hoodies. My petite frame and dark hair were similar to hers. I could be a famous movie star for all anyone knew.

Mr. Taylor ordered a bottle of wine when the waiter came. She set a glass in front of me and filled it. When she left Doug lifted the glass and set on the other side of the table.

Mr. Taylor set it back in front of me. "She needs a glass of wine. You like wine, right?"

Doug shook his head, but I lifted the glass to my lips. The Malbec was tart at first, but sweeter as it slid down my throat. Half the glass in, my leg finally stopped bouncing. When the server came back to take our order, Doug's dad ordered for us.

"You look like you can use a huge hunk of red meat." He winked at me.

"Thank you for everything today, Mr. Taylor."

"Mr. Taylor sounds too formal. Stop calling me that." He pointed a finger at me. "Chris, call me Chris."

Doug set his glass on the table. "Then what are we supposed to call my brother Chris?"

"How about CJ? That's what you used to call him as kids. He hates it, but I'm the boss." He went back to tapping on his phone.

I leaned back in my chair thinking I had no intention of calling Doug's father Chris. Doug took my hand. "How are you really?"

I shrugged. "I don't know, physically tired, but otherwise numb." I turned my head to see how close the other tables were to ours. Seeing they were spaced out of earshot, I questioned him. "How much do you know?"

"Dad told me everything. I talked to Zack too. I changed my undershirt and shirt on the plane, cleaned up the best I could. I hope it was enough."

I rested my forehead on my hand, embarrassed about my previous freak out. "You smell great, just like you. I don't know why I reacted that way to Zack. I was so disoriented."

Mr. Taylor leaned forward. "I think you're allowed. They say smells are the most potent memories."

"I dread going back to my apartment and having to sit around with my family. I don't know what to say, what to do."

"I texted Tia on the drive to update them."

"Thanks."

Doug took my hand. "You could stay at my mom's."

"Thanks but I want to be with Lila."

The food came, and the smell of the grilled meat caused my stomach to gurgle. I seldom ate such a hearty meal, but it tasted amazing.

We finished dinner and made our way back to the garage. Mr. Taylor dropped Doug and me off at my apartment. My parents, Tia, Lila, Ross, Mark, Bill, and Zack were all gathered in our tiny place. Northie greeted us before we made it a foot into the room. Doug picked him up and rubbed his head.

Lila crossed the room to hug me. "Are you okay? Did you see him?"

"It wasn't too bad."

She led me to the couch, and I sat down. Mom sat beside me and wrapped an arm around my shoulder. "We've been waiting all day for you to come back. We wanted to spend some time with you."

"Sorry, it took a long time at the station, and then we got Doug and some dinner."

"How are you?"

"Tired."

Dad leaned towards me. "You have people who've been waiting to see you."

I looked at the ceiling, tears forming in my eyes. I flashed him my best smile. "Yes, Dad, thanks."

I got up to greet Mark, Zack, and Bill, who embraced me in a tight hug.

"A little easier there," I said gripping his bicep.

He loosened his hold and leaned back to look at me. "Sorry, forgot. Ribs, right?"

"Bill, I'm so sorry. You've probably been through hell the past day. Is everything okay at the house?"

"What are you talking about? Just thinking about that sleaze-bag being in our house makes me sick. I'm glad you're okay. We're fine." He took a step back keeping one arm wound round my back. "We canceled stuff for tonight, but we're ready for the alumni barbecue tomorrow."

"Good." I turned to Zack. "Thank you for last night or this morning, I guess. And sorry about freaking out on you."

He wrapped his arms around me and squeezed gently. "All that matters is that you're okay, and they got that guy."

I shook off the thought that Peter might be out on bail within the hour and forced a smile.

Doug held Northie up in front of my face. "I can't believe this guy. He's huge."

"I know." I rubbed the dog's head.

Marissa wrapped me in a hug. "Kate came by. She said she saw you on the walk. We didn't know what to say to her."

"I know. I'll call her tomorrow."

Everyone moved to the living room, taking seats on the couches and floor. The conversation switched to the schedule for the next day. My parents and Tia and Ed had tickets for the game. They offered to skip it to hang out with me, but I insisted they keep their plans.

It wasn't an hour before Doug's dad showed up with news from the bail hearing. As expected, the judge lowered the bail to half a million and he was released. She stipulated he live at least two miles from me and the campus. The protection order required he not be within one hundred yards of campus, me, Lila, or our apartment. I was glad Mr. Taylor had thought to include Lila as I'd never seen her so upset.

As our guests filed out, I thanked them for coming. Bill hugged me. "I'm sorry for all the trouble," I said.

"Will you stop saying that?" Lila yelled. "I could hear you from across the room. Why are you saying sorry? You didn't do anything wrong."

I lifted my shoulders and let them fall. "I don't know. I don't know what I did. He chose me. I was nice to him, and he thought I would help him. When I didn't seem to, he lost it. Maybe if I told someone about the encounter at the club. But I forgot the next day and…"

She put her arms around me. "I didn't mean to yell." She stepped back and placed her hands on each of my shoulders and looked me in the eyes. "This is not your fault. You did nothing wrong. You were in the wrong place at the wrong time. Stop apologizing to everyone."

"Okay, sorry."

"Ugh—" she pulled me to her "—I love you. What is your problem? Aren't you angry? Because I'm angry."

"Thank you." I squeezed her tight. "I don't know. I'm sort of numb."

After our display, people filed out, and only Lila, me, Ross, and Doug were left.

Lila sat down beside Ross. "Sorry, I don't know what's wrong with me. Maybe I'm just tired."

"Everyone's exhausted. We should get some sleep."

Lila squeezed me and they retreated to her room. Doug and I sat on the couch, and I leaned back into him. He wrapped his arms around me and kissed the side of my head. "I'm sorry."

"Me too."

"What do you need?"

"Sleep."

Doug took Northie out for a walk, and I brushed my teeth and changed into pajamas. When he returned, he showered and sat beside me as I stared at the wall.

"Are you sleepy?" I asked, realizing it would be morning in Tokyo.

"Not really, but I'll lie here with you."

"Thank you." I kissed his bare chest, and he put his lips to the top of my head. When I looked up at him, he leaned in to kiss me. The thought of someone's lips pressing against mine made my stomach turn, and I pulled back. "Tomorrow, maybe."

He rubbed his hand along my arm. "Sorry, forgot." The corners of his mouth turned down, and I hated that he seemed upset. I laid my head on his chest, breathing in his scent, listening to his heartbeat, and using his warmth to help me relax.

Chapter 4

I woke to a silent house save the sound of Doug's breathing. The smell of coffee hung in the air, and sunlight lined the shade of my window. I picked up his phone from the table. The display read 8:09 a.m. Nearly ten hours of sleep had been interrupted only once when the pain medication wore off.

My body ached, but I got up and went to the bathroom. Afterwards, I pulled on a sweatshirt and padded into the living room.

"Morning," Lila whispered.

"Hi." I gave her a hug and sat down beside her. "I didn't think anyone was up. It's so quiet."

"Ross just left for the house." She made circles on the table with her finger.

"Everything okay?"

"I guess." She shrugged and sipped her coffee.

"Is that yes or no?"

"He wasn't happy that I wouldn't come to the house and game today." I took her hand as tears formed in her eyes. "I'm not ready to go back there. He doesn't get it." She wiped her cheek with a sleeve. "He doesn't think this should impact me. But it does, something happened to me too. My best friend called me, and I couldn't help her." I put my arms around her and pulled her to me. "What if he'd hurt you worse?"

I loosened my grip to wipe my tears. "But you did help me, and we're both safe." I squeezed her hand and stood. "And I need coffee." I poured myself a cup and returned to the table.

"We took Northie for a walk."

"Thanks." I let the coffee warm my throat.

"Kate and Elise have been texting about getting together for the game. I told her Doug and his family were here, and we didn't know our plans. I think Kate suspects something."

"Elise, oh my goodness, I totally forgot. She's only in town for two days. What should I do?"

"You have to tell them sometime."

"Should we invite them for dinner tonight? We could order take out."

"That'd be good. Everyone else will be at the alumni barbecue." She tapped a message to Kate on her phone.

"I have to get a new phone."

"Good, because I can't stay in this apartment all day."

"We could go to Doug's mom's. I know Doug wants to see her, and Michael is there."

"Are you sure it's okay for me to tag along?"

"Are you kidding? I'm not letting you out of my sight."

"Good, cause I feel the same way." She squeezed my knee, and we sat there a few minutes as if we were frozen. Eventually she let go. "I'm going to shower."

I moved to the couch, sipping my coffee and petting Northie. My side throbbed, and I got up to find some medicine before settling back on the cushion again. The sun shown in the front window just like it did any other day. How could the world outside go on like nothing had happened? A warm hand wrapped around mine, and I realized I'd been gnawing on my thumb again.

"Good morning." Doug kissed me on the cheek and lifted Northie off the couch. "How are you?"

"I feel like I got run over by a truck. My whole body hurts."

He shook his head and let out half a chuckle. "I almost wish a truck hit you."

I looked towards the window, nodding. "Me too."

He stood up. "Breakfast?"

"That would be great. We should make enough for Lila too."

"She didn't go to the house?"

"No. Is it okay if she hangs out with us? Can she tag along if we go to your mom's?"

"Course." He pointed towards his phone. "My dad said he'd meet us there. You should call your parents too. I just got a text from them."

I dreaded talking to them but sat at the bar and dialed Mom's number while Doug scrambled eggs in a bowl. She answered and put me on speaker so Dad could talk too. They wanted to know how I was, and if we could go to brunch before the game, and then meet up after the alumni barbecue. Their doting the previous day had almost driven me insane, and I requested they come after all their events.

As I ended the call, Lila joined Doug and me at the table for eggs, toasted bagels, and fruit. We ate in silence.

"What's on the schedule for today?" Both of us jumped at the sound of his voice.

I pointed between Lila and myself. "We invited Kate, Elise, Stephen, and Jeremy to have dinner here after the game, around six."

He squeezed my hand. "You're going to tell them?" I nodded. "Okay, sounds like a plan." There was no more conversation as we finished eating. I was grateful Doug had come, as our silence may have consumed us.

I took a quick shower and pulled back my hair in a high ponytail. It took ten minutes for me to get makeup on, and Doug was typing away on his computer when I came out of the bathroom. He set the device on the bed and stood in front of me. I pushed up on my toes and kissed him. His arms wrapped around me, and he touched his lips to my cheek. "You look beautiful."

"You're a liar, but thank you."

I packed my computer, extra change of clothes, and some toiletries in a satchel while he showered. We walked Northie around the border of the apartment grounds. As we circled back to my place, I saw Marissa jump out of my parent's rental car. She ran over and threw her arms around me.

"Lila told me you were going shopping. Is it okay if I hang out with you guys?"

"Of course, the more the merrier." We waved to my parents as they drove away and went to my apartment to meet Lila. Heading towards Chicago, the traffic near campus was already bad, and we were lucky to be going in the opposite direction. In the city, we parked in the condo's garage and took the elevator up to Paula's home. Inside, she wound her arms around me and stroked my head.

"It's good to see you. I worry so much."

She hugged Doug, Lila, and Marissa and then took my hand and led us into the living room. Mr. Taylor reviewed the schedule for the week. University representatives had asked to meet the next day, and Peter's plea hearing was set for Monday. "You don't have to come to the hearing. I'm just giving you information."

"You think they'll ask for a jury trial?"

"I would if I were them."

"Then I'm going."

Mr. Taylor moved to the front of his seat. "Amanda, it's not necessary. It will increase the chances of your name being leaked to the media. Actually, it will probably assure that the media will get your name."

"That's okay. I need him to know I'm not scared of him."

Lila took my hand. "But aren't you? I am."

"No." I looked at the ceiling. "Yes. I don't know." I stood and crossed to the coffee pot.

Mr. Taylor followed me. "You don't have to decide today. As far as safety goes, you're safer now than you've ever been. Like after 9/11, the safest time to fly was the next week."

Doug cleared his throat. "Dad, Amanda was six on 9/11."

"I remember it. Dad was stranded for days."

Mr. Taylor sat back down. "She gets what I mean."

Paula waved her hands in the air. "Enough about that. Did I hear we were shopping today?"

"I need a new phone."

She stood. "Well, shopping is shopping. I'm in. Who else is coming?"

Doug lifted his hand and Michael followed. Everyone except Mr. Taylor decided to join us. We got our coats and made our way down to the street. The shopping district was only a couple blocks away, and as it was a sunny, warm day, we chose to walk.

The familiar feel of his callused hand and the heat from his arm felt reassuring. The towering buildings and concrete walks were a welcome change of scenery from the tree-lined streets of Evanston. There I was anonymous. I could be anyone. There were no triggers in the scenery, and I felt myself relax for the first time in a day and a half.

Closer to the shopping district, it became more crowded, and we got stuck behind a group of smokers. I turned away from the cloud and tucked my head behind Doug's arm, trying to steady my breathing. He squeezed my hand and lifted his eyebrows when I looked at him. I covered my nose with my hair and pointed at the smoke. He nodded and guided us around the crowd.

The street was packed by the time we reached the block with the phone store. Arms from oncoming pedestrians bumped mine, and I started to feel as if the crowd were closing in on me. Had I become claustrophobic? Or was it a reaction to people touching me? I crossed my arm over my chest and held Doug's bicep, trying to dodge the oncoming wave. Thump, my heart jumped in my chest. *No*, I told myself, *this is ridiculous*. I looked up at the bright empty blue sky and exhaled.

Doug wrapped his arm around me and whispered, "You okay?"

"Yes." I shot him my best smile.

"Really? Because you're cutting off my circulation."

"Oh, sorry." I looked at my hand and the fingers were white. I stuffed them in my pocket.

"It's right here." He lifted his chin and opened the store door for me.

It was wall to wall people inside, and I wanted nothing more than to get a phone and shoot out of there. Marissa and Lila were determined that I get a cool new color and case. They picked each one up to show them to me.

I tried to be polite. "Guys, I got a new phone last month. I want the same one."

Paula wouldn't be dissuaded from getting me the upgraded gold version, and Lila picked out a clear case dotted with white spots. Once the decision was made, it didn't take them long to pull up records and reload the new phone with my old number. I watched as my text screen filled with messages. I didn't care what they said or who they were from. Engaging with the world in a normal way seemed like a foreign concept. None of the appointments or meetings mattered. I could breathe in and out, and that was enough. If you'd asked me before Thursday to go without my phone for two hours, much less twenty-four, I would've flat out refused. But with Doug and Lila there, it was of little use.

I sent a group message to my family and friends letting them know I had my new phone. We walked through a couple of other shops: a jewelry store, a shoe shop, and a clothing shop.

"I said... don't you think this is pretty." Lila grasped my arm and shook a dress in front of me. Doug shook my hand, and I looked away from the window to her face.

"Sorry." I turned my eyes to the dress. The image of my blood-soaked bandage flashed in my mind. I forced my hand towards the fabric, picking up the edge of the skirt. "Yes."

"Homecoming?" She moved her thumb up and down.

"Not red for homecoming, maybe Christmas formal? Valentine's Day?"

I scanned the room, wondering why in some moments my senses seemed heightened as if someone had turned up the volume or held a magnifying glass in front of me. In others, I felt as if they were muffled, like a plug of cotton had been stuffed in my ears, or a veil had been slipped in front of my face.

Lila turned to replace the dress on the rack. Doug giggled my hand in his. "What were you thinking?"

I shook my head. "Nothing, just looking at the sky, the buildings."

He kissed my temple. "You tired? Hungry?"

I shrugged my shoulders. "I guess." Maybe that was my problem. I did feel sapped of energy.

We found a café a couple of doors down and ordered sandwiches. I wasn't especially hungry and ate half of mine and gave the rest to Doug. Afterwards, we walked back to Paula's condo. In the foyer, Doug pulled me aside. "Would a nap help?"

"I don't want to abandon Lila and Marissa."

"They'll understand. Besides, my mom and Michael can entertain them."

Doug and I made our way back to his room. Inside, I plopped my satchel down on the bed, remembering I needed to email clients to reschedule tutoring sessions. I'd decided to take a week off to let my bruises heal. After sending the messages, I reclined on the bed, resting my head on Doug's chest.

He wrapped his arm around me. "Do you want to talk about it? You seem preoccupied."

"Not now."

He kissed the top of my head. "Did it help that Zack told us everything?"

"Yes, I feel bad for Zack, but it's easier for me."

"I couldn't sleep the whole flight worrying about you."

"When did they call you?"

"As soon as they found you."

I lifted my head and kissed him on the lips. "It's nice to have you here. Thank you for coming."

He wrapped his arms around me. "I wouldn't be anywhere else."

I rested my arm on his stomach and closed my eyes.

🐦 🐦 🐦

I woke to his hand tracing circles on my arm. Him, the room, and the condo felt safe. I moved up onto my elbow, grateful for the respite and dreading the next task of the day, telling Kate, Elise, Stephen, and Jeremy.

We drove back to my apartment, and as we neared Evanston, my leg began to bounce. I put my nail to my mouth. I was glad it wasn't dark yet, but the tree limbs forming arches above the streets were disconcerting, and my chest tightened. Doug wrapped his hand around mine and lowered it to my thigh, stopping my leg from its motion.

"You're safe."

I turned around to look at Lila. "Maybe I shouldn't tell them today. We could cancel, say I came down with a cold or something."

She leaned forward. "They're going to be upset if you wait. Plus you haven't seen Elise since June. Don't you want to see her?"

I slid my hand from under Doug's and back to my mouth, chewing on my nail. "I guess. We should wait till after dinner."

"You're going to wear sunglasses the whole meal? Like that won't be weird." She leaned back in the seat.

"I guess. You have wine, right?" I halted the motion of my leg again, and Doug rubbed his hand up and down it.

"Yes, we have wine."

Doug squeezed my leg. "I don't like you drinking with the concussion."

"I won't drink much."

"Your friends want to help you."

"This goes way beyond forming a study group."

Lila rubbed my shoulders. "We can have our own mini-therapy sessions. I totally need it after this."

We parked and took the sidewalk to our apartment. Inside, we freed Northie from his crate and attached his leash for a walk. After a loop around the complex, Doug left for the fraternity house. I was glad he'd decided to join his friends at the barbecue. Lila, Marissa, and I ordered pizza. Maybe we should've order something more formal, Chinese or sushi, but I was in the mood for a comforting staple and cheese pizza was it.

We stacked plates, napkins, and utensils on the counter, and opened the wine. As Lila poured the first glass the doorbell rang. I took the bottle, slid on my sunglasses, and let her answer the door. After greeting Lila, Elise bounded over to me, her normal peppy nature still apparent.

"You look awesome." I wrapped my arms around her, gathering her in a hug.

"Wow, I get a hug."

"Of course you do."

She stepped back. "Oh my goodness, what happened?" She raised her hand towards my face.

I ducked away from her, seeing Kate, Jeremy, and Stephen all staring at me.

"Why don't we have pizza first?"

They looked between each other and at Lila, who opened the pizza box. I grabbed the first piece and took a bite.

"Okay." Elise took a slice from the box and sat down.

"Wine?" I poured some wine into the glass in front of her.

Everyone sat down and grabbed some food. Conversation was light as we ate. They'd been to the game and summarized the highlights. Elise caught us up on her new position, and Jeremy and Stephen reviewed their summers. When everyone had their fill Elise finished off her wine and set the glass on the table in front of me. "Okay, spill, before I drink the rest of the bottle. Does this have anything to do with what happened at the house?"

I blinked my eyes to clear the tears starting to form, and removed my glasses. "The girl, the one with the long brown hair hanging from the stretcher in the papers—"

Stephen stood, hands raking through his hair. "I can't hear any more."

"That's fine. I wanted you to know before—"

Kate moved to the chair beside me. "I saw you yesterday."

"I'm sorry. I wasn't ready."

Kate paced to the other side of the room. "No, it's okay." Her hands shot up. "Who am I kidding? This is not okay. That guy—" she flailed her hands in the air "—is evil incarnate."

Jeremy pushed his chair back, turned and walked to the window, looking out. Yes, I had killed any sense of innocence my friends had. It was shocking when something happened on your campus, where you lived. But to have someone close to you hurt—I could see it in everyone's eyes. It was personal—it had happened to them too.

Stephen gripped the back of the chair. "Are you staying in school?"

"Yes."

He raked a hand through his hair again. "Okay."

My revelation could've been listed as a top way to kill a dinner party. "I'm sorry, guys. But I knew you'd find out anyway, and I didn't want to lie." Elise wrapped her arms around me and squeezed. I winced and slid away. "Ribcage."

Jeremy looked at me, his brow creased and his eyes narrowed into slits. "What else did he do to you?"

"Hit my ribs and face."

"He was charged with sexual battery."

My thumb went to my mouth, and I wondered how many details I should give them. "He tried to kiss me."

Jeremy's hand went to his stomach, and Stephen looked up at the ceiling and then back to me. "I'm guessing that wasn't consensual."

"No."

"Kate's right. This guy is evil." Jeremy crossed to the other wall and then back. "You are pressing charges."

"Yes."

Kate jumped up. "That's why Doug's dad is here?"

"He's handling my case." I stood up. "Okay, enough with the heavy. More wine?" Lila poured more wine for Elise and we moved to the living room.

Stephen plopped down on the couch. "I guess this nixes running for a while."

I sat down beside Northie on the floor. "Six weeks at least."

"Brutal. Are you starting classes Tuesday?"

"Yes, shades and all." I swiped my super-sized sunglasses from the table and put them on. "He doesn't get to win."

"The Profs probably won't like those, but I'm proud of you."

The conversation switched to lighter subjects. Elise loved her job in DC, and she was making friends. Stephen was happy with his resident assistant position and felt comfortable with the students under his watch. Kate was ready for a new quarter after interning at a chemistry lab during the summer. She was jealous that I'd gotten organic chemistry and physics out of the way. Jeremy still hadn't decided on his major after a summer of rotating positions at his dad's software company.

After my friends left, Marissa emerged from my room, and she caught me up on her first semester. She'd pledged a sorority and, not surprisingly, already had tons of friends. Her roommate was nice, and the courses were going well. Dad never had the same high expectations about her grades as he did mine, so she wasn't too stressed.

I caught myself feeling jealous of her carefree attitude. Even in high school, I'd never felt completely unbridled by responsibility. Whether it was grades during the school year or my tutoring sessions in the summer, I was constantly working.

The past summer should've been the one I floated through. My parents' constant attacks on my relationship with Doug, eating, and exercise habits made it exactly the opposite. I'd had three weeks with Doug before he left for Japan, and then three weeks tutoring and hanging out with friends. The past six weeks had been the best of the summer, but Peter had brought them to a screeching halt. I looked at the ring on my finger and thanked my lucky stars he hadn't injured me worse.

Just then there was commotion at the door, and I looked up to see my parents, Tia, and Ed entering our apartment. They stood in line to hug me.

"Hey there, pipsqueak," Ed said as he held his fist in front of me. I bumped mine into his.

"How's my favorite brother-in-law?"

"I'm good." He gathered me in a loose hug.

"I'm glad you're okay," he whispered in my ear.

"Thanks." I patted him on the back.

Doug and Zack weren't far behind my parents, and our apartment became packed with guests. Stephen, Jeremy, Kate, and Elise made their exit, with Elise promising to call before she left the next day.

When they were gone, Zack sidled up next to me. "It's great to see you. You look much better." He wrapped one arm around me.

"Thanks." I cocked my head sideways towards the deck. "Can we?"

"Sure."

We made our way outside and I closed the sliding door behind us. *Dang, stupid, orange lights,* I thought, looking out onto the grounds. "I wanted to apologize for what happened in the hospital."

"You don't need—"

I put my hand on his arm. "Yes, I do need to apologize. It was selfish of me to ask you to stay to listen to what happened.

Thank you for relaying the story to everyone. It couldn't have been easy."

He looked down at the cement and then back at me. "I don't think I'll get the image of you when you woke up or the experience of hearing you tell that story out of my head for a while."

"I'm so sorry."

The glass door slid open, and Dad poked his head out. "It's getting late, can we get a schedule for tomorrow?"

"Sure, give me a minute."

He closed the door, and I turned back to Zack. He rubbed his hands on my shoulders. "I'm glad you're okay."

"Yeah, well, okay is a relative term."

"You know what I mean. Anything you need, I'm here."

"I know. Thanks."

Inside, Dad was pacing the floor. "Okay, good. What's the plan for tomorrow?"

"We are meeting with the University reps at Paula's at one."

He held his hand up. "Why Paula's?"

"Because it's large enough for everyone to meet."

"Why not at the University?"

"It's what I want, Dad." I left out that Mr. Taylor had arranged the meeting.

He waved his hand in the air. "Okay, are we invited?"

"Yes." I told them about the brunch Paula had planned before the meeting.

"But we want some time with you, just our family." He circled his finger around the room pointing towards Mom, Marissa, Tia, and Ed."

"Okay, when are you leaving?"

"We need to decide when you want to leave for Champaign."

"I'm not going home Dad. It's late and I don't want to talk about this again."

"We need to discuss it before we talk to the University reps."

I put my hand to my head and sat down on the couch. "Why don't you come by tomorrow before brunch?"

He pointed at me. "We'll be here at nine."

Behind Dad, Zack distorted his face, opening his mouth and gritting his teeth together, and I stifled a laugh. He pointed at the door. "I'll see you guys tomorrow."

Mom, Dad, Tia, Ed, and Marissa filed out, taking turns giving me hugs. Dad was the last one to the door. He pointed at Doug. "You heading out too?"

"I'm going to stay a bit more."

"Okay." Dad squeezed my hand. "Bye, sweetie."

"Night, Dad."

He shut the door and Doug wrapped his arms around me.

"You're not leaving, are you?" I asked.

"Of course not."

"Good." I spun around to face him.

He moved my hair back and pressed his lips to my forehead. "You look exhausted."

"I am exhausted."

"You need a day of rest. Maybe we could sleep at my mom's tomorrow night. It would be quiet there. He grabbed the leash from the closet and clipped it on Northie's collar. "I'll take him out."

"Thanks." I kissed him on the lips, and he held me there for a minute. "I love you."

"I love you, too." Northie whined and tugged at the leash. "Duty calls." He pointed at the puppy.

After he left, I brushed my teeth, washed my face, and slid into bed. I pulled the covers up, shivering from the shock of the cold fabric on my skin. Doug returned with Northie, who jumped up beside me. After brushing his teeth, Doug inched in beside me, wrapping his arm gently around me. I snuggled into him, letting the warmth from his body relax me. He kissed the back of my head. "Need anything else?"

"No."

🕊 🕊 🕊

I woke to Northie jumping onto the bed. Doug sat on the bed and squeezed my shoulder. "Sorry, I took him out, and he bolted back in here."

"It's okay. What time is it?"

"Seven. Do you want me to make coffee?"

"In a minute. Can we just lie here?"

I cringed when I turned to face him. He grabbed the ibuprofen bottle and a glass of water from the bedside table and handed them to me.

"How are my bruises today?" I asked when I swallowed my sip of water.

He tilted my chin so my left side faced him. "More yellow."

"That's good. They'll be gone in a few days."

We propped up the pillows and rested against them. I looked at the ceiling, thinking about the day ahead. My parents thought I should go home to Champaign. They would argue that it was necessary. Unlike last year, I didn't feel the need to try and convince them or provide evidence that I would be okay. Still unsure of how I'd cope, I knew it'd be easier near friends and a support system.

I pushed myself up. "Okay, coffee." We walked to the kitchen and started the brewer. Doug started a bagel in the toaster. As it dinged, Lila emerged from her room.

Entering our cramped kitchen, she wrapped me in a hug, and I squeezed her tight. "Is Ross sleeping late?"

"No, he didn't come." She sat down at the table.

"Oh, I'm sorry." I couldn't remember the last time they'd spent a night apart.

"It's okay. They were drinking. He said he needed to be around the house anyway. Things are hard there."

Doug sat down beside us. "The house looked good. Better than it ever has."

I closed my eyes, trying to erase the image of the brick building from my mind. It didn't help as views of the trees, the leaves on the path, the wooden fence, and the high brick wall danced behind my eyes. I looked out the window at the blue sky and exhaled.

Doug's hand on mine startled me, and I turned back to him. "Did you have fun? You didn't tell me who was there. Anything new and exciting?"

"Just the regulars, nothing new." Doug looked between Lila and me. He slid the plate of bagels towards me. "Want one?"

"No, I'll eat at your mom's. Hey, I'd like to get out of the house. Will you come on a walk with me?"

Doug nodded.

"You want to come, Lila?"

"Yes."

"Great." I excused myself to brush my teeth and change. Back in the kitchen, I refilled my coffee cup and waited for Lila and Doug. We leashed Northie, and I donned my sunglasses.

It was nice out, sunny with a slight chill in the air. I tried not to think about the leaves or the trees and avoided walking through the piles on the path. It was stupid really, ridiculous that I should be scared of a patch of dead leaves. But I knew they would make that sound—they would rustle and crunch under my feet. I swiped a tear from my cheek. It wasn't fair.

Doug wrapped an arm around me. He kissed my cheek. "You okay?"

"Yeah, sure." I rubbed the next tear away.

Lila stopped. "We can go back. You want to go back?"

"No, let's walk over there." I pointed to the open field. *No trees, no leaves, perfect,* I thought.

"Are you worried about talking with your parents?" Lila asked.

"No, I know they want me to go home, but it doesn't matter. I'm not leaving."

Doug squeezed my hand. "How about the University reps?"

"Those people I could do without."

He swung our hands between us. "You should take advantage of everything they offer. They could really help. You don't know what you're going to need."

"I guess." I was going to have to face the irrational fears that had started to pop up. First the smells, the crowds, the orange lights, and then the leaves. I couldn't be scared of leaves. My heart thumped in my chest, and I exhaled, willing it to beat normally. I spun around to face them both. "I thought this was supposed to be fun."

Doug produced Northie's ball from his pocket and handed it to me. I bent down and let him off leash, threw the ball, and watched him chase after it. "At least he can run."

Doug pulled me to him and kissed my temple. "Only six, maybe eight, weeks, and you'll be back to it."

"You could play tennis with me. Since it's your left side, I bet you could still swing with the right."

"That's a good idea."

"See, I'm good for something."

I hooked my arm around her neck. "You're good for lots of things."

Chapter 5

Back in our apartment, we took turns showering. I washed my hair and blew it out straight. The bump on the back of my head was all but gone. I had to be gentle around the stitched area, but I made it through the drying process without too much of a headache. As I finished my makeup, I heard the doorbell.

The sounds of my parent's voices followed by Marissa, Tia, and Ed, drifted to my room. When I walked into the living room, they took turns hugging me.

"How are you?" Mom asked as we sat down.

"Good. I'm not as sore today."

Dad jingled his keys in his pocket. "I don't think that's what your mom means, Amanda."

"Okay, well, I haven't had time to process much else. It's been sort of a whirlwind..." I turned my palms up.

Mom sat forward in her seat. "We think you're going to need a lot of support. We'd like to be able to provide that."

I shook my head. "Yes, I may, and I always appreciate your help."

Dad moved to the edge of the cushion. "What we're saying is we have the means to help you."

"Okay." I cut my eyes to Doug and leaned forward, wondering exactly where they were headed.

Dad looked at Mom then back to me. "We talked to Dr. Medders. He has worked with girls in your position. He can set you up with a treatment plan. You can take a couple of easy courses at UI." He wrung his hands together.

They'd talked to Dr. Medders without my permission? The room grew fuzzy and started to tilt. I gripped Doug's knee to steady myself as my heart issued its now familiar thump. *Low blood sugar, anxiety, that's all it is*, I told myself. Yes, mixed with a huge amount of anger. I took in a slow breath.

"You talked to Dr. Medders? Told him what happened?"

Mom put her hand on Dad's knee. "Well, yes, honey. We needed to know what to do to help you."

As it was the previous summer, their help was the opposite of what I needed. I released a breath and looked at them. *They're trying to help*, I told myself. "Thank you for checking into that solution." I was proud those words had popped into my head because what I really wanted to say was: *Quit orchestrating my life!* "But, as I said before, I'm staying in Evanston. I'm starting classes on Tuesday just as I planned. I can see Sara, the counselor who helped me after the accident last year, and go from there."

Dad cleared his throat. "I'm sure you think you have all this figured out. But you don't know what you're dealing with here. You said yourself that after you attend the trial tomorrow it could be a media zoo wherever you go."

"Yes, that could happen. But I'm not letting this derail my life."

Mom reached out to me. "Sweetie, we don't want to see you struggling like last year."

Doug squeezed my leg, but my temper got the best of me. "Yes, struggling like last year when I made a 3.6, 3.8, and 4.0, fall, winter, and spring quarters."

Dad stood, and Mom crossed to sit on the corner of the sofa beside me. She picked up my hair and draped it around my opposite shoulder. "You know what we mean. It was a hard year."

I wanted to say that really the only hard part was them judging me. "My support system is here. I'm going to stay."

Dad squatted down on his knees in front of me, and I was sorry Doug had to witness the conversation. "We can't financially support any treatment we're not one hundred percent sure of."

So they wouldn't pay for anything unless it was on their terms. Again with the money! I wouldn't be dissuaded. "That's fine. I understand."

"My promise from before still stands."

His promise, as he put it, a means for making sure I was eating healthy, was to drag me home if he didn't think I was doing well.

He'd threatened to pull me from school if I didn't stay above his ninety-pound limit. It sounded ludicrous even when I said it in my head. *Ninety pounds*. At five foot two inches, I'd never weighed more than ninety-five. My weight had been steady since the injury last year, save my lapse in June. Some people ate when they were depressed, but my appetite decreased and I exercised more.

I wasn't going to be scared away from campus by Peter Scalini or my father. I looked up right into his eyes and smiled the biggest grin I could. "Of course, okay, that works for me."

Dad's eyes widened and Mom removed her arm from my shoulders, folding her hands in her lap. Dad clapped his hands together and stood. He looked around the room. "That's one tough cookie I raised there."

I stood and pointed towards my bedroom door. "I'm going to grab my boots from my room so we can get to Paula's."

Dad rocked on his feet. "We'll be here."

Crossing to my room, I glanced in Lila's direction.

"I'm going get my sweater," she said. When she was a foot from me she mouthed, OH MY GOODNESS.

I clenched my jaws together and mouthed back, I KNOW.

Doug followed me into my room. Inside, he plopped down on the bed. "Wow," he whispered rolling to face me. "You lived with that all summer?"

I grabbed my boots and sat beside him. "He didn't even get to accusing me of being a drug addict and alcoholic yet."

He put an arm around me. "You know they're just worried about you, right?"

"Yes, but they can't dictate every detail of my life." Truth be told, they governed my decisions more than I liked to admit. I was still enrolled in the chemistry-language double major program when every bone of my body knew I hated the science. But I was too scared to break away from that safety net. I wasn't sure what I would do if I decided government service wasn't for me.

He kissed me. "I love you. I think you're making the right decision. If your parents drive you nuts it won't be helpful to be with them."

"Thanks." I kissed him back.

🐦 🐦 🐦

Lila and Marissa rode with Doug and me, and the rest of my family took the rental car to Paula's condo. The sweet earthy smell of ham, rice, and beans greeted us as we entered her home.

Paula gathered me into a hug. "I didn't know you were making ham."

"Of course." She released me. "It's your favorite, right?"

She introduced everyone, and we moved into the dining room. Paula served orange juice and champagne, and I glanced at Dad to see his reaction. Looking at him from a distance, I took in his whole countenance. His still held his face taut as creases framed his eyes and his brow furrowed, but his eyes were red and his shoulders slumped. Both he and Mom looked tired, and I felt sad that their alumni barbecue weekend was tainted with Thursday's event.

We found seats around her large table, and Paula's husband, Gary, said the blessing. The meal was good, and conversation seemed to flow easily. Michael had stayed through the weekend, and Mr. Taylor would stay until after the plea hearing. Peter's image flashed through my mind, and I cut off my worry about going to the courthouse, refocusing on the brunch conversation. Chris, Doug's oldest brother, was planning a wedding for December, and Paula was reviewing the details for my family.

After the meal, we helped Paula clean up and then adjourned to their rec room. A few minutes before the University officials were scheduled to arrive, Mr. Taylor asked my family to join him in the study.

He addressed me first, "I believe they will have many options for you as far as continuing school at Northwestern. Have you thought about what you want to do?"

"I'm staying here, starting the quarter, just as I'd planned."

"Okay—" His answer was cut off by the sound of the bell.

We all walked to the foyer. I wasn't sure what I'd expected, but I was surprised to see such a big group waiting in the vestibule. Mr. Taylor had already met with them and introduced us to the Vice President for University Relations and Dean of the College of Arts and Sciences, who I recognized from the hospital, the President of the University, Sara, and Dr. Milner, Head of Mental Health Services.

I'd rather have been hiding under a rock than be in a meeting with all these University officials, but I took a deep breath, smiled, and shook their hands. Mr. Taylor led us to Paula's study. The president offered his regrets, assuring us the campus was safe and they were establishing new guidelines for reviewing applicants' histories.

I sat and listened, shook my head, and said thank you. It felt like I was in a dream state, like I was watching a movie or floating above the scene observing. The room became too hot and crowded, and I fidgeted with my sweater. It was real. It had happened to me. I was in a room with the University President.

The VP of Relations spoke next, again offering his regret and shock at the incident. "Ms. Avery, what we need to know from you—"

Hearing my name brought me out of my fog. I smiled at him. "Yes."

"Are you going public with your identity?"

I looked to Mr. Taylor and back to the VP. "I'm going to the plea hearing tomorrow. We are assuming I won't be able to keep my identity secret after that."

"Do you want to be a part of a press conference or any University statements concerning the incident?"

"No."

"We can protect your information from our end then."

Dr. Milner spoke next, reviewing her role and the department's support programs. "Have you thought about your classes for this quarter?"

"Yes, I'm keeping my schedule the way it is."

She looked at the Dean and then back to me. "You have a heavy course load." She took some paperwork from the bag she had beside her. "Organic Chemistry II, Physics II, Japanese II, Intro to Macroeconomics, Chinese Literature II, and Calculus IV."

"Yes, that's right. I need all those courses."

She looked at the dean and then me again. "Well, we have the two-week drop and add period, and then we have the six-week drop allowance period if you need it."

The injuries derailed rowing season, but I was not going to let Peter ruin my college plan. "Thank you."

"Okay." She looked around the room, reaching in her bag and pulling out a couple of stacks of pamphlets. She held a set out to me and then passed the stacks to the others. "I brought some information about our support system, how families and friends can help, and what you may experience as a victim."

I hated attention—I'd always hated attention, good or bad really—but I found myself at the center of it yet again. I wanted the meeting to be over. I stood up. "Thank you for coming." I scanned the faces of the University reps. "I really appreciate it."

Dr. Milner folded her hands in front of her. "If you have any questions, my contact information is on the back of the pamphlets."

I was amazed and grateful Dad had stayed silent. His eyes were fixed on one of the pamphlets. Perhaps the literature distracted him from his quest to have me move back to Champaign. As I was about to look away, he lifted his chin and met my gaze. For the first time that weekend, the creases around his eyes had smoothed and his jaw hung loose. He'd turned off his officer mode, and his face only seemed to hold concern.

Sara approached me and took my hand. "I'm so sorry," she said in a half whisper. "You should really email or call Dr. Milner. She'd be a good person for you to talk to."

"I was hoping to talk to you."

"I know we have a history, but Dr. Milner really is the expert in this area."

I turned the pamphlets in my hand. *Great*, I thought, *just what I want to do with my time while I'm not rowing or running.* I admonished myself for the sarcastic mental attitude. That point of view wasn't going to get me anywhere. "Okay, I'll call her."

She hugged me. "Stop in to see me whenever you need."

"Thanks." I squeezed her back.

Each of the other University representatives took turns shaking my hand. Dr. Milner urged me to email her, and I told her I would. The dean was last in the line and offered an open door as Sara had.

Watching them leave, I snuggled into Doug's arms. He held me for a moment, kissed the top of my head and released me. I turned to see Dad standing there.

He bounced the pamphlets in his hand. "I still don't agree with your plan, but I won't bug you anymore. Please see Dr. Milner and go to the support group."

"I will."

He hit his leg with the documents. "Okay, how long do you want us to stay?"

"I don't know. I could use a day of rest before classes start."

"We'll head out this afternoon then."

I felt horrible wanting them to go, but I needed space. "Thanks for coming. It really does mean a lot."

"Wouldn't have it any other way."

I snuck a peek at the brochure Dad had been reading as we walked down the hall. The first bullet point under the heading

WHAT FAMILIES AND FRIEND CAN DO TO SUPPORT A VICTIM
READ: RESPECT AND ACCEPT DECISIONS OF THE VICTIM. Victim,
the term stuck in my head. Did I feel like a victim? Certainly I
was annoyed at the disruption of my life. But I had never been a
victim. I would not be a victim. Peter did not get to win.

We joined the group in the rec room as they made travel
plans. Lila decided to get a ride back to our apartment with
Tia. I hugged each of them as they left. Mom was last in line.
She squeezed me tight, and when she stepped back, tears were
in her eyes.

"I really will be okay."

"I wish I could kiss you and make it all better like when you
were little."

"I know, Mom. I'll see you next week, right?

"Yes, Saturday." She hugged me again and planted a kiss on
my good cheek. "I love you."

"I love you too."

After the elevator doors closed, Doug pulled me to him. "You
look beat."

I covered my face with my hands. "I'm a terrible person. That
was mean."

"What was mean?"

"To send them away."

He took my hands in his. "What do you need right now?"

"I'm tired. I just want to rest."

"You're not going to be able to do that with them here. They
understand."

"I hope so. I feel horrible."

He tugged at my hands. "Let's get you a nap."

We walked to his room where he pulled the shades down. "What do you want to do tonight?"

"Can we stay here?"

"Yes." He rubbed his hand down my back. "Do you want to go to Mass?"

I took a minute to think. How did I feel about God right now? Indifferent? I'd been through the whole God letting bad things happen to good people after my accident last year. Things happen, I'd decided, and what Peter did was the same. Doug always went to the chapel when he was upset. It'd been ingrained in him since childhood. "I could wear my glasses, and could we sit in the back? I don't want to talk to anyone."

"Course, we'll sneak in at the last minute and pop out right after."

I slipped my shoes off and lay down. Doug grabbed his computer out of his bag. "I'm going to do some work."

"It's Monday morning there, right?"

"They gave me a break because I told them my fiancée was attacked and in the hospital, but I still want to check in."

"Fiancée?"

He kissed me. "You're wearing a ring I gave you. It was simpler and will give me more leeway to come see you."

"Thank you." I rested my head on the pillow beside him, wondering if I would really be able to sleep. The list of things I needed to do started growing. I'd planned on getting books on Friday, so I still had that task. And there was the trial at four the following day. I needed to email Dr. Milner, get the support group meeting time, and schedule a session with her. I had to figure out how to sit in my classes with all my bruising and go unnoticed. How was it going to feel to be on campus? When was I going to attempt going to the fraternity house?

I squinted my eyes until white spots formed in the middle of the blackness. I pulled the blanket up, and Doug tucked it around my shoulders, resting his arm on my back. I repeated the strategy I used when I couldn't get to sleep as a kid. First, I imagined my feet getting heavy and sinking into the mattress and then my legs, my torso, and my arms. I focused on each body part, and by the time I reached my head, it felt like a brick on the pillow.

🕊 🕊 🕊

When I awoke, Doug still sat beside me, his fingers pressing buttons on the keyboard, eyes darting across the screen. "You didn't sleep long." He kissed my head.

"What time is it?"

"Four, I was going to wake you in fifteen minutes."

I pointed towards the bathroom. At the sink, I brushed my teeth and freshened up. He got up and did the same, and we met Paula and Gary in the foyer. We walked the couple blocks to the church and hung back until it was time for the service to start. After the priest went in, we snuck in the back, finding seats in the last pew. It felt wrong to have on sunglasses, so I took them off and pulled my hair down close to my cheeks. The ritual of the service was comforting as it always was for me.

Doug squeezed my hand, and I realized I was in my own world, hypnotized by the wave of people moving towards the front of the church to receive Mass. I shook my head at him, and he dropped my hand, turning to join the line. Maybe I'd go to the Catholic Center on campus later in the week. Doug and I could go together. Father would serve us communion whenever we stopped by.

Confession. I hadn't been in a few weeks, since Doug left for Japan. Reviewing the three weeks in my head, under-age drinking was the only sin I remembered committing. I'd never gotten drunk, but I was rationalizing. Honoring your mother and father was a tricky one for me. Did it apply when you were an adult? They thought I shouldn't be in a relationship with Doug, which was a constant issue. Things were good between us before they left. I didn't dread texting or talking with them, which was a major breakthrough.

People from our pew approached, and I stepped into the aisle to let them take their seats. Doug took my hand as we knelt on the kneelers. The priest stored the host, and we left before the final blessing, waiting on the walk for Paula and Gary. The sky darkened, and I shivered, realizing I hadn't been outside after sunset since the attack. The blue streetlight in front of the church flickered, and Doug wrapped an arm around my shoulder.

We walked to the street as streams of people came out of the church. Paula skipped socializing with her friends, and we started back to the condo.

She took my hand. "I'm glad you felt well enough to come."

"Me too."

"Do you want to order Mrs. Chen's takeout for dinner?"

"No, I'm not that hungry. I can have soup or a sandwich. You guys can, though. Don't make choices around me."

"No, sweetie, I just knew it was one of your favorites."

"Thanks," I said, forcing a smile. Doug and I had gone to Mrs. Chen's on our first date. Linking the restaurant with this weekend would be wrong.

Back at the condo, Paula insisted on making Cuban sandwiches with the ham from brunch. It was relaxing sitting at the counter with Doug's family. After dinner, Michael and Mr. Taylor left. I sat staring at the wall, wondering what I was supposed to be doing. Then I remembered Northie. I felt my pockets and found them empty.

I grabbed Doug's arm. "Where's my phone?" Even that was an insane question. I always had my phone with me. Where was my brain?

"I think you left it in my room."

"I didn't take it to the church? Is anyone watching Northie? I totally forgot." Tears formed in my eyes, and I quickened my pace, almost jogging down the hall. What if something happened to Lila, my parents, or Marissa? What if Northie had been in his crate all day? Thoughts of the multiple possibilities of tragic events raced through my brain.

"Zack is watching Northie. I told you that."

I flung open the door and flipped on the light, scanning the room. With water pooling in my eyes, everything blurred.

Doug crossed the room ahead of me, reaching the bedside table and picking up my phone. "It's right here."

"Oh God, thanks." I turned away from him, wiping the tears on my sleeve, and swiped the screen, bringing up my messages. My hands shook as I scrolled through the texts. A tear landed in the middle of the device, and I dried it on my jeans. My reaction was irrational, but I still couldn't stop the thoughts racing through my mind. What if something happened and I didn't have my phone?

Doug came up behind me and put hand on my back. "Amanda—"

I spun to face him. "I forgot about Northie." I couldn't stop the tears from forming.

He wrapped his arms around me and pulled me into his chest. "It's okay."

I shook my head on his shirt. "No, it's not. I walk him three times a day, feed him, make sure his has fresh water, and play with him. I do it every day, but I forgot."

"He's okay. Zack is taking care of him."

I let him hold me. My chest heaved with sobs and pain shot through my side with each breath. His grip on my arms was the only thing that kept me up. Finally he slid his hands to my face and lifted my chin to look at him.

"Talk to me."

"What if I can't take care of him? Can't handle a trial and school?"

His arms wound round me again, and he whispered in my ear, "If you can't, we'll deal with it. But you can. I know you can. You don't have to do it alone. You have me, Lila, Kate, Mark, Bill, Zack, my dad, your family, and a whole University who will help you. Remember what you said? He doesn't get to win. No one is going to let him win. Whatever you need to get through this, we'll get through it together."

He was right. Peter did not get to win. People would help. I could let people help. I brushed my cheeks with a sleeve. "I'm sorry. Is it okay if we stay here?"

"Of course."

"Okay, I have to call Lila and make sure she's okay." I wiped my phone on my pants again and tapped the screen to call her number.

She answered immediately. "Hi, Amanda."

"Hi." I tried to steady my voice. My hands were still trembling, and I stuck the free one in my pocket and crossed the room to sit on the bed. "Are you okay? Is Northie okay? Doug said Zack was watching him."

"Yes, he's good. I'm good. Are you okay?"

"Sure." I wiped my nose. "I thought we might stay here tonight. I wanted to make sure you weren't alone. Is Ross there?"

"He's here. Don't worry about me. I'll be good."

"I'll text you in the morning."

"Okay, sweetie, sleep tight."

"You too. I love you."

"Love you too. Bye."

I ended the call, putting the phone on the bed. Doug sat down beside me. "See, everything is fine."

"I'm sorry. Forgetting about Northie put me over the edge."

"I think you're allowed."

"I don't want to be allowed." I picked up my phone and looked at the time. It was only after eight, but I was exhausted. "I'm going to take a shower and go to bed. Will you sit with me?"

"Are you kidding? I'm not leaving your side."

"Thanks." I squeezed his hand and looked up at him. "Oh God." I ran my hand through my hair. "I must look hideous."

"Never." He cleared the hair from my face.

"Thank you. I love you." I kissed him. He pressed his lips into mine, and Peter's face flashed through my mind.

No! He did not get to ruin this. I kissed Doug's lips again and again until I only thought of him, until the kisses felt like they used to. When I pulled back, he squeezed my hand.

"Was that okay? You seemed tense. I wasn't sure—"

"No, it was good. I love you." I kissed him again and stood up, pointing to the bathroom. "I'm going to shower."

"Okay, I'm going to shower in the guest room."

I grabbed some clothes from my satchel and went into the bathroom. I turned on the water to let it get hot, leaned against the counter, taking slow breaths until I was sure I could stand without trembling. The warm water and steam, the smell of the soap, and the blue hues of the room, relaxed me. My skin was red when I came out, and my hair had formed ringlets. My head pounded, but my psyche was more stable. I spread lotion onto my skin and dressed in my pajamas.

When I entered Doug's room, he was sitting on the bed, tapping on the keys of his laptop. I slid in beside him.

"I have to get some work done. Will it bother you?"

"No." I snuggled in close to him.

"I love you." He leaned down and kissed me.

"I love you too." I lay my head on the pillow and let the dull light from the screen and quiet rapping of the keys lull me to sleep.

When I woke, he was still in the same place, but his arm stretched across my stomach, his head beside mine. I loved to watch him sleep, breathing in and out, but I had to get up. I inched out from under him and tip-toed to the bathroom.

Afterwards, I went to the kitchen, finding Paula hovering over the coffee maker.

"Morning."

"Oh, Amanda, you're quiet as a mouse." She pointed at the pot. "It'll be ready in a minute." She wrapped an arm around me. "How are you?"

"I'm okay."

"I have to get to work, but you guys are welcome to hang out as long as you need. Use whatever you want."

"Thanks." I sat on a barstool. The pot dinged, and she poured coffee for both of us. Paula set a tray of pastries in front of me, and we sat in silence as she buttered her croissant and I picked at mine.

She got up and put her dishes in the sink. "I'll be thinking about you today. Be strong."

"Thanks."

"Are you guys staying here tonight?"

"Probably not, I have classes tomorrow."

"Okay, call me and let me know how it goes, okay?" She wrapped her arms around me, hugged me, and kissed my cheek.

I forced myself to eat half the croissant and went through my mental task list. Books, Dr. Milner, trial—that was enough for one day. I tiptoed back into the bedroom to retrieve my phone and padded back to the kitchen. There were already messages from Mom, Dad, Marissa and Tia, Lila, and Elise. It was still early, and I decided to phone Mom before she left for work. I kept the conversation short and then sent a group text to Dad and Tia.

Lila messaged she was going to be at the frat house all day and would meet us back at the apartment for dinner. I was happy that she'd decided to go to the house and texted back and forth with her for a few minutes. I replied to Elise's message and then checked my email. All my tutoring clients had agreed to skip their sessions for the week. I looked up the books I'd need for my courses and copied them to my notes file for later.

"Good morning." I dropped my phone upon hearing Doug's voice. "Sorry." He kissed my temple and slid his phone onto the counter.

"Hi, did you get enough sleep?"

"Yes, you?"

"I slept like the dead again."

"That's good." He took a mug from the shelf, poured himself some coffee, and sat down next to me. "What's up?"

"Figuring out my books."

"Do you want to go to the bookstore today?"

"No, but yes."

"Dad wants to meet at your apartment at two."

I nodded and sucked in a deep breath. "Okay."

"We should wait until after rush hour to head to Evanston."

We both dressed and then settled in the rec room. He typed away on his laptop while I surfed through the channels trying to find a movie. I passed a local news station and had to double back. A reporter stood in front of the fraternity house broadcasting. I didn't even hear her words as my eyes were fixed on the picture inset into the top left of the screen. I nudged Doug and pointed at the television. In the video, the paramedics wheeled a stretcher towards an ambulance parked on the fraternity house lawn. My face was turned the opposite way, but my hair hung at least a foot down the side. As they lifted me in, the paramedic gathered my hair and laid it beside me.

Doug ran his hand down my leg. "Dad said to be prepared. There are going to be a lot of reporters this afternoon."

I refocused on the TV. "A plea hearing is set for four this afternoon at the Evanston courthouse."

My breath caught in my lungs, and a sharp pain shot through my side. My heart thumped and then didn't. I put my fist to my chest and forced out my breath. Thump.

"Are you okay?"

"Yeah."

"Okay, I've noticed you've been doing that since I got here. What's going on?"

"I think it's anxiety, sort of like a panic attack."

"What is?"

I didn't want to tell him, didn't want him to drag me to the doctor where they would tell me nothing was wrong with me except I was going crazy. "Only a little shortness of breath."

"Like all of a sudden."

"It's no big deal. It just feels like my stitches catch or something."

"Okay, well, do you think everything is okay? When is your follow-up appointment?"

"Thursday. Yeah, I'm good."

"Do you want to talk about that?" He slid the remote from my hand and pointed at the TV.

I shrugged and raked my hair back from my face. "Your dad seems to have things under control."

"Okay." He shrugged and turned his attention back to his computer screen.

It was a little after nine, and I walked to his room to call Dr. Milner. I'd hoped to leave a message, but she answered after the first ring. She asked how I was doing and if I had seen the news. She wanted to know if I had scheduled a campus visit. I told her about my plan to go to the bookstore and be in classes the following day. The roads to those locations didn't pass the fraternity house, so I felt comfortable with the trips.

"I usually like to be able to talk to a new person before the group meeting, but we are slammed with this incident. Do you feel up for joining us tomorrow? We'll have to schedule the private session for later in the week."

Way to jump in, I thought, but agreed to attend the meeting. I'd rather be a new person at a first meeting than a new person at a second anyway. As much as I dreaded talking about the incident, it felt like a safety net to have the meetings on my calendar. I didn't want to burden my friends further.

I packed everything in my satchel and found Doug where I left him. He closed his computer and took my hand. "Want to watch a movie?"

"Sure." We found an old James Bond movie, and I snuggled into him. It was a good distraction, and it felt nice to do nothing. The movie ended, and we both stood and stretched.

He wrapped a hand around mine. "You ready to go get books."

Although hiding at his mom's condo and watching movies for the rest of the week didn't sound like a bad option, I nodded.

Chapter 6

We gathered our bags and made our way down to the deck. It was a sunny warm day for September, and he drove along the shoreline. I looked at my ring and smiled, remembering the day he'd given it to me five weeks before. As we neared Evanston, he reached out and took my hand.

"I was thinking to drive by Peter's apartment so you'll know where it is. Then you can avoid the area."

It made sense. The street name and a dot on the map hadn't helped me place the address. After a few turns, he slowed and pointed towards an apartment building.

"There."

"Okay." I scanned the area, my heartbeat echoing in my ears faster and faster, wondering what I'd do if he were outside or in a passing car. I chewed on my nail, recognizing a coffee shop where I'd met a new client last week. Even farther along was a shopping center with the sporting goods store Zack frequented. In another few minutes, Doug made a right turn. My apartment complex was only blocks from the intersection.

"Two point one miles. He's two point one miles from you and a little farther from the campus."

"That's what your dad said. Thanks." I ran my hands down my jeans and stretched my legs out straight.

"You look freaked out."

"I don't want to think about seeing him randomly." An image of his face morphing into a skull popped into my head, and I squeezed my eyes shut. I was safe. I opened them again, focusing on the blue sky and the bright sun. "I thought we were going to the bookstore."

"You seemed off. I didn't want to push you."

My hands went to the dash. "I need to get my books. Classes start tomorrow."

"Okay," he slowed and turned into my apartment complex. Pulling into a spot right past the guard station, he shut off the ignition. "Are you sure you're ready to go to campus?"

I rolled my eyes. My mantra echoed in my head. *He is not going to win.* "Yes, I want to get my books. I need my books." If I did nothing else this quarter, I would do well in my courses. I would get closer to graduating and to being with Doug.

"Okay." He put the car in reverse and backed up. He turned onto the main road, the same one I'd taken that night. In a few blocks, he turned onto the main campus. There were a couple of news vans parked on the grass, and I stopped myself from thinking about what the scene at the courthouse might be like later.

I put my hand on his shoulder. "See, I'm fine."

"Ooh, rah." He rolled his eyes.

I pulled my hand away. "What's that supposed to mean?"

"What doesn't kill you makes you stronger. You're nothing if not your father's daughter."

The comment prickled my nerves and bumps formed on my arm. "I am *not* like my dad."

"You're exactly like him. You're on opposite sides right now, so you don't see it."

He stopped the car, and I realized we were already at the bookstore parking lot. "Were you distracting me?"

"Yes."

I wasn't going to fight with him, especially about my dad. I opened the door and crossed to Doug's side of the car, scanning the parking lot. "See, I'm fine with my huge sunglasses." I slid them up my nose. "Plus, I'm wearing the same sweatshirt as every other NU student. I am nobody."

He took a step forward and pulled me into him. My stomach turned. *No,* I told myself, *this is Doug.* I forced myself up on my toes and kissed him.

He backed away, dropping my hand. "Your palm is sweaty."

I pictured a sandy beach to drive out the image of Peter's thin lips. "Quick movements may be hard for a while."

"Okay, got it, slow and easy."

He held out his hand. I rubbed mine on my pants and put it in his. Through the windows I could see the bookstore was jam packed. *Deep breaths*, I thought. No one knew who I was.

As soon as he opened the door, the smell hit me. Smoke, sweat, and cologne odors overtook my senses. Stopping, I held my breath and covered my nose with my sleeve. I felt cold and hot at the same time, and beads of sweat formed on my forehead. I turned my head, searching for his face. No, no, no, it wasn't anywhere but in my head. Someone touched my shoulder, and I jutted my arm out. "Stop."

"Amanda, it's me." Doug stood in front of me.

I wasn't even a foot into the bookstore. *Get a grip, Amanda.* I pulled my sleeve over my hand and held it to my nose.

"You okay?"

I looked him in the eyes and nodded. "Yes, I'll follow you."

"Okay." I took it his hand and we weaved through the crowd. I molded my body into the spaces. Every time someone bumped me, I jerked away and clutched his hand tighter. He looked back at me and pointed ahead. "Upstairs?"

I nodded and followed. On the stairs, it was less crowded, and he slid in beside me. "What's going on?"

"The smell of all the people mixed together..." I shuddered.

"And?"

"He smelled like smoke and sweat."

"Well, that's something to work around."

"Let's get the books and get out of here."

The literature and economics books were upstairs, but all the science and math books were downstairs. On the lower level, we fought the freshman crowd at the front of the store as we made our way to the higher level course books. He piled the big books in his arms, and I carried the smaller ones, finding the line for the cashier.

The guy in front of me reeked of smoke and sweat. Didn't people shower anymore? I covered my nose with my sleeve and tapped my foot as we waited. How was I going to be able to concentrate in a class or go to the gym if Peter's image flashed through my mind every time someone smelled like him? What a cruel element to have embedded in my psyche!

"Next." A guy behind the counter held up his hand, and Doug nudged me from behind. I stepped forward, grateful I hadn't seen anyone I knew yet. "Nice glasses," the cashier commented when I put the books in front of him.

"Thanks." I let Doug add the others to the pile. I'd have to come up with some line for those kinds of comments, an excuse to offer if I saw someone I knew, and a reason to need glasses inside a lecture room. I handed the guy my credit card when he'd totaled the books. Doug took the books, backed into the door and held it open for me as we left.

"Not too bad, Ms. Shades, you made it."

"I guess."

"What's that thing where people deal with phobias, like de-sensitization? Maybe that's all it will take for you to feel more comfortable."

Yeah, that and a total brain erase, I thought but nodded in agreement.

We made our way to the car and back towards my apartment, passing the campus entrance where even more media vans had convened. We crossed the road that led to Peter's apartment, and I started making a mental list of substitutes for the businesses on that street.

In my living room, Northie barked from his crate. Doug opened it, and Northie bounded out. I couldn't shed my sweatshirt quick enough, as it seemed to have soaked up the smells from the bookstore. I gathered the rest of my laundry and started a load of light-colored items, adding in double the amount of fabric softener.

"You want to go on a short walk before my dad gets here?" Doug held up Northie's leash.

"I have to shower." I held a handful of hair to my nose, and it too smelled of smoke. "And wash my hair."

"Okay."

"You think I'm crazy, don't you?"

"Whatever you need." He bent down and hooked the leash to Northie's collar. After he left, I locked the door behind him and went to my room to shower. It seemed too quiet, and I started some music on my phone. I washed quickly so as to have time to dry my hair out straight. By the time I had dressed, Doug was back with Northie. They both sat on my futon beside me while I blew out my hair.

As I was finishing, the doorbell rang. Doug opened the door for his Dad. I joined them at the dining table where he'd stacked his files. "Good." He pointed to me. "Nice outfit. You can wear that this afternoon. We want you to look like a normal student."

"I am a normal student." I looked down at my white tank and tan corduroys.

"Yes, well, you know what I mean. You don't need to dress up. He'll wear a suit. They have money from what I can tell. Their lawyer tells me he will plead innocent, and they are requesting a jury trial. But anything can happen."

"Okay, what do we do?" I sat in the chair opposite him.

"You don't need to do anything except give us as much information as you can." He set the police report in front of me. "You were very thorough. Is there anything else you remembered? Take your time and read through it again."

I held the paper up and took a deep breath. Doug stood up. "How about some lunch?" He moved to the kitchen and looked in the cabinets and opened the fridge. "Do you guys eat?"

"We usually shop on Sunday."

He pulled some deli meat, cheese, lettuce, and a tomato out of the fridge. "Will this do. Dad?"

His dad looked up from his computer. "Yes, thanks."

I picked up the report and walked to the window. Sitting down on the floor next to Northie, I leaned my back against the chair. Scanning the words, they came to life again, and I saw the parking lot outside the bar, his form leaning against my car. The brick fraternity house framed by trees glowed orange in the setting sun. The leaves crunched beneath my feet. His stark image danced through my head, and a skull glowed in the light of my phone.

When I finished, I set the pages in my lap and pulled my thumb from my mouth, realizing teeth marks were indented into the tip. Looking outside at the blue sky and the bright sun, I tried to purge the images from my mind. "He'd threatened other girls. He didn't say it in so many words. It's just a feeling I got from him. Why would he say you better not remember? Why would he threaten me unless he'd had success with it before?"

Mr. Taylor stood and walked towards me. "You may be right. I'll have someone look into prior cases."

"How many man hours are we talking if this goes to a full jury trial?"

"Three, four months, two to three lawyers. I'm going to put Chris and some junior lawyers on it."

"Doesn't the DA appoint an attorney?"

"Yes, but they don't have the funds to uncover everything, know everything about his life, his parents, details about any prior incidences, girls that were paid off."

"I'm not sure I can ask you to do this."

"You're not. I'm doing it without you asking. This guy deserves to be punished to the full extent of the law. I'm not letting him get away with anything less." He pointed at the floor as he spoke.

"Thank you. And thank you for helping me today."

"Either Chris or I will be here every time you have to be in court. This is not going to be easy. They're going to try to paint you as an unstable, loose girl."

I took in a deep breath, and the all-too-familiar thump radiated through my chest. I pressed my fingers into my sternum.

"Again?" came the sound of Doug's voice. I looked at him and our eyes met. "You have to get that checked out." He pointed at me.

"What's wrong?" Mr. Taylor looked between us.

"She's having these anxiety attacks." Doug motioned towards me.

"I'll be fine." I got up and handed the statement to Mr. Taylor.

"Anything else beside the other girls?"

"When he mentioned his dad, he spit the words like he hated the man."

"That's common with angry teens."

I sat with Doug and his dad at the table. Doug slid a sandwich towards me. As we ate, Mr. Taylor reviewed the plan for the plea hearing. We'd take his Mercedes and park in the back. They had reserved spots for attorneys in the garage, and the entrance wouldn't be far from the car. Afterwards, we'd take the same route out the back door of the courtroom and down to the garage.

"Wear your sunglasses into the courtroom. The judge will ask you to remove them, and it will go on record."

I wasn't sure what I was more scared of, my reaction to seeing Peter or the media circus. At least Lila's dad had insisted on her living in a gated complex. The reporters wouldn't be allowed past the guard house.

I texted my family and Lila again while we waited the next half hour. Afterwards, I freshened up and got my sweater. Looking in the mirror, I didn't like my outfit and switched it to darker pants and a beige sweater. Mr. Taylor changed his shirt and put on a vest and suit jacket that matched his pants.

We rode to the courthouse in silence. "Okay, here we go." Mr. Taylor's voice brought me out of my thoughts, and I wiped my wet thumb on a tissue from my bag and looked out the opposite window. The building's steps were covered with reporters and cameras. My leg involuntarily started to bounce.

Doug reached across the seat and took my hand. "You don't have to go in there. I can drive you home."

"No." My thumb went to my mouth again, and I yanked it out. "I need to do this."

His Dad turned into the back lot, stopped at the security gate, and showed his identification and credentials. I'd never been inside a courtroom except on a field trip in grade school and wondered if the one I was about to go in would look the same.

Mr. Taylor found a space in the parking garage, and I locked my bag with my phone in the trunk. Slipping my hand in Doug's we rode the elevator to the first floor. The doors opened to a hall packed with people.

"Follow right behind me. Don't say a thing to the reporters. Doug, you stay behind her," Mr. Taylor instructed. They formed a pocket in the crowd as we moved to the entrance. Face after face popped into my view, and hand after hand armed with recording devices were thrust in front of me.

"Are you affiliated with the Scalini hearing? Are you the victim? Do you know the victim? Are you the attorney for the victim?" My heart rate jumped, beads of sweat formed on my forehead, and my breathing became labored. *No*, I told myself, *this is okay, you are okay, you can do this, ooh-rah. What doesn't kill you makes you stronger, remember.*

As soon as the courtroom doors were closed behind me, it was quiet. The walls were painted white and the high ceiling made the chamber feel immense. My boot heels echoed as I followed Doug's dad down the aisle. Nearing the bench, he stopped and motioned for us to sit in the front row. The district attorney approached us and introduced himself. Then, Mr. Taylor joined the DA at the prosecution table.

Doug held out his hand to me when we sat down, and I slid mine into it. He looked at his watch. "Five minutes till the hearing."

I nodded, looking straight towards the front of the room at the judge's bench. It was a large hall, and we were probably twenty feet from the bench. A half wall separated us from the attorney's tables, the juror's box, and the bench.

Doug squeezed my hand. "You're trembling."

"Sorry, I'm okay."

A roar of voices came from the back of the room, and I turned toward the noise. The doors opened and four men, a woman, and Peter entered the room. The woman had her arm around his shoulders, and I guessed she must be his mom.

Doug leaned into me. "That's him?"

"Yes." I snapped my head around and aimed it at the front of the room.

The group appeared in my peripheral vision. One of the men and the woman sat down in the front row opposite us. The other three men, lawyers I assumed, and Peter took seats at the defense table. The lawyer on the end unbuttoned his jacket, stood, and crossed the aisle to shake hands with Mr. Taylor and the DA. He turned his head slightly to face me and then crossed back to his table, buttoning his jacket and sitting down again. The other two attorneys at the table huddled around Peter, talking to him.

I couldn't take my eyes off them, off him. It wasn't a bad dream I would wake up from. A boy I had been nice to, gone out of my way to talk to, cracked my ribs, punched me in the face, and left me for half-dead. My side throbbed as my breaths came in and were forced out. The room dimmed, and my hands were suddenly wet. I blinked my eyes and looked up at the ceiling. Wiping my hands down my pants, I formed them into fists. Doug had told Mr. Taylor I was good at acting as if everything were fine. He was clear that I should be natural. As tempting as it was, I reminded myself I wasn't supposed to detach.

I bit my lip and wrapped a hand around Doug's arm. His muscle was hard as a rock, and it distracted me from my panic. "You okay?"

"It's taking everything in me not to run over and hit that guy."

I turned Doug's arm over and checked his watch. "Two more minutes." Peter still hadn't looked at me, and I prayed I didn't have to see his thin lips form the smirk etched in my memory. I couldn't get the sound of his voice out of my head, and to hear it live again I feared would cement it into my psyche. If I couldn't block it out, pretend it wasn't real, I wanted it done. Mr. Taylor said it would be short—fifteen, twenty minutes at most. My leg bobbed, and Doug set his hand on it.

A door in front of us opened, and a woman in a suit and two police officers came into the room. The woman set a laptop on a table beside the bench and sat down. One police officer stood behind her, and the other crossed to stand on the other side of the bench.

I looked towards Mr. Taylor. He finished his discussion with the DA and the junior lawyer beside him, and then he turned and nodded.

"All rise for Judge Akin," one officer said, projecting his voice though the room.

Tricia Copeland

I fought looking towards Peter. Was he scared? Did he feel remorse? What would he plead? Mr. Taylor had said they would either plead guilty and hope for leniency or plead innocent and request a jury trial.

The door opened again, and a woman in a black robe stepped into the chamber. Her eyes showed no emotion, and her lips formed a tight line on her face, as she approached the bench. Stepping behind it, she appeared above it, rolled back the tall chair, and sat down.

She placed a folder on the desk and opened it. Straightening her robe, she looked up. "Counselors." She nodded towards the DA and Mr. Taylor and then to the group of lawyers at the defense table. Peter straightened his back and sat forward in his chair. I forced myself to look back at her.

Her chin lifted towards the other side of the room, and then she turned towards us. As her eyes landed on me, she sighed. She raised her hand. "Miss, I've closed this courtroom to avoid the show outside. This isn't a runway. Please show some respect and remove your sunglasses."

I looked at Mr. Taylor, who tilted his head slightly towards me. Putting a hand to the frames, I removed my sunglasses, set them in my lap, and looked back at the judge. She looked down at her papers and then back at me, moving her glasses down her nose.

"Miss, can you state your name for the record?"

My hands trembled, but I balled them into fists and swallowed. "Amanda Avery."

Again she studied the pages in front of her. She removed her glasses and leaned towards the clerk. "Please record that Miss

Avery is the alleged victim. She has significant bruising on her left cheek bone." She put her glasses back on and then sat back up straight. "Gentleman, proceed."

The DA stood. "As you can see, Judge Akin, Miss Avery has extensive bruising on her face. She sustained two broken ribs, requiring repair via surgical procedure. Mr. Peter Scalini is charged with aggravated assault and sexual battery. In addition to the witness's testimony, the state has evidence of Mr. Scalini's clothing and hair samples at the scene and on Ms. Avery's clothes. The state also has surveillance footage from the night of the crime of Mr. Scalini entering his residence hall and then leaving with a backpack. The same backpack was on his person when he was arrested in a bus station on the south side of Chicago. The state believes we have ample evidence for a conviction."

"Thank you, Mr. Maram."

The judge's eyes rose to me, and then she turned her head towards the other side of the room.

"Counsel for the accused, what does your client plea?"

I looked to Peter, who jerked his head to the front. I was grateful I didn't have to look into those small dark eyes. I didn't want to know whether they showed remorse, anger, or nothing. His voice echoed in my head. *You better hope you don't remember.*

I shivered, and Doug put his arm around my shoulder. The lawyer seated at the end of Peter's table stood. "The witness's testimony is hearsay and inadmissible. The defendant pleads innocent and requests a jury trial."

I looked at Peter, and he turned his head towards me. His face was stoic, not a muscle moved. He blinked and looked back to the front of the room, and I followed suit.

"Are there any other requests?" The judge looked towards the DA.

"No, madam," he said.

She picked up her gavel and knocked it on the desk. "Jury trial is set to begin Monday, January sixth." The knock of the gavel on the wood and her words echoed though the chamber, and then there was silence. She stood and the lawyers stood, and Doug and I followed suit. She walked to the door and left the room. The clerk followed her out, and it was done.

Mr. Taylor shook the DA's hand, and walked towards us, motioning us into the aisle. Doug moved towards his father, and I followed. He corralled us to the doors and then stopped. "Sunglasses." He pointed at me, and I put them on my face. "Ready?" I nodded.

He opened the door and slipped through, me on his heels. The foyer was quieter than before, but the chatter grew as we made our way through the crowd. Soon, we were accosted by a wall of people thrusting arms in our path. I shielded my head and my ribs seared in response. Behind me, Doug kept a hand on my back. Mr. Taylor was trying to make a path, but we were blocked.

He spun around to face me and bent to speak into my ear, "We're not going to make it to the car without them trailing us. If we make a statement now, they may leave you alone."

It didn't seem fair. The media storm was winning. They'd bullied us—me—and won. But I knew it was true. Someone would follow us, and then they'd be camped out at my apartment complex.

I nodded. "Okay."

Mr. Taylor issued a shrill whistle and held his palm high in the air. The roar of the crowd slowly subsided. "We'll take questions out front for five minutes."

The crowd parted and allowed us to walk out the doors. At the top stairs Mr. Taylor stopped in front of another small army of reporters.

"We'll take questions for five minutes," he repeated to them.

One by one the bright lights on the cameras were turned on until I could see nothing beyond the first row of reporters.

"Do you represent the victim?"

"I do. My team will be assisting the DA's staff in the investigation."

"Is this the victim? Why did she come today? What do you think about the plea?" A microphone appeared not inches from my face.

My mind reeled. I felt like a deer facing on-coming headlights. I looked to Mr. Taylor, and he leaned towards the device. "Jury trials are very common in this type of case."

"Aggravated assault is a felony, and sexual battery can be hard to prove. Do you think you can win when often these cases are based on the witness's testimony?"

"The DA's office has gathered enough evidence to support the charges, or we wouldn't be here," Mr. Taylor continued.

"The victim is a student at Northwestern. We saw your seemingly lifeless body being put in an ambulance three days ago. Will she be starting classes tomorrow with the rest of the students?" The voice was like a song in a sea of random noises.

Mr. Taylor leaned towards the microphone again, and I put a hand to his chest. Taking in a deep breath, I removed my sunglasses and stepped forward. I swallowed and projected my voice. "I will be attending classes tomorrow."

"You've kept your identity secret up till now. Why attend this hearing?"

"People, bullies, who commit crimes like this don't get to walk away."

Mr. Taylor pumped his arm into the air. "No more questions." His hand blocked me from the reporters who started to crowd us. He pointed to the doors we'd come out and we made our way inside and towards the back of the building. The doors to the chamber opened, and Peter's team of lawyers poked their heads into the space. The sea of people flowed towards the hall's entrance, leaving us space to slip into the elevators. As soon as the doors closed, the noise was cut off. I leaned against the back wall, ears ringing from the volume. I gripped the bar behind me with both hands, realizing my arms and legs were trembling. Doug put his hand on my shoulder, and I jerked away.

"Don't." Doug backed toward the other wall and I got in two deep breaths before the elevator stopped on our floor.

"You okay?" Mr. Taylor asked.

"Yes." I pushed off the rail and walked into the garage. Lifting my hair, I let the air from the garage cool my neck. The lower temperature and the dim lights calmed me, and I leaned back against the car, placing my palms on the cold surface. I closed my eyes, waiting for the tremors to stop.

"You did great out there," Mr. Taylor said. I heard one of the handles to the car door move.

I opened my eyes, and Doug stood a foot in front of me. Mr. Taylor opened his door and slid into his seat. Doug held out his hand, and I took it. Squeezing his hand, I turned towards my door and got in.

Doug slid in beside me and Mr. Taylor started the car. As we pulled out of the garage, the orange streetlights started to flicker and light up. I closed my eyes and rested my head against the seat, breathing in the scents of the car. Unlike most rental cars, it smelled new. The leather and wood smell hadn't been replaced by the scent of cleaning formulas yet.

I felt the car turn, one turn after another, and focused on the motion of the ride. "Should we get dinner?" Mr. Taylor's voice brought me out of my trance. I looked out the window, and I realized we were near my apartment.

Doug turned around. "We can get takeout from your place."

I was sick of my apartment, and they were my bubble. The I-didn't-have-to-talk-about-it-because-they-already-knew-everything bubble.

"No, that's fine. I'd rather go out."

Mr. Taylor pointed at Doug. "Call that fish place from last time."

Doug called the restaurant. "You should text Lila and your family. Let them know how it went."

I got my phone out of the bag and turned it on. It repeatedly buzzed with receipt of text after text. Ignoring them, I opened the message application, entered the names of my family and friends, and then typed: HE PLEADED INNOCENT, REQUESTED JURY TRIAL SET FOR JAN 6, PROBABLY ON THE NEWS :-(, GETTING

DINNER NOW. I closed the app and held the button to cut the power.

It was selfish to shut people out. But I needed a break from thinking about the trial. Doug took my hand and I remembered I only had three more days with him. At least something good had come out of the horrible situation, I got to see him. He shouldn't have come. He was missing work. Points were probably being deducted from his performance score each second he spent away from the office.

I would make the most of my time with him. I gripped his hand tight. He folded his other hand on mine and I picked it up and kissed it. "Thank you for being here."

"There wasn't any question about me coming."

We pulled up to the valet stand. "Guys, come on. Later. I'm hungry." Mr. Taylor put the car in park, shut off the ignition, and got out when his door opened. Doug's door opened, and I slid out behind him.

Still in my sunglasses, the host showed us to a table in the back. The waiter came and took our drink order. If we'd been nearer to campus, he would have carded both Doug and me. But Mr. Taylor went into lawyer-in-charge mode, and the waiter didn't even bat an eye when he asked for three glasses with the bottle of wine.

"Thank you for everything," I said to him as the waiter left with our order.

"I'm glad to see you back to your normal paleness. That blue hue you took on back at the courthouse was a bit scary."

I flicked my hands in the air. "It's done. I'm fine."

He held up his glass. "I'm going to let you live in that world tonight."

The two glasses of wine I had with dinner did exactly what I wanted them to do. When we were done, I wasn't bothered by Peter, or the trial, or my aching ribs. Doug had again protested my consumption of alcohol, and Mr. Taylor had again defended it. He drove us back to my apartment, and we said goodbye to him in the parking lot. Lila, Ross, and Mark were waiting in the living room, and Northie bounded up to me right away. I sat down and he jumped onto my lap.

"So?" Mark started.

"So?"

Lila stood. "You looked good on TV. You should see it. You sounded strong."

"Thank you." I set Northie on the floor. He flipped belly side up, and Doug and I rubbed his stomach.

Mark hit his knee. "You should call your parents. They've been calling."

Ugh, I picked up my bag and found my phone. I didn't have the energy to deal with talking to them and let the device drop back into the satchel.

Mark stood. "Are you buzzed? Have you been drinking?"

"Mark, don't judge, you're not twenty-one, and you drink all the time."

"I didn't have surgery four days ago." He shook his head and picked up his jacket. "I'll see you guys tomorrow."

He closed the door behind him, and Lila got up. "Don't mind him. He can't wrap his brain around all this."

I extended my arms straight up towards the ceiling and lowered them, setting my palms on the floor. Rummaging through my bag, I found my phone. "I'm doing my best. I don't know what to say to people. Do I tell them I'm fine? I feel fine one second and not the next. I can't even predict it."

Doug stood up. "Everyone is worried about you. Just reply to the messages. I'll take Northie out." He went to the pantry and found the leash, snapped it on the puppy's collar, and walked out the door.

I slid onto the couch beside Lila. She extended her arm around my back as I started opening my messages. Mom, Dad, Tia, Marissa, Zack, Elise, and Bill had all left similar messages, so I sent a group reply: Had a nice dinner with Mr. Taylor and Doug in Evanston. Back at my apartment now. Ready for classes to start tomorrow.

I held the screen up in front of Lila's face. "Okay?"

"I guess."

I opened Kate's message and replied to her. She and Jeremey had planned to hitch a ride to school with me, and I confirmed it still worked. Afterwards, I laid my head on Lila's shoulder and stared at the wall.

"What did you guys do today?"

Ross pointed at her. "This one made it to the house." He rubbed his hand down her leg.

She shook her head. "You could eat off the floor in that house now. Everything is perfect. The yard, the parking lot, the floors." She put her hand on my leg. "Bill wants you to come by and see the new lights and security cameras."

I closed my eyes, trying to clear the image of the brick façade of the house lit by the orange streetlights. "Maybe I'll go by with Doug tomorrow. I'll text Bill."

"Well, text me too, and Mark, so we can be there."

"Okay." I had no idea if I really had any intention of going to the house the next day. I did have a two-hour break between classes in the afternoon. The block was after lunch, and the house would be nearly empty. Perhaps it would be a good time to go. I didn't feel up for looking into the faces of all the brothers and seeing exactly what I saw in Mark's and Ross's eyes. Their wide-eyed expressions made it hard to pretend nothing happened.

I leaned into Lila and wrapped my arm around her back. "I love you."

She patted my hair. "I love you too."

I gave her a squeeze and released her. "I have to put together some notebooks for my classes." I heaved myself off the couch as Doug came in the door with Northie. "We're going to turn in." I pointed towards my bedroom.

"Okay, sleep well."

"You too."

I got two glasses of water from the kitchen and met Doug in my room. He started a shower, and I found spiral notebooks and labeled them for the next day. When he finished, I changed and joined him on the futon where he was working on his computer.

I rested my chin on his shoulder. "What are you going to do tomorrow?"

"I thought I would go to campus with you and work at the house while you're in class."

I slid my arm around his stomach. "Kate and Jeremy are meeting us at nine fifteen to go to campus. Do you have a lot of work to do tonight?"

He closed his laptop and set it under the futon. "Yes." He wrapped his arms around me. "But I'll do it tomorrow." He kissed the top of my head. "Are you really fine like you told Lila?"

I kissed his cheek. "Most of the time."

"What time is your group tomorrow?"

"Five fifteen. It's only an hour. Do you mind meeting me after? It will be dark."

"Course not, we can pick up dinner."

"Okay, I'll let Lila know."

I laid my head on his chest and then looked up at him and kissed his lips. He rubbed his hand down my back, and I rolled up onto him and kissed him again.

"What are you doing?"

"Kissing you."

"You've been drinking. You should take it easy."

"I want to be with you. I'm not going to waste the gift of having you here."

He kissed me but pulled back. "Are you sure?"

"Yes." I kissed him quickly. "But go easy on the ribs."

"I can do that." He smiled and traced his finger down my arm to my leg. He sat up and kissed my neck, my chin, and brushed his lips on my bruised cheekbone. He laced my arms under his, and I kissed his lips again and again until we were lost in each other.

Chapter 7

When I woke, my head still lay against his warm chest. I took in a deep breath, inhaling his scent and wishing we never had to be apart. Maybe I'd quit school, move to Japan. I had the perfect excuse to ditch the glorious CIA career path Dad had planned for me. My parents would probably flip out, but it was my life, and I could do what I wanted. Goodbye chemistry, goodbye physics, goodbye calculus—all of them would be gone. I'd take linguistics, education, and speech development. I could live on my tutoring money. Of course, school was expensive. I'd probably have to take out loans, and those would suck to pay off. But any escape would have to wait till the trial was finished.

Doug rubbed my head and kissed my neck. "What are you thinking?"

I rested my chin on his chest. "I could come live with you in Japan."

"That would be awesome. Sort of a waste of your scholarship though. What happened to not letting him win?"

I sat up, and Northie jumped on the bed. "The two are completely unrelated."

"You haven't said anything about moving to Japan before. I thought you were happy here."

"I am, or was, but that doesn't mean I haven't thought about it."

He rubbed Northie's head. "Your family would freak out."

"I know." I stood up and walked into the bathroom.

When I came out, Doug had on his jeans. "I'll take Northie out."

"What time is it? I'll come."

"Seven, but you don't have to. I'll do it."

I took a pair of exercise pants out of my drawer. "I do it every day. I want to go with you. I had four days of weirdness. It'll be good to get back to my routine."

I changed and we walked outside. The sun had just come up, and dew was still on the grass. It felt good to be moving, and we took the path around the complex. When we neared the front of the grounds, we stopped short. Gathered outside the gate were three news station vans with cameras and lights aimed in all directions.

"I think they found you."

"I guess."

We retraced our steps back to my apartment. *Well, that sucked*, I thought. I'd get to add that to my list of stuff I couldn't do anymore.

"You're quiet," Doug commented as he got Northie's food from the pantry.

I shrugged. "Just frustrated."

He crossed the room and took my hand. "I'll make breakfast if you want to get a shower." He encircled me in his arms and kissed me.

"Ewww, too early." Ross came out of Lila's room.

I turned towards him. "Please, like you didn't walk around here shirtless for the past month."

"Whatever. It's nice that you're not all doom and gloom, I guess. And I hear your boyfriend makes good eggs."

"Thanks, I think." I went to my room and took my shower. I dried my hair out straight while Doug took his shower. Lila was packing her backpack, and she gathered me into a hug when we started towards the kitchen.

The doorbell rang, and Ross got up to open it. Zack poked his head into the doorway. "I'm headed to campus and wanted to check in." He and Doug made plans to meet up later in the day.

When the eggs were done, we sat around the table. "So, campus, courses, how are you feeling about everything? Doug said there were TV vans at the gate." Lila shoved a bite into her mouth.

"We need Mr. Taylor's car again."

"They'll get bored," Ross said. "Hey, are you coming by the house today?"

My food caught in my mouth as I stopped chewing mid-bite. Swallowing the lump, I pointed at him. "I told you last night I would text you."

He held his palms up towards me. "Okay, just making conversation."

"Sorry." I poked the eggs. Didn't I have enough to think about with the reporters and every student and professor who watched the news yesterday? "Hey, did anyone look at the school newspaper? Doesn't the first edition of the quarter come out today?"

Lila set her fork on her plate, and Ross picked up his mug and downed a gulp. I looked at Doug. "Well?"

Lila put her hand on my arm. "Your picture wasn't in it." She looked down at her meal. "Well, not one someone could recognize you by."

I grabbed my phone, opened the Internet browser, and found the paper's link. They had a picture of the fraternity house, and the one of me being wheeled into the ambulance. My name was in the text, but the major part of the article stressed safety.

Replacing the phone on the table, I took a deep breath. "That's not good for the fraternity I guess."

Ross abandoned his mug and got up. "No, it's not." He pointed to Lila and then back to himself. "We should get going."

"I'll try to come by the house after one. I'll text you guys."

Lila got up and wrapped an arm around me. "I'll be in class. Don't push yourself. If it's too much, don't worry about it."

"Thanks." I squeezed her arm.

We cleaned up the breakfast dishes, brushed our teeth, and packed our bags. Then we took Northie out to the field for a few minutes and put him in his kennel. As I was finding a jacket, the doorbell rang.

"Check the keyhole." Doug pointed at me.

"Okay," I said, thinking I'd have to make more of a habit of it. We'd relaxed our security habits with our friends stopping by all the time, often leaving the door unlocked. I stood on my toes and saw Kate and Jeremy waiting outside.

As they came in, Kate hugged me, and I stiffened. "Oh, sorry." She backed away. "You look good."

"You don't have to lie."

"Well you look a lot better than before."

"I'll give you that." I stepped back, and Jeremy wrapped an arm around me.

"You're like semi-famous."

Kate put her hands on her hips. "Jeremey, don't."

"It's okay. I already looked at the school paper. At least it didn't have a recognizable photo."

Jeremey scratched his forehead. "You didn't see the local coverage?"

Doug came out of my room. "I'm ready, you guys good?"

I retrieved my keys, glasses, and phone from the table and slid them in my bag. "Do college kids watch that?"

"I do."

Kate opened the front door. "I don't."

I waved my hands in front of my face. "It doesn't matter. It's not going to change anything. Let's go."

Opening my shades, I fitted them on my face. I could assume my incognito persona anytime I wanted.

Doug drove and I sat in the back with Jeremy so I'd be behind the tinted windows.

"See," Kate said as we inched past the news crews outside the complex. "They're not looking for a Hispanic guy or Asian girl."

Local station vans were parked on the grass fields at the entrance of campus too. I guessed the administration must be going nuts doing damage control with the media circus. We parked in the lot and passed the student union to get to my class. Reporters littered the steps, interviewing students. I tightened my grip on Doug's hand as my chest felt heavier and heavier. He wrapped an arm around my shoulders.

"You have a six three bodyguard, and a few more waiting in the wings if you need them."

"Thanks, it's stupid. I'm just anxious. Like the beginning of the quarter isn't stressful enough with new professors and getting the syllabi."

"Do you have a plan for the lecture rooms? Your classes are much smaller than last year's."

The anxieties rumbled through my mind. What if someone smelled like him or looked like him? What if the classroom was packed and reeked of body odor? What if someone touched me? What if the professor called me out? Surely they'd been prepped, right?

Doug stepped in front of me and put a hand on each of my shoulders. I looked up and realized we were at my building.

"You're going to be fine. Do you want me to walk you to your room?"

"No, I'm good." I looked past him to the students getting in the last puffs on their cigarettes before class. I put a finger to my sternum. "I'm good. I love you."

"I'll be right here when you get out."

"Okay, thanks."

He kissed me on the lips and squeezed my hand. "Have fun in calculus."

"It should be amazing." I shoved myself off with my toes and walked towards the building, phone gripped tight in one hand. Covering my nose with my sleeve as I approached the doors, I ducked my head and held my breath till I was inside. A crowd of students was waiting for the elevator, and I turned towards the stairs. The stairwell was dank and dark, and my stitches pulled with each step. *One floor*, I told myself as I counted the stairs. There were nine and then a landing, four steps and then nine more stairs, and three steps to the door. In the hall, I saw a group of students entering the room, and I hung back, checking the time on my phone.

I let the rest of the students file in, and then I found a seat at the end of the back row. It was a small lecture room with only three rows of seats. A lot of the majors required three calculus classes, but only science and engineering students took the upper level math courses. Most of the seats were filled, and I scanned the room for familiar faces. I noticed Justin sitting in the middle of the front row and recognized a few others.

The professor cleared his throat, and the chatter subsided. I opened my notebook and took out my pen. It'd never bothered me before that my name was usually near the beginning of the list, but my palms were sweating. I rubbed them on my pants and took some deep breaths. What was the worst that could happen?

"Adams, Jonathan," the professor called and looked up, moving his head along the rows of seats. A kid in the second row raised his hand and called out. The professor nodded and punched a key on his laptop. "Avery, Amanda."

It was as if a tiny electric current had been cast through the air. I tried to decipher if I was being paranoid, but kids craned their necks left and right. Justin's turned to the left and then back to the right until he found me. There was no way out of the awkward situation. *Peter doesn't get to win*, I told myself.

"Here," I called without moving any other muscles.

The professor looked at his computer and back up. His hand tapped on the desk in front of him. "I'm sorry. Miss Avery?"

I inched my hand into the air.

"Ah, thank you." He pointed towards me. "But this is not California or a Hollywood set. Please remove your sunglasses, Miss Avery."

How many times did he have to say my name? Didn't he watch the news, listen to the papers, or read his email? "I'm sorry, my eyes are sensitive today."

"If you have a medical note, I can take that now or you can remove your glasses."

Before I could respond, Justin spoke up. "Sir, I think she said she had a problem with her eyes."

The professor leaned forward. "If either of you have an issue with the behavior requirements of this class—"

Thump. The arrhythmia was back. *Damn, Peter*, I thought. *He did not get to win.* What did it matter anyway? Yes, I was the girl whose picture was strewn across all media channels.

I took a breath and projected my voice. "Sorry, sir." I removed my glasses and set them on the table and looked up at him. The whispers died for a second and then rose again.

Thump, thump. I pressed my fingers into my sternum. He cleared his throat and looked down at his computer and tapped on some keys.

I took some slow breaths, keeping my eyes on the professor. He looked up at me. "Sorry, thank you." He called the next name and the next until he was done with the roll call. All the while the room hummed as the kids tapped away on their screens. He got to the last name and requested all devices be turned off and placed towards the front of the desks.

He brought up the syllabus and began the lecture. After forty-five minutes, we had a five-minute break. My bag was packed save my notebook, and I tucked it inside, slid on my glasses, and shot out the door as soon as he released us. When I passed the stair-well, I fought the urge to bail on the last part of class. I didn't want to have to talk to Justin or anyone else. At least five times forty people probably already knew Amanda Avery had Calculus IV at 9:45 a.m. on Tuesdays and Thursdays. What if reporters were gathering outside the building? *Get a grip, Amanda*, I told myself. Being paranoid was not going to get me anywhere.

Shades on, I made it to the water fountain. I walked to the bathroom and washed my hands to kill time. Finishing, I made my way back to the classroom. Trailing behind several students, I pretended to check messages on my phone. When the kids walked into the lecture room, I could see Justin leaning against the wall. *You're going to do this a hundred times, get used to it*, I thought.

I took a deep breath and approached him. "Oh my goodness, Amanda." He wrapped his arms around me, and I froze, arms positioned straight down my sides. Why did people all of a sudden feel like they could hug me? Kate, Jeremy, and even Justin all felt a new need to hug me. "Sorry." He released me and took a step back. "I don't know why I did that. I saw the news and was so worried about you."

"Yeah, crazy, I know, but I'm good."

"That guy was freaky. His picture made my skin crawl."

The image of Peter's face transforming to a skull flashed in my mind, and I squinted, trying to clear the image away.

A hand gripped my arm. "Hey, are you okay?"

I pulled his hand away and stepped back. "How's football?"

"It's good. We've been winning."

"I went to the games. I saw you playing." The dimming of the lights in the lecture hall caught my eye, and I pointed into the room. "I think he's starting."

He rested his hand on my shoulder. "I'm glad you're okay."

For goodness sakes, why is he touching me again? "Thanks."

The lecture was a review of the major principles of Calculus I, II, and III. I was happy to have a refresher since I'd planned on recapping the past weekend. After class ended, I walked outside to find Doug waiting ten feet from the building door. He held a cup of coffee and brown bag in one hand and wrapped the other around my waist. Him holding me, I liked.

"How was class?"

I shook my head.

"That bad?"

I took the cup from his hand and took a sip. "He started with, 'You're not in Hollywood.' Justin tried to defend me, and the professor didn't like that any better than my eye problem excuse, so I had to take off my glasses." I scanned our surroundings but found no reporters or cameras. "I would bet thirty times thirty people know I had calculus this morning."

"All the reporters got cleared out."

"Really?"

"Yep, the University is privately owned, and campus is private property."

"Nice." I exhaled and leaned into him.

"You want to go to the student union and grab a table?"

The building would be packed. "What about the courtyard? The one you would follow me to last fall?"

"I was not following you. You were stalking me."

Out of the corner of my eye, I caught sight of a figure hurling towards us. I turned to see Vivian in a half-sprint, bag bouncing against her back, running towards us.

She stopped and took a few gasping breaths. Then her hands clutched my shoulders, and she pulled me to her. With my free hand, I wrapped my fingers around her arm, peeled it from my back, and stepped away.

"Vivian, how are you?"

"Oh my gosh, I was so worried about you."

"Well, no need." I raked my hair behind one ear and lifted my cup in the air. "Here I am. You remember Doug?"

"Yes." She smiled up at him. "I saw you on the news last night. What happened?"

The question was blunt. But leave it to Vivian, my shares-too-much-personal-information class friend, to flat out ask. I tucked my hair behind my other ear and gathered the rest in my hand. "You know I only have ten minutes till my next class, and I need to eat." I held up the bag. "Maybe we can talk later."

"Of course. What classes do you have?"

"Macroeconomics next, and then Chinese lit later."

"I'm in economics. We can sit together."

"Sure, I'll see you there."

"Okay." She squeezed my arm. "Ten minutes, I guess."

My eyes darted to Doug, and I took a step back. "See you in a few."

Doug took my hand, and we started towards the picnic benches. "I didn't realize you guys were on hugging terms?"

"It's the newest rage—let's hug Amanda." I shook out my hair, thinking I might need to come up with an anti-hug strategy. Maybe I could step a foot away from anyone who approached me.

"I'm not crazy? You noticed it too? I mean, I want to hold you every second to make sure you're okay. But what's with everyone else?"

"I have no idea. Justin hugged me too."

He stopped. "Justin?"

"You remember my friend from the football team?"

"Yes."

"It was freaky." I trembled, shaking off the feel of his touch.

"I really don't like guys hugging you."

"Believe me, I don't either." My skin seemed to hold the imprint of each embrace. I already felt like I needed to go home and take a shower. I stopped when we got to the courtyard. Half of it was occupied by smokers. I put my sleeve to my nose. "Let's try the library."

At the building, I tucked my coffee in my bag, and we went straight to the elevator. On the fifth floor, we found a deserted table. I leaned against the tabletop and slid my arms around his waist.

"Are you eating?"

"I'm going to eat at the house."

I sipped my latte and opened the sandwich wrapper but folded it back up and placed it in my bag.

"You're not hungry."

"It's still early. I might eat it at the next break. We only have a few minutes. Remember when we used to come up here last winter?"

"I do." He smiled and kissed me on the lips. My alarm buzzed.

He ended our kiss. "Darn."

"Macroeconomics." I rested my head on his chest, and he planted a kiss on the top of my head.

He lifted my chin so we were looking at each other. "You up for this? You don't have to go."

I stood up straight. "Yep, I'm good." We made our way back down the elevator and to my building. I caught site of Vivian walking in the door and turned to kiss Doug goodbye.

He wrapped his hand around my neck. Peter's face flashed in front of my eyes, and I stripped his hand from the back of my neck. He backed away, palms in the air.

My hand was trembling as I reached out to him. "I'm sorry. It's not you, when you grabbed my neck..."

"It reminded you of him? If you would tell me everything, we wouldn't have these issues."

My phone dinged, and I grabbed his hand. "I don't even know my triggers." I hoped he understood. I wouldn't get through everything without him.

"Okay, go."

"I'm sorry."

"We'll figure it out. Go."

I turned and walked as fast as I dared towards the building. My class was on the first floor, and I made it inside as the professor started calling names. Vivian was in the back row and motioned me towards a seat beside her.

The professor graced over my name when I called out I was present even though he'd looked up to locate the other students. My sunglasses stayed on my face, and there was no drama. Afterwards Vivian walked outside with me, detailing her summer as an intern at her uncle's company. Sighting Doug, I said goodbye to her and navigated around the other students to him.

"How was it?"

"Fine. The professor barely even looked at me."

"Good, what now? Lunch? Are you up for visiting the house?"

I took his hand. "Sure." It was going to have to happen sooner or later, and I'd rather be with Doug when it did. Unlike the night I was attacked, the sun was high in a blue sky.

"Walk or bus?"

"We can walk." We made our way to the house, and I stopped on the sidewalk in front of it. It looked the same but different. The trees still hung above the roof, but there was not a single leaf on the lawn. I scanned the walls. New lights and cameras were fitted on the corners of the building under the gutters. I opened my hands and wiped sweaty palms on the legs of my pants.

Doug took my hand. "You good?"

I nodded and took a step towards the front door. As we passed the path that went round the back, the path I'd taken that night, I kept my eyes facing front. Even so, my heart fluttered with the arrhythmia I'd seemed to have acquired. I swallowed hard and stayed my course.

He opened the door for me, and I stepped inside. I thought about the nights I'd spent socializing with the new freshman and how I'd made a point to talk to Peter since no one else seemed to be. He was a mean person, evil to the core. It didn't make sense how he could be capable of hurting someone to bend their will. I shook off the thoughts as we made our way to the back of the house where Bill, Mark, Zack and Ross were playing pool.

"Don't you guys ever do any work?" I called to them.

"Well, you'd know that if you'd ever come around." Mark let his cue drop to the table and walked towards me. "Hi." He wrapped both arms around me.

"Hi." I smiled at him when he stepped back. I'd known Mark since I was a kid. He and Zack were the only people who hugged me besides Lila, Doug, and my family.

Bill approached us. "It's good to see you."

"Sorry it took a while." I tucked my hair behind my ears. "There was a lot of stuff going on."

"Are you kidding? Don't even think that."

Ross shook his phone. "Lila had class."

"I know, thanks."

Bill pointed to the ceiling. "You want a tour? We've upgraded the whole security system."

I followed his gaze, seeing a security camera in the far corner near the ceiling. "No, I'm good. You guys go back to your game."

The room was big, but the stairwells and halls were tight, and I could already feel the walls closing in on me. It wouldn't do for me to go into a full out panic.

"Do you want some lunch?" Doug asked, sitting at the bar.

I shook my head. "No, I'm good."

"You going to stand there?" He pulled a bar stool towards him. "Sit down."

"No, I'm good." I looked between him, and the other guys, my chest tightening by the second.

"Do you want the sandwich? Here, I'll take your bag." He slipped his fingers under the strap on my shoulder.

I grabbed the handle and tugged it away from his grip. "No. I can't stay here."

His palms went up. "Sorry?"

I studied the balls on the table. They blurred and my breathing became labored. I repeated the motion of raking my fingers around my ears, taking slow breaths. I'd tried not to think about enjoying a game of pool like a normal person. Outside the window the tree limbs overhung the roof and I was back in Thursday night. The leaves buried my feet and the walls became brick. His face flashed before my eyes.

Zack rested a hand atop each of my shoulders. "Hey, you okay in there?"

I shifted my weight between my feet, making sure my knees weren't locked. "Sure." I turned to Doug. "We should go. I have that thing now, remember?"

He squinted at me. "What thing?"

"You know, I told you, that meeting." I slid my hand down his arm and slipped it in his palm.

"You guys are going already? You just got here." Zack pointed a pool cue at me.

"I have to go. Doug you can stay." I dropped his hand and walked towards the front exit.

"Wait." Doug jogged towards me.

"Bye, guys." I spun and took the longest strides I could to the door. It was irrational, but a chill, fear, panic—I didn't know what to call it—descended, and I had to get out of there. I walked through the doorway, tears spilling down my cheeks, and jogged to the road and across the street.

"Amanda!" Doug yelled my name.

I froze, realizing I hadn't even looked before I crossed. In a few seconds, he was beside me. "What was that?"

I bent down, hands on my thighs. "I don't know. I couldn't be there anymore."

"Well, you can't bolt across a street. You could've gotten hit."

"Now you're mad at me? Great!"

"No, you scared me."

"Okay." I sucked in a breath. "I'm okay now. Can we take a walk? Off campus or something?"

"Are you sure you feel up to it?"

"I can't be here."

We walked to the edge of campus and crossed the street. "You should eat something." Doug stopped in front of a café.

"Okay." I motioned towards the door. Inside, we moved to the front of the line, and I ordered a small double shot latte.

"You can't live off caffeine," Doug said as we waited for our order.

"It's got milk and will hold me till dinner." I made my way to a table at the back of the restaurant and sat with my back against the wall.

He sat down opposite me. "I didn't fly halfway around the world to watch you self-destruct."

"I'm not self-destructing. I'm in survival mode. And who are you to judge anyway? When did you become my dad?"

"If being worried about you makes me your dad, then that's me right now."

"Well, I don't like this version of you."

"If you'd let me in, then maybe we could work through things together. What happened back there?"

I stared at my paper cup. "All I could see, hear, smell, were the trees, the leaves a foot deep, the fence on one side of me, the brick wall on the other, his face, his voice, his odor."

He cleared his throat. "You're moving to Arizona to live in a stucco house that has a cactus in the yard?"

"Maybe." I half-laughed. "But I'd rather move to Tokyo."

"That's the second time you've said that."

"Would you want me to live there with you?"

"Are you kidding? Of course."

"Okay, then, what's the problem?"

"No problem, I guess." His watch beeped. "Are you going to your last class?"

"Yes."

We walked back to campus. For my next lecture, the professor was the same I'd had in the spring for the first course in the Chinese literature series. The class was small, and I didn't have high hopes for remaining anonymous.

In the hall, I sipped my latte, waiting till the last minute to find a seat at the back of the room. I was the only one in the back row, and it probably seemed strange and anti-social, but the only other free seat was in the front, and I wasn't going to pass every kid to get to it.

The professor counted us instead of taking roll and seemed satisfied everyone was there. "Okay—" he motioned for us to move forward "—everyone get up and come sit down here." He walked around the podium to the wide steps on the side of the room. "I hate these lecture rooms. They're too antisocial. Come on." He stuck out his hands and pulled them to his body again.

Students got up and started to form a cluster on the stairs around him. "Face each other, people." He used his finger to make a circle in the air.

I got up and made my way to the back of the group and sat down behind the row of students.

He clapped his hands together. "Good, I wanted to start out by getting to know each other. Many of you already do from spring quarter, but that was a while ago, so let's start off with your name, what year you're in, your major, and one cool thing you did this summer." He proceeded to tell us about his trip to China and then pointed to the girl on his left. "You go next."

I tried to pay attention, but as it got closer to my turn, my anxiety grew. I hugged my arms to my chest and wondered what to say. I still had my glasses on, and I didn't really want to speak. Maybe I could crouch behind the kid in front of me and they would forget me. Maybe I'd say pass. That would probably draw more attention though.

The boy in front of me introduced himself, and then the boy next to him jumped in. The professor pointed towards us. "Hold up, sorry, in the back, can you introduce yourself?" The two boys parted so that there was a space between them, and I had a direct line of sight to the professor. He looked down at his tablet and then back at me. "That is if you're comfortable with sharing." He cleared his throat.

He'd given me an out, but being recognized was inevitable. I kept my sunglasses on. "I'm Amanda." I looked around the room, waiting for recognition of the name, but there was none. I exhaled again. "I'm a sophomore. I took Chinese Literature I in the spring. I double major in International Studies and Chemistry, and I learned Japanese this summer."

A boy to my left coughed and cleared his throat. "Right."

The professor spoke to the group in Japanese. "How many of you know more than one language?"

I was the only one to raise my hand, and he repeated the phrase in English. All the other kids raised their hands.

"How many of you know more than two languages?" he asked in Japanese. I kept my hand up, and he repeated the question in English. Only two other kids held their hands up.

"Thank you." He pointed to the boy who had coughed. "Mr.?"

"Bates."

"Mr. Bates, I believe you owe Miss Amanda an apology."

"Sorry, Amanda." He waved at me.

"Thank you. Proceed." He pointed to the boy at my left. We finished introductions, and he began with the first reading selection. After fifty minutes of sitting on the hard steps, my body ached and I was grateful when he called for a break.

As we stood up, the professor called out. "Miss, Miss Amanda." Waiting until the other students exited, I followed him to the podium. "Amanda, I'm glad to see you in class. From the description in the paper, I had assumed you would be taking some time off. How are you?"

"Thanks, I'm okay."

"Okay, well I'm glad to see it."

"Thanks." I pointed to the back exit and made my way up the steps. In the hall, I ducked around the other students to the restroom. Back in the lecture, the second half of class seemed to fly by. My next meeting, the assault support group, had me distracted, and I forced myself to write down all the professor's comments.

Outside, Doug was waiting on a bench beside the walk. "This must've been the most boring day for you." I told him when he gathered me into a hug.

"Are you kidding? I got to hang out at the house and get some work done while everyone is sleeping in Japan." He took my hand as we started towards the administration buildings.

"Do you have a lot of work tonight?"

"Not much. What do you want to do for dinner?"

"Lila mentioned getting takeout for the three of us."

My anxiety grew as we neared the administration building. I chewed on my thumb and I wondered why I was going. Skipping the first week wouldn't be a crime. No one would slight me. I didn't have to do everything in one day.

"Have you replaced biting your lip with biting your thumb?"

"I'm anxious about this meeting."

When we reached the building, he stopped. "Who wouldn't be?"

"What are you doing for the next hour?"

"I'm going to get the car and meet you back here."

"This totally sucks."

"I get to see you." He leaned into me. "That's a good thing."

"I can't think of any others."

"I love you."

"I love you, too." I stood on my toes, kissed him, and then watched him walk away. Bringing the information for the room number up on my device, I took the elevator to the second floor. Most of the rooms were dark, so it was easy to spot the right one.

"Oh my God, these are awesome." I heard a voice from inside the room. Four girls were gathered around a counter that held a tray of donuts. My stomach knotted. Really? Eating? I stood in the doorway unobserved, thinking I could leave.

"Amanda, glad you made it," came a voice behind me. I turned around to see Dr. Milner. I was trapped.

"Thanks." I took a sideways step into the room to let her in, and the smell of fried dough and sugar encompassed me.

"Have a snack." She pointed towards the back of the room. I clutched the strap of my bag, thinking I was going to hurl if I ate anything. It was not where I wanted to be or how today was supposed to go. I should've woken at six, walked Northie, gone to rowing practice, come home, showered, walked Northie again, attended my classes, had a tutoring session in my break, caught my last class, taken Northie on another walk, made dinner with Lila, and then hung out and studied the rest of the night. Instead, I got an abbreviated walk to avoid reporters, humiliated in organic chemistry, accosted by Vivian, survived a dash across a busy street, received a lecture on safety and nutrition from Doug, and had to attend an assault group therapy session.

I clenched my jaw and made myself move towards a group of chairs in the center of the room. A girl sat in the circle, and I took the seat beside her. She studied the screen on her phone, and I took out mine. Any distraction, even reading worried parent messages, was a welcome relief. I typed a reply to mom's text and hit send.

Dr. Milner closed the door and sat down in a chair opposite me, calling for the rest of the girls to join us. Carrying napkins piled with donut holes, they made their way to the circle. The girl who sat beside me had a napkin stacked with pastries. A new wave of the sweet scent flooded my senses, and I fought covering my nose.

"Do you want one?" She held her hand out towards me.

"No, thanks." I looked up at the lights on the ceiling, thinking I might puke. The sugary greasy odor mixed with the musty smell of the building was going to put me past my limit. I sucked in a slow breath through the fabric of my sleeve. What was with me? None of these things bothered me before.

Dr. Milner called the group to convene, and I focused on her image. Why was I there? It was the last place I wanted to be. My eyes circled the room, seeing the other girls smiling and joking with each other. Save the girl beside me, they looked like happy people, people that could pass a smoker without gagging, enjoy the changing colors on the trees, and go about their normal lives.

"We have some new people." I scanned the faces, and all the eyes were trained on me. Looking down at my feet, I tucked my hands under my thighs. "I thought we'd start with introductions. Why don't we go around and say a little about ourselves."

A hand on my right went up. A blonde girl licked her fingers and then rubbed them on her pants. "I'm not saying anything. We don't even know who she is. She hasn't even taken off her sunglasses. She could be a dude for all we know. This isn't a safe place." If looks could kill, she would've been burning a hole through my skull. The other girls nodded in agreement, save the girl beside me who didn't look up.

"Change can be scary," Dr. Milner said. "I will go first. I'm Dr. Milner, but for the purposes of this group, you can call me Nina. I am the head of psychological health here at Northwestern, and my goal is to help all of you be successful students despite challenges you may face. Who wants to go next?"

No one moved. After what seemed like minutes of silence, the girl beside me looked up for the first time. "My name is Addie," she began. Addie was a junior drama major and had been in the group since last fall.

"Thank you," Nina replied when Addie had finished. "Anyone else?"

No one spoke for at least a minute. "We're not talking." The blonde crossed her arms over her chest. Why did I come to the group? I could get up and walk out, pretend I didn't freak out every time I smelled smoke or sweat, and pretend I was fine with fall leaves and orange streetlights. I bit my lip and tears formed in my eyes. I blinked them again and again, trying to clear the tears.

My indecisiveness turned into anger. Did she have to be mean? Still, I took the high road. I slid my sunglasses off my face. "Sorry." I held the glasses out and folded them in my lap.

"No apologies are necessary," Dr. Milner said.

I stretched my feet out, pointing my toes towards the floor. "My name is Amanda. I'm new, obviously." I twirled my hand in the air and looked at my legs. "I'm a sophomore."

"Wait." The blonde flung her arms out into the middle of the circle. "I knew it. You're the chick from the papers." She pointed at me and then to Nina. "She wasn't even raped. He was charged with aggravated assault and sexual battery."

My heart pounded in my ears as his image flashed through my mind. I put my fist to my sternum.

"We're all here to support each other." Dr. Milner looked over her glasses at the blonde.

"This is a rape support group." She pointed at me again.

Really? I wasn't even good enough to be in their group because I hadn't been raped. I took a slow deep breath, my heartbeat pounding in my head. The rhythm missed a beat, and I pressed my thumb into my sternum harder.

"This is an assault support group," Dr. Milner responded.

"Give her a chance," Addie said. "I was new last year, and you didn't like me either."

The blonde folded her napkin and crossed her arms on her chest again. "That's different. I'm not saying a thing in this group."

"That is your choice." Nina looked around the room. "Does anyone else want to introduce themselves?"

One by one the girls said their names and year in school. The blonde, Misty, went last.

"Great, thank you. Should we talk about our summers?"

Addie raised her hand and proceeded to talk about her break at home. The rest of the girls followed with some of them describing their vacations or jobs but others hinting at challenges with anxiety and relationships. My summer and the challenges with my parents seemed like a lifetime ago.

"Amanda, would you like to share a little more about yourself." Nina smiled and nodded towards me. Her smooth voice sounded kind, too kind, and I could feel my eyes starting to mist up. I was *not* going to cry. I dug my nails into the underside of my thighs.

"Misty is correct. I'm the girl who was assaulted last week. I had a sucky first quarter here last year when I got hurt in a volleyball accident. I got through that but had an even suckier summer at home with my parents. I was happy to be back here with my roommate and friends but then..." My voice cracked and water formed in my eyes again.

Motion from my right caught my attention. Misty was shaking her head. "Weren't you dating like the Greek Council President?"

"Did you go to classes today, Amanda?" Nina asked.

"Yes." I wiped my cheeks with my hands.

"How was that?"

I shook my head, trying to stop the tears. "They got the reporters to leave, so that was good." I looked at the ceiling again, thinking I'd rather be anywhere else.

Nina ended the meeting and asked us to stack our chairs in the corner. As we carried our chairs, Addie leaned towards me. "She doesn't like new people, or Greeks, or men. But she'll come around. She did the same thing when I joined the group. Don't get scared off. This group really helped me."

"Thanks." We retrieved our bags from the floor. I wasn't sure how the group could help me. I wasn't even sure how I felt except that within the span of an hour all my dread had turned to anger. I couldn't row, or run, or play co-rec football. Instead, I'd spend my time in a support group with mean girls, in individual counseling sessions, and in discovery meetings with lawyers, all because some slacker boy had to prove how tough he was.

Addie and I took the elevator down together. "Misty really is more bark than bite. It's all a tough girl act."

"Thanks, it was nice to meet you," I told her as the doors opened. Through the front window I could see Doug leaning against his car. The only thing I wanted was to be in his arms.

Looking at the sky, I was grateful it wasn't quite sunset. I crossed the lot to him and buried my head in his chest. He didn't ask anything, didn't say anything. He just held me. I heard the doors to the building open and the group of girls from the meeting talking. Then their chatter stopped. I turned my head toward them.

Misty shook her head as she passed us, her eyes boring into me. "Dude, not cool, not cool."

The group moved on, and I looked after them, mouth agape.

Doug released me. "What was that?"

"I have no clue." I tapped the tire with my toe.

"Hey, you okay? You ready to go? I told Lila we'd pick up Chinese food."

"Are you kidding? No, I'm not okay. I have to go to these stupid sessions with mean girls. I can't row. I can't run. My head is pounding. My side hurts. There are probably reporters camped outside my apartment complex. And I have to see a counselor and be interviewed by lawyers who are going to ask me how many people I've slept with. So, no, I'm not okay."

I flung my bag off my shoulder and walked around the car to my door, waiting for him to unlock it. He pressed the remote button and the locks disengaged. I pulled the handle up and slumped down into my seat.

He got in beside me, and I buckled my belt. "Don't say anything. You wanted me to open up."

He held his hands above the steering wheel. "I wasn't going to."

I hit the radio button and crossed my arms over my chest. The lamp in front of us flickered on as we pulled out of the space. *Damn lights*, I thought putting my thumb to my mouth. I looked out my side door window as the tears streamed down my face. I wished I could stop them, but I couldn't. As he pulled into the restaurant parking lot, I wiped the tears from my face.

He stopped the car. "Do you want to come in with me?"

"No."

He got out, and I took out my phone and messaged my parents.

CONGRATS ON GETTING TO YOUR CLASSES, THE HOUSE, AND THE MEETING. GOOD JOB, my dad replied when I told him about my day. Congrats? Good job? Like I had achieved some goal? I didn't need to be patted on the back for doing normal stuff.

Marissa could usually be counted on to have some dramatic incident in progress, and I needed distraction. HOW R U? I sent to her.

HOPE YOUR DAY WAS BETTER THAN MINE. MY ROOMMATE ATE ALL MY FOOD, Marissa replied.

MY ROOMMATE COULDN'T EAT MY FOOD BECAUSE I HAVE NONE. I HATE MEAN PEOPLE. WE'RE PICKING UP CHINESE.

SWEET. I'M GOING TO ORDER OUT TOO.

The car door opened, and Doug handed the food bag to me. I took it and lifted it into the back seat. I messaged back and forth with Marissa as Doug drove.

"You might want to put your glasses and a hat on," Doug said as we neared the apartment complex.

The lawn around the entrance was littered with news vans and I slid glasses on my face. "How long are they going to be here?"

"There aren't as many as there were this morning."

"That's a good sign. Maybe they'll be gone by tomorrow."

"All you need is another distracting story. Closer to the weekend they'll have game coverage."

We turned into the main entrance and stopped at the gate, punching in the required code. I'd slid down in my seat and sat up once we were out of sight of the reporters. When he parked, I looked towards my apartment. The last thing I wanted to do was to have to report on my day to anyone. I just wanted to not think. All this fueled my anger again, and I pulled the handle and thrust the door open with as much force as I could. Grabbing my bag, I slammed the door shut.

"I'm going to take a quick shower before we eat. If you're hungry, you don't have to wait for me."

"I had a good lunch. I can wait," Doug said as he caught up to me.

At our door, I turned the key in the latch and opened the door. Lila was sitting on the couch, and Northie jumped from her side and ran towards me. I dropped my bag and sat down beside him, rubbing his head, his back, and his belly. He stretched his front paws out straight and stuck his butt in the air. Then scurried to a toy and brought it back to me.

Playing tug with the dog, I forced myself to be nice to Lila. "How are you? How were classes?"

"Overwhelming as usual. I heard you went to the house."

"Yeah, sorry I missed you."

"No worries. Our schedules are completely opposite."

"You want to eat?"

"I thought I'd grab a shower first." I pointed towards my room. "If you're hungry, go ahead."

"I can wait."

"I'll make it quick," I told her, walking towards my room. I really had no intention of taking a short shower. What I wanted was for the warmth of the water and smell of my soap to seep into every crevice of my body until they blocked out every other sensory input. Fortunately for Lila, our hot water heater wasn't big and fifteen minutes was as much as I'd ever gotten.

Doug followed me to my room. "I kinda wanted to be alone."

"Oh, okay." He turned to go.

"I'm sorry."

"Your life sucks right now."

"Wow, thanks."

"No, I mean you have every right to be angry."

"I'm not sure you want angry zombie me."

"Anything zombie is better than black hole zombie."

"If you say so." I opened a drawer of my chest and found a clean pair of leggings, tank, and underwear. "I won't be long. We don't have that much hot water."

"Okay." He caught my hand as I passed by. "I love you."

"I love you, too." I forced a smile. At least I had him and my friends. I couldn't imagine what it would be like to go through a traumatic experience if didn't have anybody close.

In the bathroom, I turned the faucet and let the water get hot. I put up my hair and stepped inside the shower, letting the beads pound on my skin. Soaping the bath mitt, I scrubbed every inch of my skin. I spread shaving cream and ran the razor along the length of both legs. Then I stood there, taking in the heavy moist air and letting the smells penetrate my lungs. When the water temperature dropped, I turned off the stream.

Wrapping in a towel, I wiped the condensation from the mirror. I washed my face and dressed. Better, I felt better. I looked at myself in the mirror and released my hair from the bun. I gathered it back up and made a ponytail. In my room, I found a sweater, slipped into it, and joined Lila and Doug in the living room.

"Food?" Doug asked when I sat next to him.

"Yes, food." I stood up and held my hand out to him. Lila got glasses, filled them with water, and we sat at the table. We chatted about classes and all the gossip Lila had heard at the house.

Once full, I realized how exhausted I was. All I wanted was to curl up in my bed and sleep. Doug walked Northie, and I brushed my teeth and slid between my covers, pulling up the blanket to my chin. My mind raced as I thought about the day ahead and another set of professors and students to face. I got up and opened my computer, checking my schedule. Organic chemistry was at ten, followed by physics at eleven, physics lab, and then Japanese at three. The professors were all new to me.

Doug came in while I was staring at the screen. He sat down wrapping an arm around my waist, and kissed me.

"What are you looking at?"

"My schedule." I closed the laptop. "Just dreading tomorrow."

"What would make tomorrow better than today?"

"For the professors to accept me wearing sunglasses and people not to hug me."

"Email your professors and friends."

Okay, that was a brilliant idea. I could be proactive and have some control. I opened my laptop and sent emails to my professors. The next question was which friends to email. All of my close friends I'd talked to, but it was people like Justin and Vivian who felt like wild cards. Who else would approach me? The list included friends from rowing team, Spanish club, and the mentoring group. Please don't hug me seemed like an odd request. The whole thing seemed weird, and I ditched the idea. I'd have to deal with talking to people as it came up. As it was, I had a list of unread text and email messages. I didn't have the energy to respond to each of them individually and a group message seemed impersonal, so I let them sit in my inbox.

"I need a personal assistant or public relations person."

"It'll get easier." He rubbed his hand in circles on my back.

Chapter 8

Being exhausted had its advantages as it allowed for a wonderful night's sleep. I awoke to lines of sunshine peeking around the blinds. Doug was already up, and Northie was gone too. Reaching for my phone, I checked the time. The screen read eight twenty. Eight twenty? I'd set my alarm for seven. I threw the covers off and jumped up, flinging open the door to the living room. Lila was at the table studying.

"You let me sleep till eight twenty?"

Doug sat on the couch, his laptop open, Northie beside him. "You were exhausted."

"I set my alarm for seven."

"I turned it off when you didn't wake up."

"Well don't, that's when I wanted to be up."

"Okay, got it."

Crossing to the kitchen for a cup of coffee, I wondered if it really mattered and felt bad for snapping at Doug. But I had my day planned out. I'd get up, walk Northie, and have time to get some reading done before class. I was going to be behind if I didn't start on my coursework soon. The spines of my books hadn't even been cracked. It wasn't Doug's fault though.

"Sorry, I'm anxious about everything." I lowered myself onto the cushion on the other side of Northie.

Doug looked up from his computer. "It's okay. I get it."

"I shouldn't complain."

"It's okay."

I hated when I was allowed to be mean. Getting up, I went to the kitchen for a bagel and sat down opposite Lila. "How are you?"

She looked up from her book. "Good."

"Was Ross here?"

"No, he stayed at the house last night."

"Everything okay?"

"He doesn't get that I'm still a little shaky from last week."

"All of this sucks."

"Yes, it does."

Doug joined us at the table, and we talked about the schedule for the rest of the week. I didn't like thinking about him leaving in two days, but it was me who insisted he did. He needed to get back to work, and I couldn't use him as a crutch forever. Doug invited Lila to come to dinner with Doug's mom and step-dad in the evening, and I was happy she accepted.

Once I was dressed, Doug and I walked Northie around the grounds of the complex. When we approached the front entrance, I stretched my hood up to cover my hair. There were fewer news vans than the day before, but it still angered me that they were there at all. Didn't they have better things to do? We cut our walk short and looped back to my apartment.

Inside, I changed and gathered my books and computer. Lila rode with us to campus, sitting in the front seat, with me in the back behind the darkened glass. The reporters and cameramen moved closer to the drive when our car approached. Lila rolled down her window.

"What are you doing?" I asked, shrinking down in my seat.

"I am sick of these guys." She waved her hand out the window. "Hi, news people, will you please go home?" The reporters shook their head as Doug pulled out onto the main road. I stifled a laugh, and Lila started giggling. "Too bad it's not January. They'd be freezing their butts off and gone in a day. Instead of happy-we-get-to-be-outside reporters, they would be frigid reporters on a stick."

An image of little reporter people on Popsicle sticks popped in my head, and I full out laughed. Lila turned around.

"What's so funny?"

I described my vision, and Lila laughed too. By the time we got to campus, we couldn't stop giggling at her impressions of the frozen-popsicle reporters. More reporters were gathered on the sidewalk and Lila leaned out the window again.

"Go away Popsicle people," she yelled, throwing me into a laughing fit I couldn't stop until we parked.

We stumbled out of the car, me gripping my side. "We have to stop."

"I've had it up to here with them." She made a line across her neck with her finger.

I gathered her into my arms. "I know. I'm sorry."

She wriggled away and pointed a finger at me. "If you say that one more time, I'm going to hit you."

"What?"

"You keep telling everyone you're sorry. Stop, it's not your fault."

"Guys—" Doug corralled us with his arms "—there are other people here."

I glanced around to see several kids gawking at us. Lila wrapped her arms around me. "It's not your fault. He doesn't get to win," she whispered in my ear.

"I love you."

"I love you, too."

The three of us walked towards the main campus, and Lila split off for her class. Doug escorted me to the chemistry building.

"Okay, that was the weirdest thing I've ever seen you do."

"Laughter is a good thing, right?" I leaned into him and looked up at his face.

He wrapped an arm around me. "I guess. It seemed like you were about to cross the line between sanity and insanity."

"Believe me, I am closer to sanity than insanity after that episode."

"If you say so."

"I love you."

He kissed me on the lips.

"It's Tavery two point oh." I heard a voice behind me.

"God, I hate him," Doug whispered in my ear.

I spun around to see Jeremy standing there, hands on hips. "Two more days." I held up two fingers.

"And then you'll be a normal lonely person like the rest of us again?"

"I guess."

"I'm going to the chemistry, Organic Chemistry one like normal people. You're with the geeks in two right?"

"Yep."

He lifted his phone in front of his face and held it out to me. "Well, it's time."

"Okay." I turned back to Doug. "I have a string of classes. You don't need to meet me after each one."

"Okay, well text or call me. I'll be at the house."

"Okay, I'll see you at four." I stepped towards the building, but he grabbed my hand. When I turned back to him, he closed the gap and kissed me.

"I love you."

"I love you too."

"Thank God for only two more days of this," Jeremy said behind us.

Doug wrapped his arms around me. "I really do hate him."

He grasped my hand and kept hold until our arms stretched between us and he let go. I waved to him as I turned towards the chemistry building.

"Really, Jeremy, do you have to be annoying?"

"Do you remember me at all?"

"I guess."

The entrance was packed with students, and I found myself dodging between them, trying to keep up with Jeremy. He stopped inside the door. "Kate said she'd meet me here."

"Okay." I stood beside him, scanning the crowd. A trail of smoke wafted past my nose, and standing with my back to the wall left me feeling vulnerable. I tugged the fabric of my sleeve over my hand and covered my nose, breathing in the lavender scent. I took slow breaths trying to convince myself that I was safe, but it didn't work. I felt too exposed and pointed towards the stairs. "I'm going up. I'll try to find you guys after class."

"Okay," he said, not budging from his post.

I took the stairs to the third floor. The class was in a small lecture room, and I slipped in and took the last seat in the back row nearest the exit. Students I recognized from other classes started piling in, and Justin appeared in the doorway. I reached down to retrieve my book and pad, but when I sat up, he was walking towards me.

He took the seat next to me. "Hey, how are you?"

"Fine, good. I didn't thank you for trying to rescue me yesterday. I appreciate it."

"Sorry I wasn't successful."

"I emailed my other profs, so hopefully they'll be more lenient." He hadn't tried to hug me, and I liked that he was sitting beside me. He was a buffer between me and all the other students, a known rather than an unknown. I thought back to Doug and Zack's assessment of Justin and his friends. A super testosterone-hyped jock was how Doug had described Justin. I cut my eyes to him, wondering if he was really a good person. He'd been in a lot of my classes last year, and we shared a residence hall, but I knew little else about him. I made a mental note of my latest psychosis, paranoia.

The professor entered the room and opened his laptop. He looked up and tilted his chin first to the right and then towards us. His eyes went back to his computer, and he started calling students' names. Mine was the third name. I called out present, he moved to the next name, and I breathed a sign of relief.

It turned out Justin had lab with me and we paired up. The lab period was abbreviated as the teaching assistant only reviewed safety protocols and handed out the syllabus. As we left the building, I texted Doug. He and Zack met me at the sandwich cart.

Zack started in right away. "Everyone on the rowing team wants to see you."

The last thing I wanted was to look at more sympathetic faces. "I can barely lift my arm above my head. I can't row."

"You could come by practice tomorrow. I'm roping Doug in too."

I took Doug's hand. "You can go if you want. I have my fol-low-up appointment in the morning anyway."

"No, I'm definitely going with you for that."

"Lila can go. It's a five-minute thing."

He kissed my hand. "I'm taking you." We moved to the front of the line and ordered our sandwiches. "Want to go to the house to eat?" Doug asked.

"Let's grab a table outside."

"Well, I'm going to the house." Zack split off towards the fraternity building.

As we walked towards the courtyard, my phone rang. The screen indicated it was Dad, and I answered the call.

"Why haven't you called your mom?"

"What? I don't usually talk to her during the week. I texted her last night."

"Well, you could call tonight maybe."

"Okay, how are you, Dad?"

"I'm good. I'll be home tomorrow, and then we'll be up Friday night. We thought we'd stay the whole weekend. Have more time with you. We won't be in till late though. We'll meet you for breakfast before the game."

What I wanted was time alone to decompress, but there was no point arguing with him. I agreed to meet them for breakfast and dinner Saturday and then brunch on Sunday. Doug and I found an empty table and unwrapped our meals.

"My mom said she was cooking tonight and tomorrow. Mi-chael will be joining us tomorrow. Do you mind if we stay in the city? You can take me to the airport from there."

"That sounds fine," I told him between bites.

My appetite was poor at best, and I slid half my sandwich to Doug. Afterwards we found an isolated path that wound through the administrative buildings. The warm sun felt good after three hours of lectures under the ultraviolet lights.

"I could come to your Japanese class with you. I know the professor," Doug said when my phone alarm sounded.

"Thanks, but I don't want more attention than I already get."

He spun to face me. "Okay, I'll see you after." He kissed me on the lips. It was going to be hard when he left.

🐦 🐦 🐦

After the lecture, Doug, Lila, and I met at the car. At our apartment we walked Northie then piled in the car for the drive into the city. There were only two news vans in front of the apartment entrance now.

"Only two to go," Lila formed a gun with her thumb and finger, pointed it at the reporters, and curled her finger as if to pull the trigger.

"Lila!" I scolded.

"Well, they're annoying."

"They'll be gone by tomorrow."

"And back Saturday for the game." Doug pointed out.

"At least I won't be the story."

"You didn't know they covered it last week?"

"They did?"

Lila turned around to face me. "Sorry sweets. The team wore black armbands for you, so of course there were questions. You should find the interviews online. The football players were so sweet saying they were going to smash Peter's face."

It felt good to know people were on my side, wanted more than a dramatic story, but I hated the attention. I called Mom from the car and promised to phone her again the next day after my doctor's appointment. Dinner at Paula's was nice, and we were back in our apartment by nine. Ross arrived, and Doug and I retired to my room. I didn't like thinking we only had one day left together.

"I was thinking I would come back for homecoming," Doug said as he rubbed my shoulders.

"Can you really do that? Do you have that much time off?"

"I figure I'll come home for Homecoming, Thanksgiving, the wedding, and then the trial."

"That's a lot of traveling. It's really expensive, and you'll be exhausted."

"I want to be here for you."

"I have a lot of friends."

"Like Zack, who you obviously feel more comfortable talking to than me."

I pulled my hand from his. "What?"

"I saw you pull him out to the deck the other night. You won't talk to me about the attack but you will Zack?"

Standing, I put my hands to my hips. "I was apologizing for subjecting him to the story. It was wrong of me to ask him to listen to it."

"But you hardly talk to me about it at all. All I get is that you don't like trees, or leaves, or brick walls, the smell of smoke or sweat, and the orange streetlights."

"I used Zack to retell my story because I couldn't. It really wasn't my intent in the beginning. I just wanted someone there I felt safe with."

"And you felt safe telling the story in his presence and not mine."

"No, if you'd been there, it would've been you."

"Are you sure about that? You and Zack have this relationship that I'm not privy to."

"That's not true. I tell you everything."

"You won't tell me how you feel about the attack."

"You're jealous of a fictitious relationship. I don't tell you because I don't want to relive it. And up until yesterday, I didn't feel anything. Now I'm angry at everything."

"But you're not talking to me. This is a huge red flag."

"Are you reading psychology books now?" I swiped my phone off the bed. "This is me compartmentalizing. I want to enjoy time with my boyfriend, not have a therapy session with him. I see the counselor on Friday. Can't you just entertain me? Zack was right. You do have to fix things. Well I'm not a broken vase that can be glued back together. Why can't you let me be?"

I stomped out of the room to a wide-eyed Ross and Lila. She stood and pulled Ross off the couch. "We were about to turn in."

"Oh, sorry." I looked back towards my room, realizing they could hear our whole discussion.

"It's all good." Ross went into Lila's room.

Lila hugged me, but I stiffened in her arms. My heart raced, and I felt my blood boiling in my veins. "It'll be okay. Everyone's on overload."

Right, I thought, *so why couldn't Doug let me be?*

I slumped down on the couch and opened my messaging app and typed in Marissa's number. I hated conflict. Doug and I never fought. But I was too worked up. I couldn't go back in there and apologize. I was right after all. He was coercing me into feeling something I wasn't. I put all of my thoughts into a message to Marissa. She texted back immediately.

Didn't you used to fight with him all the time before you started dating?

But I didn't like it.

He's worried about you.

I don't want it to be like this with him.

You want perfection.

Can't he let me have a bubble? Distract me?

She texted about her roommate drama, and my heart rate went back to normal. After a few minutes, Doug came out of my room. "Are you coming to bed?" I looked at the clock on my phone, which read ten after ten.

"I guess I could sleep out here."

"No, come on. Let's talk."

I got up and joined him in my room. He patted the futon cushion. "I'm worried about you."

I sat down beside him. "Well, you need to stop. I want to enjoy you being here. It's the only good thing to come out of this."

"I'll try to let you be."

"Thank you." I rubbed my palms on his scruffy face and pressed my lips to his. We kissed until it wasn't enough. He helped me lift my shirt over my head, and I slid my hand along smooth chest. No video chat could replace his smell, the warmth that emanated from his body, or the tingling sensation on my skin when he touched me.

※　※　※

Beep, beep, beep. My phone sounded, waking me from a deep sleep. I'd set my alarm for seven and made Doug promise not to shut it off.

I reached for the device with my wrong arm, and a searing pain shot through my side.

"Can I get it now?"

"Yes, thank you," I said through gritted teeth. "That's going to set the incision healing back a week."

"It's been going off for five minutes but I didn't touch it."

"Thank you." I inched to the bathroom. There wasn't any blood around the incision, and I popped some ibuprofen in my mouth. I brushed my teeth and washed my face. Northie was in front of the door, tail wagging, when I finished. "That's my boy." I patted his head. Doug laid on the bed, computer in his lap. "Are you coming on a walk with us?" I asked, sliding on a pair of yoga pants.

"I need to get some stuff done. You okay alone?"

"Sure," I said, realizing I had no idea if I actually was. *Suit up,* I told myself, *don't be a wimp. You're going to have to get out there sometime.* Crossing the living room, I hooked Northie's leash on his collar and slipped on my shoes. I tucked the mace and my keychain, which included a pocket knife, compliments of my dad, into my pockets along with my phone.

Looking right and left, I stepped out the door and onto the sidewalk. The sun was coming up and all but a few of the lights had turned off. *I can do this,* I told myself. *He doesn't get to win.* Pressing my thumb to my sternum, I made my way to the path that ringed the grounds. Northie stopped to smell some bushes and bent to do his doggie business. I scooped it up and we headed towards the end of the property.

There were leaves on the path, but I ignored them. *Leaves are natural inanimate objects, they can't hurt you,* I told myself. But my heart rate quickened, and I scanned the area behind me. It was empty. I didn't like how the leaves crackled under my feet. They were too noisy. I wouldn't be able to hear someone behind me, and it made me even more nervous. *Paranoid. You're being paranoid.*

Halfway around the circle, a guy with a dog entered the path ahead of me. It was a big shepherd, and I slowed my pace. Even so, my breathing became labored causing my side to ache. He stopped to let his dog smell the grass, and I had no choice but to walk past him. *You idiot, you do have a choice. Run the other way. No, that's being paranoid. Pull it together.*

"Hi." He smiled and nodded.

Hand around my mace, I did the same, taking long strides to widen the gap between us. He followed behind, and I couldn't help but glance back every few seconds. By then I was speed-walking, my left hand glued to my incision and the right one pumping back and forth, propelling my body forward. Not caring if I looked like a complete freak running a puppy, I switched to a jog. I kept running until I couldn't see him anymore. *That's fine. You did what you needed to do*, my mental pep talk continued. It wasn't fine, I wasn't fine, and I knew it. Fine was a cop-out word for imbeciles, and I didn't believe it for one second.

At the apartment, I doubled over outside the door, trying to catch my breath. It wouldn't do to have Lila and Doug think I freaked out because there was a person on the path. After a minute, my breathing evened out. My side burned still, but I took a last long breath and shoved the door open. I unhooked Northie's chain and crossed to the pantry to fill his food and water bowl.

When I turned around, Doug stood in front of me, egg skillet in hand. "You're out of breath."

"Just winded, I was walking fast."

"Why?"

"It's chilly out."

He put a hand to my face. "You're sweating."

"I jogged a little."

"Are you nuts?"

"No, I can jog if I want." I maneuvered around him and stomped to my room. It wasn't any of his business anyway. I could run if I wanted.

He followed me. "Why are you being defensive?"

"Because—" I threw my hands into the air "—you're interrogating me. I feel like I'm under a microscope."

"You're mad at me for being worried about you?"

I put my hands on my hips. "Yes."

He kissed me. "Really? I guess you don't want eggs then."

"Don't pull that on me. Don't be flippant. I'm mad."

"At me? Okay, give me your best shot."

"Leave me alone." I poked his shoulder, and he backed out into the living room.

"Fine." He held his hands up. "I'm eating."

Where had that come from? Yes, I was mad, but not at him, at myself for being paranoid, running, and—I lifted up my arm and saw that spots of blood had soaked through my bandage— ripping my incision open. I took off the soaked dressing and got in the shower. The incision didn't really look much different once the bleeding stopped.

I dreaded the whole day, and that angered me too. Nothing was right. Nothing was good. I forced myself to take slow deep breaths and let the hot water and steam flood my senses.

There was a knock on the bathroom door and someone cracked it open. "Are you almost done? You have the nurse's appointment for your incision check in thirty minutes. I need a shower too."

"Yeah," I said, angry, feeling like I'd been robbed of the only part of my day that I looked forward to. My evening with Doug and his family would be nice, but that even seemed bittersweet since he had to leave the next day. It was too soon. I didn't want him to leave. Why did he have to live halfway across the world?

Wrapping the towel around me, I wiped the condensation from the mirror. I had to get my emotions under control. Being a basket case wasn't going to help anything. A tear formed in my eye and I swiped it away, grinding my jaws into each other. I grabbed the toothpaste, squirted it on my brush, and scrubbed my teeth till my gums hurt. I combed through my hair and applied some gel. Air-dried curls and a no-makeup look would have to do. My bruises had progressed to green, but those would be covered by my glasses.

Clutching my towel, I entered my room and sat down beside Doug. "I have to get dressed."

The corners of his mouth turned down. "I need a shower." He closed his computer and got up.

He got to the door, and I regretted being short with him. "I'm sorry. I'm overwhelmed."

"I know. It's okay."

"It's not okay. I'm sorry."

"I made you an egg sandwich. It's probably still warm."

"Thanks." I dressed and went to the kitchen to eat. Finishing the sandwich I went back to my room and packed my bag for a night at his mom's. We crated Northie and made our way to the parking lot.

"Do you want to talk about it?" Doug asked as he started the car.

"No, it's stupid. There was a guy on the path, and it freaked me out."

"That sounds legitimate."

"Really? Because it feels crazy."

"Not for someone who was attacked a week ago."

"I guess." I chewed my finger.

"Are you nervous about the appointment?"

I slipped my hand in my pocket. "No. I pulled the incision when I went running though. It was bleeding."

He rubbed his hand along my thigh. "You have to take it easy. Ask Lila or Kate to walk Northie with you or for you."

"I can do it. I want to do it."

"I know, never mind." He shook his head.

"What?" The question came out too loud, and water formed in my eyes. "I'm sorry. I'm angry. But not at you."

"I'm glad to see you feeling something. The whole stoic, blank, empty thing was starting to freak me out."

It seemed strange he'd experienced me as emotionless when I felt like everything was heightened. I exhaled and sucked in another breath slowly, willing the tears to stop. I wiped them on the back of my sleeve. "I'm sorry. Thanks for the sandwich. It was really good."

"Tomorrow we'll have breakfast in bed."

"That would be awesome." He pulled into a parking spot at the hospital, and I kissed him on the cheek.

"I love you."

"I love you too."

🕊 🕊 🕊

I was right about the incision. It wasn't healing as it should be. The nurse was sweet and told me the rib cage was a hard area.

She covered it with a special tape and scheduled an appointment with the surgeon for the next week.

The campus wasn't far from the hospital and Doug walked me to the classroom building. After a day of long lectures, he met me in the courtyard. He wrapped his arms around me, and I sank into him. "You look beat," he whispered into my hair.

"I am wiped out."

"Maybe you can take a nap."

We walked to the car and drove to my complex. The news crews were missing, and I hoped they were gone for good. Inside the apartment, I shed my shoes, grabbed the blanket, and sank down on my bed.

Doug kissed me on the cheek. "I'm going to walk Northie."

"Will you come back and lie down with me."

"Yes."

I was out not minutes after I laid my head down, and it seemed like only seconds before I felt a hand rubbing down my arm.

"Amanda, we should get into the city."

In the bathroom, I dowsed my face with cold water and brushed my teeth. We petted Northie goodbye and headed out. I pulled my phone out of my bag, realizing I'd left it off all day. It buzzed time after time with receipt of at least ten text messages and three voicemails. The last one from Mom read: OKAY, I FINALLY GOT IN TOUCH WITH DOUG. HE SAID YOU WERE OKAY AND HE WOULD REMIND YOU TO CALL ME AFTER CLASS. PLEASE JUST LET ME KNOW YOU'RE OKAY.

For goodness sakes, I was brain dead. I couldn't remember anything. I called Mom and then sent text messages to the rest of my family. Doug's phone rang and I answered for him. Bill was calling about a Light Up the Night event on campus. The university had planned an assault prevention awareness night that evening. I felt hot and cold at the same time. Why wouldn't everyone go about their business like nothing happened? And if they couldn't, why didn't anyone give me a heads up? Really, I shouldn't be mad. There was probably an email I didn't read.

Finishing the call, I turned to Doug. "Why didn't you tell me about this?"

"You were exhausted. I was waiting till you felt better. You're mad."

I said I wasn't mad, but in my mind, I was yelling at the world. "When did you find out about this?"

"This afternoon. Bill asked me to see if you would come by the house tonight."

My leg bounced. "I'm not going to campus tonight."

"Whatever you want to do is fine. I told Bill we were having dinner with my family. He understood."

"Okay." I opened my email app and scanned for communication from a university representative. I read through all my accounts, finding nothing but a campus wide announcement in the regular weekly email. Opening my notes app, I started a list of what I wanted to discuss with Dr. Milner the next day. I titled it: What I Need. First I listed: communication from University admin.

Next, I sent a message to Bill thanking him for thinking of me and then to Mark and Lila to check in. Lila's reply read: WE'RE GOING OUT AFTER THE LIGHT THING. WISH YOU WERE HERE AND WISH YOU COULD COME. NEXT WEEK MAYBE?

MAYBE, I replied, feeling guilty I wasn't going to the event with her.

I looked at Doug. "Maybe I should go to that light thing."

"Why are you rethinking it?"

"Lila is going. I feel like I should be there with her. What do you think?"

"It's your call."

"What time does it start?"

"Eight."

"I'll think about it. We could go back to your mom's after."

"Mom will understand if we don't stay the night."

I didn't like the thought of being in a room with lots of people. But unlike me, who was stuck in some sort of twilight zone, my friends were trying to move on. It was what people did after a tragedy. They came together, mourned, let it go, and started anew. I had no idea where I was in that process. My mind felt like a fuzzy, tangled web of goop.

As we pulled into the parking garage at Paula's condo, I sent text messages to Lila, Mark, and Bill saying I planned on coming to the house.

"You sure?" Doug asked when I told him my decision.

"It might be good for me."

"You don't have to push yourself."

"I'm not," I told him, but it was a lie. I wanted the whole thing to be finished. I wanted it to be six months from then. Japan sounded like a perfect spring break destination.

Paula, Gary, and Michael were waiting for us up in the condo. Paula had ordered take out from Mrs. Chen's Chinese restaurant. It was a nice haven from campus, and I found myself relaxed and unguarded for the first time in a week. No one looked at me with those huge sad eyes I'd grown accustomed to from Lila or my other friends.

After dinner we started a game of pool. Halfway through, Michael pointed the cue at me. "Hey, did you get pictures for me?

"Of what?"

"Bones, baby." He pointed to his rib cage.

"Oh." I looked towards Doug. "No, I saw the nurse today." It was then I realized I wasn't sure even what the doctors had done. They'd said something about pins but I wasn't sure what that meant. I put my hand to my forehead. My brain was such a mess.

Doug wrapped an arm around me. He kissed my temple and turned toward Michael. "I don't think you're getting pictures this time."

"Sorry, poor taste. I guess I shouldn't have had that second beer."

I laughed. "You're a cheap date."

"It's seven thirty," Doug whispered in my ear.

We cut the game short said goodbye to his family, planning to be back at seven the next day for breakfast. In the car, Doug took my hand. "Are you okay?"

"Sure," I told him, entering into my phone on my notes app that I needed to see my rib X-rays. We rode the rest of the drive in silence, me trying to formulate a plan of action rather than reaction. What did I want? What did I need? Most of the list included things I didn't want in my life, but many of those were beyond my control.

It was before eight when we turned into campus. The only lights came from news crew vans splattered on every major building's lawn. My hands got sweaty, and I rubbed them on my pants. What if there were reporters at the fraternity house? It was a prime location, and if I were covering the story, that was where I'd be. Why hadn't I thought about the press earlier?

"Maybe we should go back to my apartment."

"We may be able to get in the back door at the house. Do you want me to drive by?"

"I guess." My leg twitched and my thumb went to my mouth.

I sent a text message to Lila. She said the front lawn of the house looked like paparazzi central, but the back was clear. We turned into the rear lot, taking a spot along the drive. As we got out of the car, the lights from the house, and every other building, came on. Bill hadn't lied. With the new spotlights, it looked like afternoon on the back lawn, if sunlight had an orange tint. The hue of the green grass mixed with the orange light made the blades look brown. My heart thudded in my chest, and I shut out Peter's image by focusing on Doug's face. I wouldn't see his dark brown hair, his honey skin, or his deep blue eyes for another four weeks.

Beyond Doug, my eyes found the corner of the building Peter must have walked around that night. No leaves littered the path, and a giant light illuminated the side yard. A security camera was mounted near the gutters. An image of his face with thin lips pursed into a smile flashed through my brain. *He is not here. He can't hurt me. I am safe*, I repeated to myself.

Pressure on my hand made me refocus on Doug. "You ready?"

The back door was in front of us. I took a deep breath and closed my eyes, trying to reset all my senses. It was quiet. There was no sound of traffic, music, or activity save the hum of the camera crew's generators. A gust blew hair onto my face, and I opened my eyes. I didn't want to be there, didn't want to be a poster girl for a cause. I wanted to go back to my life and be a normal person. But I couldn't. Summoning my dad's Navy spirit, I chanted ooh-rah in my head. *What doesn't kill you makes you stronger.*

I looked at Doug's face. "Yes."

He turned the doorknob and opened the door. At first it seemed like a normal night at the house. Guys were playing pool and darts. When we got halfway through the room, the activities subsided. The brothers congregated around us. I gritted my teeth and forced myself to look at each person. I was surprised to see their eyes were different. Gone were the wide-eyed stares, and in their place, I saw creased brows and hard stares. Determined was the emotion I would have attributed to their features.

One of the brothers held out his hand to me as we passed, and I tapped his palm with mine. The other brothers followed suit, and by the time we reached the main room, the guys were packed into a line, their arms stretching into the aisle formed for us. I fought the instinct to flinch away from each one, stiffening my spine, raising my chin, and smiling at each face. I clenched Doug's hand, trying to take slow breaths in through my nose and out through clenched teeth. *Wide open spaces*, I repeated to myself as the wall of people began to close in on me.

In the front room, all eyes were glued to the big screen TV mounted above the fireplace. In the middle of the image, the president spoke from the steps of the main administration building. I followed Doug as he wound his way through the crowd until we reached the front. I found Lila, tears streaming down her face, and slid my arm around her shoulders. She kissed me on the cheek and turned back to look towards the screen.

"We at Northwestern University are dedicated to the safety of our students. We want our community to be a place where everyone feels safe. This Night of Lights symbolizes our University family's commitment to security. We want to thank the City of Evanston for its support." The president waved a hand at the cameras, and the reporters started to shout out questions.

The public relations woman stepped up to the podium. "The president will take a few questions." She pointed towards a woman reporter.

"How is the victim, Miss Avery? Have you talked with her? How is she feeling?"

The president leaned into the microphone. "We met last weekend, and she seemed in good spirits. She's a strong young woman. Her professors tell me she's been at every class this week."

"Do you know if Ms. Avery is participating in the lights event tonight?"

"I do not."

I dug my fingernails into my palm. The professors were reporting back to administration about my attendance? How creepy was it to have people watching like I was a lab rat. Why didn't the PR lady email me?

"What is Mr. Scalini's status?" Hearing his name, I refocused on the screen.

"Mr. Scalini has been suspended pending the outcome of the criminal trial."

The screen went black. "I think that's enough of that." Bill turned to face me. "I'm glad you came. Thank you."

"Of course." I squeezed Lila's shoulders and released her.

Mark gathered me in his arms. "Where have you been hiding? I haven't seen you since Tuesday."

"Hey guys, look out front!" someone called out.

The crowd moved towards the windows. A line of people walked along the sidewalk, holding up lit phone screens.

"It's Father," Doug said. "And all the people from the campus parish."

The group stopped in front of the house, and reporters gathered around them. My face grew flush, and then I felt a chill. I gripped Doug's arm for support. It was all too much. I hadn't even thought about praying or God since Mass on Sunday. To go talk to Father, who'd been such a support the previous year, hadn't even crossed my mind. And there he was with all the students from the parish in front of the house, showing support for me and my friends. Tears started to form in my eyes, and I wiped them away.

Doug tugged on Bill's arm. "You should probably go out and make a statement."

The edges of Bill's lips turned down. "Any chance you want to be the president again for fifteen minutes."

"None."

Bill looked up at the ceiling, took a deep breath, and then looked at me. "I can thank them from the fraternity and you. Is that okay?"

"That's a good idea, thanks."

"Okay, here goes." He spun towards the door and made his way through the crowd.

As soon as the door opened, the cameras panned towards him. He walked slowly to the sidewalk, sliding one sleeve and then the other up past his elbow.

He held up his hand as microphones were thrust at him. Someone turned the television on, but I kept my eyes on Bill. "Our chapter would like to thank you all for the support shown tonight. The members appreciate the compassion for our fraternity family."

"Is Amanda inside?"

"No comment. Thank you." He turned and walked back to the house, reporters trailing him. Halfway back to the building, he stopped and raised both his hands in the air. "We would appreciate if you could give our chapter and the students here a chance to return to their lives. Thank you."

The reporters dropped their mikes, and he walked back into the house. Outside, the crowd grew until the street was almost completely blocked by pedestrians, each person holding their lit screens in the air. We watched until nine when the lighting returned to normal. I tried to let it be what it was, a show of support, of solidarity, of strength. It would have been nice to be able to take in all the empathy shown in the event, but all I felt was anger. My life was a circus, and I was in the center ring.

Almost every brother found me and hugged me. By the end the imprint of all the arms didn't leave when they withdrew their arms. "I'm so sorry" and "I'm glad you're okay" rolled out of every mouth, and I tried to shut down my frustration. It wasn't their fault. There were no other words.

It was after ten before the street cleared and we felt comfortable getting the car through. Zack caught a ride with us, and I ducked down in the back seat so my head was below the door as we passed the camera crews. I was grateful they were all on campus and our apartment complex was quiet.

As soon as we were inside my place, Doug wrapped his arms around me. "I'm proud of you."

It was the last straw. I put my hands to his chest and stretched my arms out straight between us. "Don't touch me. Proud of me for what? Breathing? You can't be proud of people for breathing. Winning a race, acing a test, those are things to be proud of people for."

He stepped back. "I know you didn't want to be there. It was nice of you to go for the fraternity."

I bit my lip, regretting my reaction. "I didn't want to be there. But I'm glad I went. It was the right thing. I wanted to curl up in bed and be alone with you. Now I'm exhausted and feel like I need a shower."

"No worries. I could use one too."

"You can get mad at me."

"For what? Are you mad at me?"

"No, but don't say you're proud of me."

"Got it. Go shower. We still have all night."

I stayed in the shower until I was too hot, letting the steam, water, the heat of my skin, and smell of my soap block out all other sensations. After I toweled off, I found a tank and leggings and lay down on my futon. Doug returned from a walk with Northie and showered.

"Better," he said as he dried his hair.

"Yes. I wish you didn't have to go though."

"Me either. I'll be back before you know it. Your family will be in town this weekend and you have—"

I put my finger to his lips. "Don't try to cheer me up." I kissed him. "I just want to be with you."

He pointed at my ribs. "You have to watch that."

"I will." I smiled and leaned towards him, pressing my lips into his. I stripped my tank off, traced my fingers on his chest, and then pulled him to me. His skin was still hot from the shower, and the scent of his soap seeped from his skin. Those were the images and smells I wanted etched in my brain.

We stayed up till nearly two, kissing and talking about his next visit, the holidays, and the spring. We had the next six months all planned out, and it felt good to have something look forward to. I fell asleep on his chest, listening to his breath and the pounding of his heart.

❦ ❦ ❦

Our alarms sounded at six. I pushed up onto my elbow and stopped the ringing. Doug was already in the shower, and I went to the kitchen to start coffee. Waiting for it to brew, I checked my messages. Those from my family and Doug's were generally the same, and I sent a group reply to all of them: EVENT WAS NICE. IT WAS GOOD TO BE AT THE HOUSE WITH MY FRIENDS AND THE BROTHERS. LATE NIGHT AS IT WAS HARD TO GET OUT OF THERE. DRIVING DOUG TO THE AIRPORT THIS MORNING. LOOKING FORWARD TO SEEING EVERYONE THIS WEEKEND. LONG DAY OF CLASSES AHEAD.

I hoped that would satisfy everyone enough and that I could focus on my coursework for the rest of the day. The day would be broken up by the appointment with Dr. Milner and I was not looking forward to that.

Doug came out of my room dressed in slacks and a button down shirt. He'd shaved his face clean. I handed him a mug filled with coffee.

"You look nice."

He tugged at my shirt, his, which I was wearing, and kissed me. "You do too."

"I'm keeping this."

"I wouldn't have it any other way."

I hooked my fingers through his belt loops and put my head to his chest. "I'm going to miss you."

He kissed the top of my head. "I'll miss you too."

"Okay." I looked up. "I'm showering. Can you walk Northie?"

"Course." He kissed me on the lips. I slid my arm around his waist.

"Don't do that. We'll never get out of here."

"That would be nice."

I took a step away from him. "I love you."

"I love you too."

I hurried through my shower and blew my hair out straight. Wanting to look nice to see Doug off, I chose a pair of cords, tank, sweater, and boots.

"You look pretty," Doug said when he came in with Northie.

"Thanks."

He wrapped his arms around me. "I love you. Please take care of yourself."

"I will. We'll talk twice a day like before."

"Good." He kissed me. I held his face between my hands, hoping I would never take him for granted.

We rolled his bag out to the car, and I drove him to the airport. When I pulled up to departures, he kissed me and jumped out of the car with his suitcase. I watched him walk into the building and pulled into traffic. It was good I had a running list of things that needed to be done as it distracted me from thinking about him being gone.

I got to campus with enough time to grab a bagel and another cup of coffee from the sandwich cart. Entering the lecture hall, I saw Justin seated in the last row. Fortunately I had timed it so he only got time for a hello before the professor started the class.

"Hey, you look good today," Justin said as soon as the lecture ended.

"Thanks." I packed my book and tablet in my bag.

"This seems like a pretty tough class."

"The prof got bad reviews too."

"Do you want to start a study group? I don't really know anyone else in the class."

"That would work." I stood, smoothing my pants and hoisting my pack onto the shoulder on my good side.

"How about Sunday afternoon?"

"That should be okay."

He pulled out his phone. "Give me your number and I can text you. Where do you live?"

"I can meet you at the library." I held out my hand, and he gave me his phone. I entered the numbers in, and he called me so I could store his number.

In the hall, I pointed towards the stairwell door. "I'm taking the stairs. I'll see you later."

"Oh, I'll walk with you."

He asked about Doug and my summer, and I asked him about his. We crossed the courtyard, walking towards the physics building. Inside, he walked straight to the stairwell door and held it open. "After you."

"Thanks." I was glad he wasn't being too nosy about the stairs thing. The closed space of the elevator with strangers who might be smelly wasn't something I wanted to brave. *Baby steps*, I told myself. It made me mad that I liked having someone to walk with. I liked being independent and felt like I was using him. He was a known in a sea of unknowns. I didn't have to think about scanning crowds for potential dangers.

At the restrooms, I stopped. "I'm going to take a break."

"Oh, me too." He entered the men's room a few feet down.

My phone buzzed, and I answered the call.

"Hi, love."

"Doug, are you on the plane?"

"Yep."

"Have a good flight. I love you."

"I love you too. How was your class?"

"Good. Justin walked with me to the physics building."

"The football guy?"

"Yes."

"That was nice. I have to go. I love you."

"I love you too. Text me when you can."

"Will do, bye."

"Bye." I ducked into the bathroom. Justin stood in the hall when I finished. Again it made me angry that I liked having him there. "You didn't have to wait."

"Do I seem like a stalker? I thought you might want someone to walk with. Your boyfriend is usually here."

"I do actually. Thank you." Tears formed in my eyes, and I was glad for the huge dark glasses I wore. In class I had a chance to wipe them with my fingers when I leaned down to stow my bag under the table.

"I could use a study group for this too." Justin pointed towards the podium.

"I'm not sure how much help I'll be on either. They're not my strongest subjects."

"Aren't you a chemistry major? Didn't you have a 4.0 spring quarter?"

"I guess."

"You guess, or you did?"

"Yes, I did."

"I'm thinking two brains are always better than one." He tapped his temple with his pen.

The professor started the lecture, and I tried to type every word. I had no idea what he was talking about. Getting in a lot of study time was a must that weekend. After class, Justin and I took the stairs down to the main level.

"Where are you headed now?" he asked as he held the door open for me.

"The library."

"Okay." He turned in the direction of the building. "Hey, were you on campus last night. Did you see the lights? That was really cool."

"Yes, it was nice." I lied, thinking it was horrible to hate something that was a gesture meant to show me support. It was nice, but it reminded me how gross my life was. Probably it was more that the University was trying to save their reputation anyway. I wondered how many applicants they would lose that year.

"Hey, the team is wearing teal armbands this week."

I stopped. "What?"

He rubbed his nose and then looked at the sky and back at me. "Teal armbands for, umm, assault prevention awareness. The black ones were morbid."

My heart thumped in my chest, and I dug my nails into my palm. "Oh, right. That was nice of you guys."

He rubbed his nose again. "That was before we knew who had gotten attacked and if you were okay."

I tucked my hands in my back pockets to keep them from trembling. "I didn't see the game but Lila told me." I mentally added armbands to the list of things I hated.

"Oh, well, should we?" he motioned in the direction of the library.

"Sure." We resumed our walk.

"Are you rowing? I haven't seen you at the athletic center."

Was he nuts? I reeled in my anger. He clearly didn't know anything about my injuries. "No, broken ribs kind of nixed that."

"Oh man, that sucks. You can't even coxswain?"

"Can't swim. Can't be on the boats."

"I'm sorry. Well maybe you could come by, and we could do weights or something else."

"Okay, maybe," I told him, having no intention of going to the gym to work out with him. If I had to hear one more person say they were sorry, I was going to blow my top.

Chapter 9

It nearly killed me to sit in the library trying to study, feeling unfocused and waiting the hour before my appointment. I'd never harbored so much anger, and I had no idea what to do with it.

I continued typing my list on the phone, hitting the screen with my fingers. Things I hated: autumn trees, fall leaves, orange lights, Peter Scalini, the smell of sweat, the smell of smoke, deserted walkways, being infamous, black armbands, teal armbands, oversized sunglasses, concealer, broken ribs, healing incisions, Light up the Night events, administration that was keeping tabs on me but didn't bother to communicate, people who thought they could hug me, people saying they were sorry, empathetic eyes, a boyfriend who was literally halfway around the globe, parents who were too involved, not being able to row, not being able to run, reporters, TV crews, news vans, and last but not least, heart arrhythmias. I erased the heart arrhythmia in case she decided to send me to the medical center.

Noting the items didn't really abate my anger, but it was all I could do for then. I set my alarm and opened my organic chemistry book. My leg bounced, and I chewed my thumbnail as I read and re-read the first chapter. The bell on my phone sounded, and I jumped. Stuffing my book into my bag, I made my way outside and to the administration building. Dr. Milner's office was on the third floor, and I took the stairs.

In the office, a woman sat behind a desk. I indicated I had an appointment, and she asked me to wait in one of the chairs placed along the wall. While I waited, my phone dinged, indicating receipt of a text.

I swiped my screen, revealing a message from Stephen. SOME OF THE RESIDENCE HALL ASSISTANTS ARE TAKING CLASSES TO TEACH AN ASSAULT PREVENTION COURSE. THE CLASS STARTS NEXT WEEK. I WAS THINKING YOU MIGHT WANT TO COME AND BE INVOLVED. I THOUGHT IT MIGHT BE GOOD FOR YOU AND THE PARTICIPANTS.

I jammed my fingers into the screen. NO, NO, AND NO, I typed. In what world and why did he think I would want to take the class. So I could prevent it from happening again? To coach others, help them not make the same mistakes I did? I'd taken those courses before. Dad made sure we were up on our safety skills. I'd tried to run, to scream. My mace and keys were inaccessible. All I'd been able to do was connect with Lila. He may have done something much worse if it weren't for her fast thinking. But I couldn't write that to Stephen. I hit the delete button until the message field was clear and sent: THANKS FOR THINKING OF ME. SEND ME THE SCHEDULE AND I'LL SEE IF IT WORKS.

I bounced the phone on my thigh. Would I ever be a normal person again? Or would I be forever remembered as Amanda, the girl who got assaulted at the fraternity house sophomore year. "Slap, slap, slap." My phone pounded the fabric of my pants as my leg jostled up and down. The door to the inner office opened, and Dr. Milner followed a girl to the desk in front of me. I held my phone screen in front of my face pretending to study the images. It sucked that I had to be there. I figured the girl thought it did too. While I wore huge sunglasses, she didn't, and I wanted to give her as much privacy as possible.

When she was gone, Dr. Milner turned to face me. "Hi, good to see you. You can join me in my office now." The pitch of her voice was high, and she smiled like it was a happy occasion.

I stood up, secured my bag on my good shoulder, and slipped my phone in my back pocket. *Here goes nothing*, I thought. I followed her into a room with green walls. I imagined the color would be called seafoam. Of course a psychologist's office would be painted a soothing green.

She sat in a chair in front of her desk, and I took the one opposite her. Crossing one leg over the other, she picked up an electronic tablet off her desk. "For notes." She held it up to me.

"Sure." I produced the best smile I could muster and wiped my wet palms on my pants. To be studied, reported on, like my professors had, that's what I wanted.

She set the device on her lap and folded her hands on top of it. "How are you?"

I bit my lip, fighting the scream that threatened to emerge from my vocal chords. Examining the rest of the room, I moved my eyes back to her. "Okay."

A smiled formed on her face. "Okay?"

"Well, yes and no. I am okay, or mostly okay, physically. Although I pulled my incision open running away from a dog walker on a trail. He was probably harmless, so I'm pretty sure I had a paranoid anxiety attack. But, if you want to know how I feel, I feel so angry I can't even see straight." I gazed at the ceiling, tears forming in my eyes. Swallowing hard, I slid my phone out of my pocket and held it out to her. "I made a list of things I'm angry about, and it's really long and only getting longer by the second. Every time I turn around there's something else to be mad about. Like this RA friend who texted wanting me to be the poster child in their assault prevention classes."

She handed me a box of tissues, and I patted my face dry.

"Being angry is a good thing. You should be angry. What happened to you shouldn't have happened."

"It feels horrible. For the past two days, I've been angry about everything."

She lowered her head to look at my phone screen. "Many of these things we can't control, but some of them we can do something about."

She handed me the device and circled around the desk, pulling her desktop phone closer to her. She tapped on her computer, lifted the phone's receiver, and punched the speaker button. She called the public relations person about communicating the University's plan for events relating to the incident. The PR person agreed to have me copied on all correspondence and included in meeting invites.

She took the seat opposite me again. "Okay, that's at least one item checked off the list."

"Thank you."

"What did you think of the group Tuesday?"

"Misty hates me."

"Why do you say that?"

"In the parking lot, she looked at me and said, 'Not cool.' I think it was because my boyfriend picked me up. But what was I supposed to do? Walk home alone?"

"Misty is a very protective person. Don't give up on the group though."

We chatted about my experience as a freshman, and I told her about my summer at home. She talked about the process of mentally recovering from a violent assault, which was a little like losing a loved one, or more like my experience after the previous year's accident. The good news was that I was sort of already on stage two—anger.

I left her office exhausted and overwhelmed, almost even more emotional than I'd entered. Now I had much more to process than my anger. I surveyed the sky, the trees, the buildings, and students on the walk, wondering what to do next. I hadn't eaten since breakfast, but all my feelings formed a huge ball in my stomach.

The library seemed again like the perfect haven, and I retraced my steps back to the same table on the second floor. Taking some long deep breaths, I unpacked my Japanese book and started to read. I popped my headphones in my ears and started the audio that accompanied the book. When my alarm sounded, I'd finished the lessons from the past two lectures.

Walking to my class, I added up how much study time I needed. The calculations included six classes times two hours each for a total of twelve hours, two good days of coursework. I hoped my parents would leave early Sunday so I could have some focused time.

❦ ❦ ❦

Leaving Japanese, I mentally put that class along with Chinese literature in the things I liked column along with Friday afternoons and an evening of free time. At my apartment, all hopes for a quiet night under my covers studying vanished as I walked in the door.

"Amanda, you look great." Mom wrapped her arms around me before I could even shed my backpack.

"Wow, you're here already." I wriggled away from her.

"Your mom took off work early so we could come take you to dinner." My Dad gathered me into his arms.

Mom took my backpack and set it on the floor. "We already took little Northie here for a walk." She held his face in her hands and kissed his mouth.

I tucked my hair behind my ears and made bug eyes at Lila who shrugged her shoulders and ducked into the kitchen. "Wow, thanks. I'm going to unpack and freshen up." I pointed towards my room.

"Take your time, sweetie."

I carried the books to my room and closed the door behind me. Exhausted, entertaining my parents was the last thing I wanted to do. I took my time storing my things and brushing my teeth.

When I joined them in the living room, they were already reviewing restaurant choices. "Tia and Ed won't be in till about seven. Do you want to wait for them or go out earlier?" Mom asked.

"Either way is fine. I'm hungry, but I can grab a snack." I moved towards the kitchen, and they followed, taking seats at our table.

"We can go anytime."

I grabbed a vitamin drink and sat down beside them. "I'm really tired. Maybe we could get takeout."

Mom took my hand. "Of course, whatever you want, sweetie."

I wondered if I could get anything I wanted. Maybe it was a good time to bring up the possibility of switching majors. Of course Dad would probably advise me against making any major decisions, and then we'd be back to square one.

"I've been sitting all day. Do you guys want to take another walk?"

"Oh sure." They both stood and followed me into the living room, and I hooked on Northie's leash.

We walked around the perimeter of the grounds. I shared about the previous night's event, the armbands, the assault prevention course, and finally being in the loop with the campus admin. They were concerned when I told them my incision was slow to heal, but I assured them the nurse said it was a hard spot.

After our walk, we phoned an Italian restaurant, and Dad and I drove to pick up the order. The main thing I'd been worried about with their visit was the constant dialog that I always felt I had to maintain. I loved my parents, but having to skirt around all the issues drained me. We couldn't talk about Doug, or classes, or grades, and it left us with topics like football, the fraternity, my friends—who I knew nothing about these days—and Northie.

When Ed and Tia arrived, we went through the same subjects again. "Well, I am taking you to the spa on Sunday," she said.

"Wow, that's nice. I would really love to take you up on that, but I have at least twelve hours of study time to get in this weekend."

My dad stood and hiked his belt up. "How did you get that behind on your coursework already? I'm sure Doug being here didn't help."

I squinted and lifted my chin towards the ceiling, trying to keep my eyes from tearing up. "It was a busy week." I stood and stretched. "And I am really tired. The game is early tomorrow. Do you guys want to meet up for dinner afterwards?"

"We can come by for breakfast too."

Mom stood and looked at her watch. "Charlie, give her some space. It's late. You should have said you were tired. But we'll bring you some breakfast before the game. You don't have anything but eggs and bagels in your fridge."

Dad lifted his coat off its hook. "We'll help you get groceries Sunday before we leave."

Slow breaths, they're trying to help, I thought. "That'd be nice."

"Okay, then." Mom slid her arms into the coat Dad held up for her. "We'll see you at eight."

They filed out, and I leaned against the closed door. Northie sat beside me, muzzle up and tail swishing. He needed to be walked so I called Kate. She and Jeremy came by, and we walked

Northie around the complex. Gazing up at the trees which were illuminated by the orange lights, I fought the impending sense of déjà vu. I dug my nails into my palms and reminded myself that I was safe, that Peter was not around the next bend. Kate grabbed my hand and pulled me toward her.

"You okay?"

"Sure." I blinked to reset my thoughts. "How are you guys? Jeremy, what's the latest gossip?"

Kate and Jeremy always knew interesting stuff and kept me entertained the rest of the walk.

"Thank you," I told them as we got back to my apartment.

"No worries, any time," Kate said.

Jeremy pretended to punch me on my bicep. "Hey, you around this weekend? We're inviting people to our place after the game."

"My parents are here, but maybe I'll stop by for a little. I have a ton of studying to catch up on. Thanks for inviting me."

"Course, you're always invited."

"Thanks." I closed and locked the door behind them. Checking my messages, I saw that Lila had texted.

Hey U OK if I stay with Ross 2nite?

I was exhausted and doubted I'd be awake very long. Sure. Exhausted, no worries. Parents descend at 8 AM 2morrow FYI.

Oh, good 2 know. Thanks. Goodnite. Love U!

Love U 2!

In my room, I peeled off my clothes and changed into pajamas. Washing for bed, I slid under the covers. They were cold, and I wished Doug were there to warm them. Picking up my phone, I dialed his number.

"Hey," he answered. "I was about to call you."

"Well, I beat you!" We talked for more than half an hour, and although it was only ten, I could barely hold my eyelids open.

"You going to be okay alone?"

"Are you kidding? I have waited all day to be alone."

"I would have left before if I knew you didn't want me there."

"You know I didn't mean you."

"I hope you would tell me if you needed space."

"I would."

"Good. I love you."

"I love you too." I ended the call and set my alarm for seven the next morning. By then the covers were warm but only in the small space I occupied. I pulled them up around my chin, and Northie snuggled next to me. It was quiet, and my mind wandered through my to-do list. How was it that I'd been sleepy talking to Doug, but the next minute, my mind raced with thoughts? I laid my arm on Northie and tried getting to sleep the way I had as a child. First, I imagined my feet getting heavy and sinking into the mattress, then my legs, torso, arms, and finally my head.

His thin lips curved up on one side. "Hi, princess. Miss me?" He swaggered towards me. I spun around, seeing gnarled trees blocking my escape. I glanced up to see a single orange streetlight directly above my head and down to see leaves, burying my feet up to my ankles. "Nice to see you here. I've been waiting for you."

The branches reached out and wound round my wrists, and the leaves became quicksand around my legs. I opened my mouth and forced air through my vocal chords, but no sound came out. His fingers found my throat, and he squeezed them into my flesh. I could smell his hot breath on my face. "I told you this would happen."

I flailed my arms and legs with as much force as I could muster. A high-pitched scream erupted from my throat, the force engulfing my ribs in flames.

I opened my eyes to Northie's teeth barred not six inches from my face. I sucked in a breath, and my side seared with pain. My hand shook as I held it out towards Northie.

"It's okay boy. It's me." I could barely pet him for the convulsions rocking my body. Sweat covered me and goosebumps lined my arms. I stood and yanked the blanket off the bed, encasing it around myself. I picked up my phone. The screen read 2:02. Finding the light switch, I flipped it up and went out into the living room and did the same. Still trembling, I curled up on the couch.

"It wasn't real. I'm safe," I said again and again as I stroked Northie.

I turned on the TV, but all the commercials were for Halloween horror movies, so I started the movie *Pretty in Pink* with Molly Ringwald from mom's collection. I watched almost the whole thing before I became relaxed enough to doze off.

❦ ❦ ❦

Northie woke me at six by pawing at my leg. I got up and went to the bathroom and checked my incision. There was blood on the bandage, and I cleaned the area and got a new one. I found some yoga pants, jacket, and Northie's leash. The sun was up, and it was light enough outside that the parking lot lights were off. Still, I went straight to the meadow, walked Northie for a few minutes, and retraced my steps back to my apartment. Halfway through the parking area, I heard my name.

"Hey, you were up late last night. Wild party?" Zack walked towards me, gym bag on one shoulder.

"No, couldn't sleep."

"You okay?" He bent down to pet Northie.

"Had a nightmare."

"Brutal."

"Why were you up so late?"

"Work hard, play harder."

"Where are you headed now?"

"Duh, rowing."

"Oh, right."

"Hey, everyone says hi. You should come by, maybe Tuesday."

"Maybe, I'll see."

"You going to the game?"

"No, catching up on studying. Everyone will be here later if you want to come by."

"Okay, chief, will do."

"Chief?"

"That's what I got today." He spun around me and backed towards his car.

"Have a good one."

"You too." He waved and turned to his car.

Back inside, I showered, texted Marissa, and confirmed my client tutoring sessions for the week. I was glad I already knew my five clients. I'd worked with each of them for almost a year.

Mom, Dad, Tia, and Ed arrived after eight with breakfast sandwiches from my favorite spot. The food was good, but I could only get half of a sandwich down.

"Are you sure you won't come to the game?" Mom asked. "I worry about you being alone."

"I'm okay alone. I have a lot to catch up on."

"Seems like you should be there to support the cause, what with the team wearing the teal bands and everything." Dad stood up and took his plate to the kitchen.

No, I thought, this was their cause, not mine. "I'll watch on TV."

Mom got up and cleared the table, and I put the rest of my meal in a container for later. They had friends to meet for tailgating and stayed only an hour. After they left, I retreated to my room and stacked all my books on the futon. Choosing physics first, I got in two hours before Northie started whining.

I put on my shoes and jacket and took him outside, trying to decide on a good route. We walked around the meadow, and then I took the path to the street. Before I realized it, we were standing on the corner of the street that led to Peter's apartment. Crossing the street, I walked along the sidewalk to a coffee shop. I tied Northie to a table outside and went inside to get a coffee. It felt good to be outside doing something normal, and I sat in the sun and sipped my coffee before walking back to the apartment.

Inside, I turned on the television and sat on the couch, studying calculus and then macroeconomics. At halftime, they replayed the pre-game footage, and Justin was front and center in his teal armband. I turned the volume up to hear him over the background noise.

"Why did the team choose you as a spokesperson for this cause?"

No, no, Justin, I thought, but he did it anyway. "I know the victim. This is personal to me."

"Stop, Justin," I screamed at the screen.

"You know Ms. Avery? Can you tell us a little bit about her, how she is?"

"Amanda is a beautiful strong girl, and she will be great."

I slapped my hand to my head.

"It sounds like you think very highly of Ms. Avery."

"We all do." His face flushed, and Justin looked into the camera. "We love you, Amanda." He blew a kiss.

The players behind him followed suit, screaming into the microphone. "Amanda, we love you. Be strong." They pointed at their armbands, blew kisses, and held up two fingers to form a V shape.

My feelings vacillated between anger, embarrassment, and appreciation. I turned on my phone and found a string of messages from Lila, Marissa, and Tia. ARE U WATCHING? DID YOU SEE JUSTIN? DOES DOUG HAVE ANYTHING TO WORRY ABOUT?

Ignoring the texts, I turned off my phone and continued studying, finishing Chinese literature and economics by the time my family returned from the game. The Wildcats had a decisive victory, and everyone was in a good mood. Mom started in on chores right away. I had to admit I hadn't thought much about cleaning. It annoyed me that she darted around the house, but I was too tired to fight her. I needed the help anyway. Tia pitched in and helped me start my laundry. My ribs still hurt from the night's incident, and I could barely move that side without feeling like I was tearing the skin, so I was grateful for their help.

Dad and I took Northie for another walk. I dreaded being alone with him as I knew the inquisition would start. Was I eating right? Was I keeping my appointments with the psychologist? Was I going to classes?

He didn't disappoint, but after my six hours of study time, I was able to report I was almost caught up, and he had little to condemn.

"I'm proud of you—"

"Dad, don't say that. Don't—"

He held his hand up. "But I am. I suspect there was a bit of a honeymoon period when you were in shock. I don't know where you are in that process, but you look angry to me."

My mind couldn't form words. "How could you tell?"

"I can see it in your eyes, your jaw. It won't do you any good to hold it in."

"But most of it is misplaced. I can't be angry at Mom for helping clean or you for buying me groceries. Those are nice things to do."

"I'm watching you. At the first sign this is going south, you come home to Champaign with us."

Really? That was his go to? We were having such a nice conversation and then, wham, back to the threats of carting me home. I bit my tongue and studied the sky. "I'm doing everything I'm supposed to be doing. Why do you need to threaten me like that?"

"It's not a threat. It's a promise. I see you wincing when you stretch, I see you cover your nose with your sleeve, and I see you scanning the area as we walk. You can stay, but you have to show me you are successful, that means grades, that means socially, that means emotionally."

"Yes Dad, my side hurts. I had surgery and the incision is still sore. Yes, I make sure I am safe by checking my surroundings. Anyone in my position would do the same."

"I think it's a good idea for you to participate in those assault prevention classes. Maybe you and Lila could do it together. She could probably use some psychotherapy too."

Great, he'd added one more thing I was expected to do. If there was one way to make me not want to do something, it was to have Dad want me to do it. We circled back to the house where Tia and Mom were writing a shopping list. They had included a huge number of items we would never eat. Reeling in my anger, I flipped the page and wrote: fruit, lettuce, broccoli, low-fat vanilla yogurt, quart of skim milk, shredded mozzarella cheese, vinaigrette dressing, eggs, pasta, and bagels. After being in the apartment all day and cooped up with my family for two hours, I was ready to get out, and we phoned a restaurant for reservations.

Mark, Lila, and Ross joined us for dinner, so it was quite a big party. I liked having the distraction of new conversation topics and being in a big group where I could be anonymous. Later,

Mom, Tia, and I went food shopping and then met up with everyone else back at my apartment. Zack and Bill also showed up about nine.

Bill folded his arms around me. "We missed you at the meet this morning."

"How did it go?"

"Not as good as when you were there."

"Sorry, I had to catch up on studying. I'll try to make the next one."

"You should come by practice Tuesday."

Zack pointed at me. "That's what I told her. Should I drive you?"

"Yes, I guess." There was no sense in prolonging the inevitable. Knowing Zack, he'd already come up with an exercise plan for me.

"Hey, I thought of a bunch of workout options for you."

"Are you inside my head?"

"What?"

"I seriously just thought you were doing that."

"I was born to be your trainer. Can't let those muscles go to waste." He held up my right arm. "No wimpy allowed."

"Ooh rah," I said and snagged a sip of his beer.

"Hey." He grabbed it back but then held it out to me. "If anyone deserves this you do."

The crowd was starting to thin around ten with Zack, Bill, and Mark heading out. I made plans for brunch with Mom,

Dad, Tia, and Ed, and we said goodbye in the parking lot. Ross and Lila joined me on my walk with Northie.

Lila linked her arm in mine. "Hey, your dad was saying something about a self-defense class?"

"Stephen messaged me about it."

"Would we get to hit anyone?"

"I don't know."

"If so, I'm in. I was already thinking we should learn karate, or Jiu Jitsu, or something. Your dad had you take self-defense in high school, right?"

"Yeah, a lot of good that did."

"Hey, don't say that."

We circled back to the apartment, and Ross and Lila retreated to her room. It wasn't until then that it hit me. It was night time, and I was going to be alone again. In the bathroom, I washed my face and brushed my teeth. Finding my laptop, I called Doug.

"I thought you'd never call, your phone was off all day." He smiled into the camera. "I miss you."

"I miss you too."

We talked about our days. I couldn't believe he'd only been gone thirty-six hours. It already felt like a week. After half of an hour, exhaustion caught up with me, my eyelids started drooping, and we said goodnight.

I slipped under the covers with my socks and jacket on, rubbing my limbs on the cold linens to warm them. Northie jumped up on the bed and circled, curling up beside me once I'd settled in my position. I didn't normally sleep with a light, but I left the lamp on, figuring it might keep any nightmares away. Anxious about repeating the dream from the previous night, I turned on my phone and started making lists. First, I typed in all my expenses and marked ones to discuss with dad. Next, I completed a to-do list and week's schedule, sending confirmation emails to my tutoring clients. I messaged Stephen about the self-defense program. Finally there was nothing else to do, and I turned off my phone and slid it onto the table.

Northie sidled up to me, and I rested one arm on his back. Thinking I'd jinxed myself the previous night, I closed my eyes and waited for the flashes of light on my eyelids to dim.

Running on a path lit by a line of glowing jack-o-lanterns and deep with leaves, I stumbled on a root. My palms, chest, and chin hit the cold wet ground, and I looked up to see the carving on a pumpkin form his image. Scrambling back, I slammed into a rough tree trunk. The heads in front of me began to levitate and circle around me, increasing their speed until they were a ring of orange light. Then, they broke formation and hovered in front of me, changing positions in a seemingly random manner until they stopped and his thin lips formed the words.

"Hi, princess."

At first I was too scared to think, and then my brain kicked in. Scream, it told me.

My eyes flew open, and I woke to see my lamp knocked over, covers strewn all over the floor. With a cold sweat pasted on my skin, I retrieved my covers and set the light upright. My door flew open, and I spun around, lifting the lamp out in front of me like a sword.

"Stop."

Lila and Ross stood in front of me, her in a t-shirt, and him in boxers.

"Oh my God." I covered my eyes with my free hand.

"Amanda, are you okay? We heard you screaming."

"Yeah, I had a nightmare." Peeking at my table, I set the lamp down in front of me.

"Okay, everything's good, no intruder. I'm going," Ross said.

"He's gone." Lila wrapped her hand around my fingers and tugged them away from my face.

"Sorry." I slumped down on my bed.

"What happened?"

"I was having this dream. There were glowing pumpkins, and they formed an image of his face and talked."

"Peter? Oh my God, that's freaky."

"I had a nightmare last night too and ended up sleeping in the living room with the lights on."

She wrapped her arms around me. "You're safe."

"Thanks. I'm okay, you can go back to sleep."

"You sure?"

"Yes." I patted her arm.

"Okay." She got up. "I'll be in my room if you need me."

I didn't want to keep them awake, so I started a movie on my computer. I chose *Sixteen Candles*, another Molly Ringwald romantic comedy from mom's collection.

Northie woke me a little after six, nudging me with his wet nose. It was starting to get light out, so I slipped on my boots and jacket and walked him to the field. I stood in the sun, letting its warmth engulf me and wondering how long the dreams would last. Remembering my nightmares from last year, I shuddered. Was being killed by a maniac worse than falling to your death? I wasn't sure. I walked to the street and stayed on the sunny side, going about a mile up and back.

With plenty of time before meeting my family, I showered and started studying. By the time Lila and Ross were up, I'd already read through my Japanese, which only left calculus and physics. It wasn't how I was used to operating. Normally, I would've already read ahead for the next lectures, but I reminded myself I had the rest of the day to prepare.

I drove to the restaurant to join my family for brunch. Mom was concerned that they should stay longer, but I reminded her of all the studying I still had to do and the dinner we had planned for that evening. As we finished the meal, I broached the subject of the medical and psychotherapy bills with Dad. The health insurance would cover eighty percent of the costs, and Dad agreed to pay half of the remaining hospital expenses. With the psychotherapy, he dug in his heels, not agreeing to help since I wasn't heeding their advice and taking a quarter off. The bills would set me back thirteen hundred dollars, more than two month's rent. Hopefully, I could increase the number of tutoring clients with the extra time I had. Otherwise, my funds were going to run low. At least Mom had paid for my groceries the previous day, and I hoped the self-defense classes would be free.

We said goodbye in the restaurant parking lot. There wasn't a home game for another two weeks, but Mom said they'd decide Thursday if they'd come the next weekend. I felt guilty for thinking it but prayed they wouldn't feel the need to visit. I could use a solid weekend for studying, chores, and extra work. Not to mention a break from Dad's critical eye.

Back at my apartment, I walked Northie around the complex and started a load of laundry. Lila and Ross had gone to the house, and I started reading material for the next day's lectures. By late-afternoon when Lila, Ross, and Mark arrived, I had talked to Doug and was ready for Monday's set of classes.

As I put away my books, my phone rang, and I answered it.

"Hi, Amanda, this is Chris Taylor," Doug's brother began.

"Hi, Chris."

"I was calling to talk about scheduling discovery. We have some new developments with the team, and I was wondering if you could meet tomorrow afternoon."

"I get out of class at three, but I have a tutoring session at four."

"We're going to need several hours. Can you cancel your meeting? Can we meet at three thirty?"

"Sure."

"Dad said I should pick you up."

"I'll have my car. I'll meet you."

"Okay, I'll text the address." He asked about my schedule, and I realized committing to tutoring sessions was premature, as he wanted me free every afternoon that week. Thinking my funds were going to be in serious jeopardy, I ended the call and plopped down on my bed. Spinning my phone in my hands, I stared at the wall.

Suck it up, buttercup, I told myself, swiping a tear away. I opened my computer and emailed my tutoring clients. It wasn't fair for them to miss so much time, and I offered to find other tutors if they needed. Silently, I prayed they would resume the sessions. *One thing God, just let one thing go my way this week*, I thought.

Thinking of God, I realized I hadn't talked to Paula or thought about attending Mass. Mass was another item I could put on my early morning schedule. Checking the time, I realized Paula would be at church, and I created a reminder to call her.

Dinner with our friends was fun. Stephen was happy to hear Lila and I were interested in the self-defense class. I didn't mention that my only motive was keeping Dad happy. Hitting things sounded good, but although there was a physical component, he couldn't promise we would be punching anyone. Zack and Bill made me promise to go to rowing practice with them on Tuesday.

Afterwards, we finished the dishes, and Mark walked Northie with me. When we returned to the apartment, Lila plopped down on the couch, wine bottle and two glasses in hand.

"So, nightmares, right?"

"I dread going to sleep." I rested my head on the cushion behind me.

"This—" she held the bottle above my head "—is the perfect cure."

"Drinking?"

"You probably have to drink enough to fall asleep."

"That's not a healthy solution."

She lifted a finger off the bottle and pointed it at me. "But it is a solution. We have class early, and I was going to stay with Ross, but I'm worried about you."

"And getting me drunk and leaving me alone is a solution for that too?"

"Yes, it is. You'll sleep like a baby. You're a lightweight. It'll probably only take two glasses max."

"I don't feel like drinking."

"Come on, have one glass with me."

I held my pointer finger in front of her face. "One glass."

She poured the rest of the bottle into the glasses, filling them three-fourths full. I lifted one up in front of me. "That's a big glass of wine."

"You said one glass."

"Touché." I held the glass out, and she clinked hers against mine.

Mark was seated in front of us. "I am not going to be a part of this. Amanda should not be drinking." He slapped his knee and got up.

"Come on, Amanda is fun when she's drinking." Lila took a sip from her glass, and I followed suit. It was good wine, and I let the flavor saturate my mouth. The liquid warmed my body, and I shivered.

Mark put his hands to his hips and then held a hand towards Ross. "Are we leaving?"

"I'm with her." He pointed at Lila.

"Sit down, Mark. Have some wine." I slid my glass towards him.

He sat down but left the glass. "If your curdling screams sound anything like they described—" he pointed between Lila and Ross "—I can't imagine what you were dreaming about."

I quivered as the image of the pumpkin heads flashed through my memory. "Yeah, it was that bad."

"After January, this will be done. He will be locked away, and you won't have to worry anymore."

"Hopefully."

"He's not getting away with this."

Lila squeezed my thigh. "He doesn't get to win."

Chapter 10

The wine helped me get to sleep easily, but I woke myself with screams again, having been thrown over a cliff into a pit of leaves by Peter. It was four, and there was no use in trying to go back to sleep, so I started studying. As soon as it got light out, I took Northie on a mile walk and made breakfast. Afterwards, I called Doug. We didn't talk about the case, school, or me, but about spring break and what we would do when I came to see him.

Not a morning person, I'd never considered scheduling tutoring sessions early. But with free hours when I would have been at rowing workouts, it seemed like a good option. I emailed all my clients again, giving them the option for an early morning session. Two of the five replied within a half hour and were able to make those times. Thinking to pick up more clients, I edited my advertisement on the tutoring website.

I showered and dressed, choosing a more formal outfit than the jeans and sweats that were my go to the past week. I took Northie out again and messaged Mom, Dad, Marissa, and Tia as we walked around the field. I sent a text message to Lila, reminding her about my schedule for the evening and asking her to take care of the pup.

Back in the apartment, I packed my bag for the day and crated Northie. Pulling up to the exit of the apartment complex, I noticed a news van parked in front of the entrance sign and wondered if there was a new development that had them scouting me out again. It was cloudy, but I slid my glasses onto my face and tried to act like I didn't see the reporters. It wasn't like they had any idea what type of car they were looking for. I dialed numbers for the University PR person, my counselor, Lila, Mark, Bill, and Ross until I got someone. Ross picked up.

"Hey, is there anything going on? Anything on the news? There were reporters in front of my complex."

"I just got out of class. I haven't seen or heard anything."

"Okay, thanks," I told him, thinking I was being paranoid. It was probably a slow news day, and they had nothing else to report on but last week's story. Hopefully they were putting some twist on it. Maybe they were doing an informational piece on safety. Perhaps it was linked to the assault prevention training campaign Stephen said they were launching on campus. Local news stations loved to run those stories.

There was one more news van at the main campus entrance but none at the student union. I made it to class right on time, taking a seat beside Justin in the back row.

"Hey, did you see the game?" he asked as soon as I sat down.

"I did." I shook my head. "Why were you the one on camera?"

"Cause I said I knew you."

"I really wish you wouldn't—"

"Class," I heard from the front of the room. The professor called the students to order before I got a chance to finish.

As soon as the lecture ended, Justin spun to face me. "I know you're a private person, but you have a kick ass legal team now, so you can't really be mad."

"What do you mean? How would you know anything about my attorneys?" I stood up and set my chair under the table.

"You're meeting with my dad's attorneys this afternoon. They're going to be the local counsel on your case."

I walked out into the hall and turned to face him. "I don't know what you are talking about."

"Really?"

"Yes, really." I continued down the hall to the stairs and opened the door to the stairwell.

"We're on the fourth floor. You're walking four flights?"

"I don't do elevators."

"Okay." He followed me down the first flight. "But you don't know anything about this? Your attorney didn't tell you?"

"Tell me what? I'm supposed to meet the team this afternoon."

"Don't you listen to the news, read the papers?"

"No." I stopped on the last landing.

"My dad is a state senator. He is giving you his legal team. It's the story of the day."

"Your dad is a state senator?"

"Yes, and he's going to make sure this guy gets what he deserves."

"Justin, what did you do? I don't want more publicity. I want to be left alone."

"But these lawyers are good. They don't come any better. That's what you need, right?"

"I guess." I clenched my fists together. "I can't think about this right now. We have class."

"About the study group. Sorry I didn't call yesterday, but I got tied up with my dad."

Did I remember we were supposed to study?

"But I figured since you were going to be busy with this discovery phase you could take advantage of the tutors at the athletic department with me. I already got approval from the coach for you to sit in on my sessions."

His phone rung, and he apologized and answered it. I was glad for the reprieve and walked ahead, leaving him behind. Who did he think he was scheduling tutoring for me? Why was everyone trying to swoop in and help me? When I needed help, I would ask for it. What I wanted was for people to give me complete information and let me be. I took slow deep breaths and cupped my hand over my nose as I passed the smokers on the benches. The physics building was off from the center of campus, and the number of people started to thin out. As there were fewer and fewer students on the paths, my heart rate quickened and my breathing grew labored. I slipped my keys out of my bag and gripped them tight in one hand, while the other held my phone.

I scanned behind me and to each side and then looked ahead to see the entrance not twenty feet away. *You can make it*, I told myself. When I got to the door, Justin jogged up to me.

"Wow, what are you like a speed walker or something?"

Don't be mad at him. He's trying to help. Instead of telling him I hated every idea he had, I held up my phone. "I thought we were going to be late." I pressed the screen button. "But we have five minutes. I'm going to run to the restroom. I'll meet you in class."

In the bathroom, I tried to reach Chris and Mr. Taylor via phone. Chris was still on the plane, and Mr. Taylor was in a meeting. My phone alarm buzzed, and I made my way to the classroom. Thoughts swirled through my brain. My paranoia was not misplaced. Those reporters were probably reporting on my new legal team. I wondered what the afternoon would be like. At least the meeting would be free of media involvement.

After class, Justin walked outside with me. "I'm grabbing a sandwich before lab, want to join me?" He pointed towards the main campus area.

"No, I'm good. I'll see you in lab."

I found the snack cart and got in line. It wasn't a nice day, and there weren't many people out. Smelling smoke wafting back from the person in front of me, I surveyed the small crowd, realizing they were mostly smokers. I pulled my sweater past my wrist and cupped the fabric on my nose, thinking I'd have to start adding double the fabric softener to my laundry. The guy in front of me wore a leather jacket, and I fought the urge to abandon my lunch plan. He pointed his face to the sky and blew out a huge cloud of smoke. *Not the same*, I told myself, *not the same*, as my heart skipped a beat. But the smell permeated my sleeve, and I couldn't stand there any longer. I raced to the building, finding a bathroom in time to hurl into the toilet. The smell wouldn't leave, and Peter's image floated through my memory.

Get it together, Amanda. He doesn't get to win. I rinsed my mouth and patted my face dry. Fluffing out my hair, I stood in front of the blow dryer, trying to clear my nose of the smell of cigarettes. Back in the hall, I used the vending machine to get a coffee and made my way to the lab, inhaling the scent of beans as I went. I barely got in half the cup before I had to toss it to start the class.

Justin and I finished the lab assignment without difficulty. I was grateful he stayed on task, and we finished early so I could stop at a café before meeting Chris and my new legal team. I'd dreaded the meeting before, but since talking with Justin, I was almost petrified. How weird was it for my friend's dad to give me lawyers? I was already uncomfortable with Doug's dad volunteering his services, but suddenly I also had someone I didn't even know, a senator no less, gifting me his team.

Approaching the law office, traffic came to a standstill and I inched forward, glad I had allowed extra time. I craned my neck and saw that the police had stopped traffic. Opening the map app on my phone, I saw the slow zone cleared past the meeting location. Hoping the accident wasn't too bad, I waited. Eventually the cars in front of me started moving, and I was able to see the building. News vans and camera crews lined the sidewalk in front of the entrance, and there were two squad cars parked in front.

My stomach lurched, and I regretted eating the half of a chicken wrap and not having Chris pick me up. I flipped on my right blinker and turned into the parking lot for the building. As I did, a wave of reporters streamed towards my car, almost blocking the entire drive in front of me. Rummaging through my bag, I found my glasses. The news people were close to the car, and I feared hitting someone. I prayed for a parking deck to escape into. When I got to the last car, I realized there wasn't a garage. The sea of media people crowded my car. When I turned off the motor, they thrust their cameras in front of the windows. Shielding my face with one arm, I dialed Chris's number.

I could barely hear him with the commotion outside. "Amanda?"

"Chris, I'm trapped in my car in the parking lot."

"Okay, hold tight. I'll be right out with some police officers."

There was no way I was going to be filmed walking into the building escorted by law enforcement. I would look like a criminal for sure. "No police."

"What?"

"No police. Get out here."

I could hear their voices through the glass. "Ms. Avery? Are you Ms. Avery? What do you think about the senator's offer to help with your case? Have you met the senator before?"

I laced my fingers together atop my head and dropped my chin to my chest like we used to do in a tornado drill in school. The drone of their voices echoed through the car. For the second time that day, my heart thudded, paused, and then restarted. Why did everything have to be so hard? Couldn't people leave me alone? Didn't I have any privacy? I willed my breathing to even out. Yes, my apartment was my space. It was safe, and I'd be back in it in no time.

There was a knock on the window, and I heard Chris's voice. He stood outside with two other men in dark suits and ties. He pointed at the lock, and I slid my bag onto my shoulder, unlocked the door, and opened it. The roar of voices hit me, and I plastered my back to the door.

Chris put an arm around me and yelled at the other guys. "Make a path." He pointed ahead of us. I covered my head with one arm and followed the dark suit in front of me as we squeezed through the crowd to the building.

Once the doors were closed behind us, there was silence. What I wanted to do was run and imagined dashing for a secret back exit. Chris squeezed my arm. "Are you okay?"

I fought jerking away from his grip, straightened my back, and jutted out my chin. "Yes, that was crazy!" I faked a laugh and smoothed my pants.

"We have someone who would like to meet you," one of the men said, motioning towards a group gathered a few feet away.

An older gentleman walked towards me, hand out. I took a few steps forward and extending my hand to grip his.

"Amanda, it's nice to meet you. I'm Senator Russell."

"Hi, Senator." I wasn't sure what else to say.

Chris stepped forward. "Should we talk in the conference room?"

I followed him down a hall to a large room. Two other men and one woman were already seated around a rectangular table that took up most of the room. The senator held a chair out for me, and I sat down. When everyone was seated, he reiterated what Justin had told me and introduced his legal team.

I thanked the senator for his offer and asked to speak to Chris. When they were gone, I got up and walked to the window. "I'm not sure I like this. I can't have this—" I waved my hand towards the pane "—everywhere I go."

"It won't be like this. They're here for a promo with the senator. He has a good team, and they know people here. They would be a really good asset."

"What does your dad think?"

"He feels the same way, or we wouldn't be here."

"And when did you guys know about all this?"

"Senator Russell contacted us yesterday."

"A heads up would've been nice."

"I offered you a ride."

"It could've been offered with a warning. I want to know what's going on in real time."

"Okay, got it, we can do that."

"Thank you."

"So I can let them back in?"

"Yes."

The senator didn't stay long. I thanked him and acknowledged Justin's role in bringing the team together, even though I secretly hated the whole thing. The meeting with the legal crew progressed with reviewing my statement and everything I could remember about Peter.

It was eight thirty before Chris concluded the meeting. He stood and laid his palms on the table. "Okay, we made good progress, and we'll see everyone at three thirty tomorrow."

I tugged on his jacket sleeve. "I have class until four thirty tomorrow."

He put his fingers to the bridge of his nose, sat down in his chair, and rolled it towards me. Leaning his head close to mine, he whispered, "We have to get this done. Is there any way you could skip some classes?"

"I guess I could meet at one thirty."

He nodded. "Good." He stood again and rapped his knuckles on the table. "Amanda, can meet at one thirty. Let's be ready with all the questions we have for her. We'll start at nine tomorrow morning."

I couldn't imagine how they slept at night. How they went home and had normal lives after hearing stuff like what happened to me every day. Somehow they turned it off. I could see it in their eyes. They weren't thinking of me as a person, a victim of a violent crime. Instead, I saw their eyes bouncing, neurons firing in their brains processing each answer, formulating more questions, and deciding on strategy as they tapped all my responses into their computers.

As for me, I felt like an anxious pile of mush, and in my mind, I was huddled in a corner, knees to chest, rocking back and forth. They'd asked about all my interactions with Peter, twice, and I swore I could hear his hissing voice and smell the sweat- and smoke-infused leather of his jacket. My hand trembled as I reached for my bag, and Chris hefted it onto his shoulder before I reached it.

"You should have had some of those cookies. Let's go get you some dinner. Dad says you like red wine. Not sure we should be buying a minor alcohol, but I'm guessing Doug spoils you with the good stuff."

A huge vat of wine sounded like the best thing in the world, and I followed him out to the parking lot. He held up his keys and squeezed the car remote. "Let's leave your car here. We'll get it tomorrow."

Part of me thought to protest, to say I needed the car, but I doubted I had the capability to drive. I slid into the leather seat when he held the door open. On the drive, I turned on my phone and scrolled through the messages, responding to Mom, Dad, Marissa, Tia, Lila, and Doug. It was mid-day in Tokyo, and Doug would be at work. I longed to be held, to sink into his arms, and feel warm and safe.

When I looked up, we were pulling into a valet station in front of a steak restaurant. The attendant opened the door for me. Chris grabbed my bag and met me in front of the door. I was anxious about spending time with him. We hadn't spoken much, and I knew little about him. Doug was closer to Michael than his other brothers. It was good Chris was getting married so I had a conversation topic.

We sat in the back of the restaurant, and he ordered an expensive bottle of Malbec, steak and potato for himself and a pasta dish for me. They brought the wine and some bread right away. The wine calmed my nerves and the bread my stomach.

"Where did you go to school?"

"Northwestern."

"Is Michael the only one who didn't?"

"Yep, they had ten years of Taylors at that fraternity."

"Wow, that's cool."

I asked him about his major, law school, his cases, his fiancée, and her career. When the food came, I'd already finished one glass and the waiter poured another for me.

"You don't like meat?" Chris asked as we started our dishes.

Truth be told, I love rare steak, but I didn't want to see blood leaking from a piece of meat today. The potato smelled good but my pasta was the perfect comfort food. Finishing a bite, I took the last sip of the second glass of wine. Chris held the bottle out towards me, but I waved him off.

It was almost ten when Chris walked me to the door of my apartment. Four in the afternoon, Tokyo time, I thought as I thanked him for the dinner. It would be another two hours till I could talk to Doug. Like the previous night, Lila and Ross walked with me and Northie to the meadow. *Wine is a good thing*, I thought, staring at the trees and the starry sky beyond.

In my room, I washed up for bed. Zack had sent a message saying he would pick me up at eight. Only half an hour left, and then I could talk to Doug. I read my organic chemistry and physics notes till my phone dinged.

"Hi." I smiled into the camera on my computer.

"You look better than I thought you would after today."

"Chris bought me dinner and wine."

"That was nice."

"He owed me."

"Why's that?"

"He didn't bother to tell me about the senator yesterday."

He talked about his day, and I talked about rearranging my tutoring sessions and appointment with Zack at the gym the following day.

"Three weeks," he said as we were wrapping up our conversation. "Three weeks until I see you again."

"I can't wait! I love you!" I kissed my fingers and blew my breath on them.

"Love you too. Let's talk in the morning."

"Okay, bye." I ended the call.

I lay back on my pillow, and Northie snuggled in beside me. As with the previous night, sleep came easily, but I was screaming into my pillow when Lila shook me awake.

"Amanda?"

I pushed myself up with my arms to see her flipping the light switch up.

I threw my pillow onto the floor. "He was about to get me. I hate this."

She sat down beside me and wrapped her arms around me. "You're safe. It's just the process. You're working through your fears in a safe way."

I nudged her, reaching for the tissue box beside my bed. "Were you reading some psychology article or something?"

"Maybe."

"I'll be fine. You can go back to sleep."

"You think we can get the memory of the sounds of your screams out of our heads?"

I covered my eyes with my fingers, tears running down my face. "I'm sorry. I don't know what to do."

"When do you see the counselor? You could call her, right?"

"Crap, I have the recovery group meeting tonight and a session with the lawyers that will probably last till eight again."

"You need to focus on you. Get them to cut the meeting short."

"Okay." I wiped my cheeks with the tissue, thinking one thirty to five would be three and a half hours. "I'll be fine."

She squeezed my hand and stood up. "I'm here if you need me."

"Thanks."

I opened my computer and emailed my Chinese literature professor, the dean, and the counselor. Then, I read the material for the calculus and economics lectures. Finally, it got light out and I took Northie for a walk. Lila and Ross emerged from her bedroom as the coffee pot finished filling, and I poured everyone cups.

They sat down at the bar. After a few sips, I started to apologize, but they wouldn't let me finish my sentence. I was too tired to argue with them and headed to my bedroom to dress for the gym. I packed an extra bag with some pants, a sweater, and my makeup for afterwards and texted with Doug while I waited in the living room for Zack.

Within a few minutes, there was a knock at the door, and I peeped through the keyhole. All I could see was an eyeball. I turned the lock and held the door open for him to come inside.

"Come on, we're late already." He hitched his thumb in the air in the direction of the parking lot.

I crated Northie, grabbed my bags, and yelled goodbye to Lila. As soon as we were out the door, he swiped his hand down my face. I stopped, but he didn't remove his hand. I fought the instinct to bite him and took a step back.

"Don't touch my face."

"I always do that. It's my thing." He spun around to face me. "You look like hell."

"Thank you."

He started towards the car again. "See, that's why I'm here. Comic and stress relief all in one package." He held his arms out.

"I'm not sure how coercing me into going to the gym is stress relief."

"What's wrong with the gym? Exercise will be good for you."

"The exercise part I'm game for. It's the people part I'm not sure about."

He started the car. "Oh, I didn't realize you didn't like people anymore."

"Not you, other people. Leave me alone, Zack. I'm coming to the gym like you wanted." I reclined my head on the cushion behind me.

"You think this is for me? This isn't for me. This is for you."

"I can't even stand in line behind someone who is smoking without hurling. There are going to be a hundred sweaty people in that gym. Do you remember when I woke up?"

"The athletic gym isn't as bad as the student gym. That's why I suggested it. You can at least give it a try."

"I *am* in the car with you."

"That's what I like about you." He squeezed my thigh. "You are one tough cookie. You just keep on keeping on."

I slid his arm off my leg. "Ooh-rah."

In the gym lot, droves of students were filing into the building. As we got out of the car, I could see rowing team members congregated at the entrance. Zack put a hand on my back and massaged a shoulder. "Happy thoughts of warm beaches and sea breezes."

"A beach would be nice right now."

As we approached, the crowd moved toward us. Most of the girls and some of the guys hugged me and said they were glad I was back.

Bill hooked his arm around my shoulder. "You're here! Awesome! You have to train our new coxswain."

As soon as the doors opened, the smell hit me. I swallowed hard, pulled the fabric of my sleeve over my hand, and cupped it on my nose. The group moved up the stairs to the training floor, and I tried to take slow even breaths. Coach was waiting on the second floor with the rest of the team.

"Avery, good to see you. Nice shades." He pretended to punch my shoulder.

"Thanks."

He called the group to order and reviewed the training drill for the day. After the crowd broke, Bill introduced me to the new coxswain. She wasn't as little as me but had a small frame, so I could see why they picked her. As the guys started training, I watched her count and gave her some pointers, my hand covering my nose. It got warmer, and the smell of hot bodies permeated the air. Scanning the room, I made my way towards Zack.

"I need to go." The fluorescent lights buzzed and started to dim.

"You look a little pale. Let's get you some air."

We walked down the stairs and outside. Around the corner, I doubled over, taking in a large breath.

"You get any exercise in?"

"No."

"Let's try the weight room."

"What's this, like desensitization training?"

"Yep, come on." I followed him back inside and up the stairs. He pointed to the leg press. "Try this."

I sat down, and he adjusted the weight. "Go for it."

When I started to extend my leg, the muscles in my torso pulled and my ribs screamed at me. Stopping mid-way, I put my hand to my side. "That's not going to work."

He looked around the room. "Okay, let's try that one." He pointed to a weight machine that worked the calves. I got on and tried it but with the same result.

Walking seemed to be the only exercise where I wasn't moving my core muscles. My body was going to be mush, and I was going to end up a fat blob. I could sense the tears starting to form. Back of my hand to my nose, I pointed to the stairs with the other.

"You should stay and get a workout in. I'm going to go get some breakfast."

"You can spot me."

"Zack, I'm going. I'll see you later."

"Hey." He grabbed my sleeve.

"Let me go, Zack."

He slid my glasses from my face and leaned down so we were eye level. "We'll figure something out."

I took my glasses and fitted them on my nose. "Okay." I swallowed hard, fighting tears.

Outside, I started towards the edge of campus. The walk calmed me, and I ordered a water and muffin at a coffee shop. Needing to change before meeting with the lawyers, I made my way back to campus and found a bathroom in the math building.

In the lecture hall, I studied until a form plopped down beside me. "My dad was super impressed with you. He wants you to come to Sunday dinner this weekend."

Ugh, the trial thing again! But I smiled. "That was nice of him. I'll check my schedule."

"There's a tutoring session tonight at the athletic center for science and math. Want to come?"

"What time?"

"Six to nine. I could pick you up."

"That's okay. I'll be on campus anyway. Text me the room number, and I'll meet you there." I figured if I was going to miss classes, I needed all the help I could get.

After my lecture, I found Chris waiting in the Mercedes in front of the building just as he'd said. "Do you need lunch?" he asked as I slid into the car.

"No, I ate a few hours ago."

"Okay, I'll order sandwiches later." He pulled into traffic.

"I have to be back on campus for a something at five thirty."

"I thought we could work till eight thirty again."

"This is sort of important. I can take Doug's car."

The meeting was as intense as the day before. They picked through every aspect of my life back through high school. By the end, they had a list of all my friends, everyone I'd dated, all the potentials I'd talked to the week before the incident, Peter's roommate, and all the fraternity brothers I even remotely knew to interview. I'd picked at a sandwich, but it wasn't even a fourth gone when Chris wrapped it up and stuffed it in my bag since I was leaving.

"Please, eat it at some point."

"Okay, I'll see you tomorrow."

"Twelve thirty?"

I nodded and slinked out of the room, feeling guilty the others would probably be there till midnight. The traffic was bad, and I inched through, thinking I was trading one horrible event for another. I parked in the lot at five thirteen and made my way up the stairs to the meeting room. As before, they were huddled around the counter. A sweet tangy scent hit my nose as I entered and saw they were dipping chicken wings in ranch sauce.

"These are amazing. I can't believe you made these," Misty exclaimed, dunking another orange bone in the sauce, and stripping the meat off with her teeth. I added barbecue sauce to smells I would avoid and sat down beside Addie. Looking back at the group standing around the food, I saw Misty toss a bone in the trash and snatch a napkin. Rubbing her fingers on the paper, she walked straight to me. She stood above me, hands on hips.

"Seriously, you're back after you brought your boyfriend last week."

I let my bag drop on the floor, stood up, and jutted my chin up to face her. She took a step back, and I balled my hands into fists. My heart raced, and I took a slow breath, thinking I could hit her. One jab to the nose and all my anger would be released.

"I'm not sure what I did wrong, but I have as much right to be here as you do."

She chuckled and looked back at the other girls, who seemed frozen. She waved her hand in the air in front of me. "You cannot have someone pick you up like that. It compromises all of us."

"It won't happen again."

Her shoulders rose and fell. "You bet it won't."

"What won't happen again?" I heard Dr. Milner's voice behind me.

Misty took a step back and looked at the floor, and I turned to face the counselor. "My boyfriend picked me up last week. I didn't realize it was wrong. We were clearing things up." I slid into my seat beside Addie, wishing I could disappear.

"I don't think we've established that as a rule." Dr. Milner sat down, and the other girls filed into the circle, taking chairs. "You had every right to have someone pick you up."

I didn't look towards Misty. I imagined steam coming out of her ears. I tried not to glance in her direction, but eventually it was her turn to share about her week. Her eyes were red, and my heart automatically went out to her. "I don't want to be mean. I've worked so hard, and I feel like it's one step forward and two steps back."

My turn was last. I felt spent and empty and had nothing to report other than that everything sucked and I was angry all the time. Would the meetings ever do anything for me? Did it help to see Misty still struggling after two years? I felt a bit of relief because most of the others seemed stable. A few of them shared how they felt after their incidences, and at least, I didn't feel quite as crazy.

As we had the previous week, Addie and I stacked our chairs and rode the elevator down together. Exiting the building, I realized the sun had already gone down. Orange lights illuminated the parking spaces. I stopped outside the exit, contemplating the walk to my car at the far end of the lot.

"Do you need a ride?" Addie asked.

I cocked my heads toward my car. "My ride is on the other side of the lot. Having someone to walk with would be nice." I bit my lip, fighting tears and feeling like a paranoid freak.

"I'm that way too. You were really brave to stand up to Misty that way. She slapped a girl one time."

Her admission frightened me, and I reminded myself to think twice before standing up to people. "I pictured myself punching her."

She laughed. "I could tell. Hey, I do kickboxing if you're interested in trying it once you're all healed up. Great for getting all that anger out."

"Boxing? Like with gloves and everything?"

"Yep, gloves and everything."

That sounded like the best thing ever. "Thanks." We exchanged numbers when I got to my car.

"Call or text anytime."

"I am really busy right now—"

She placed her hand on my forearm, and I froze. "Sorry." She moved her hand away slowly. "No obligation, I'm here if you want to talk."

"Thanks." Water started to form under my lids. "Okay, bye."

I unlocked my doors, slid into the seat, and locked them back. Arms out straight, I gripped the steering wheel, waiting for the tears to stop. I wiped them away and took out my phone, messaging my parents and Lila.

It was almost seven when I pulled into the athletic lot. Contemplating walking through an empty lot, I texted Justin, and he met me at my car. Before we entered the building, I moved my sunglasses down to cover my eyes and cupped my hand on my nose. If I'd looked in the mirror, I would've probably thought I was a poster child for a crazy person. Ignoring the thought, I followed Justin to the elevator. Upstairs, the study room didn't smell like the rest of the building, and I slid off my glasses and sat down at one of the round tables beside him. Even though I was starving and exhausted, I was glad to get the extra study help.

"Every night, six to nine," he told me when we reached my car afterwards. "I'll text you the schedule of subjects."

"Thank you for everything. I probably didn't seem very grateful before. This is a lot to deal with."

"No problem, I totally get it. My sister went through the same thing. Guy got off with nothing. My dad nearly lost it. That's why he's so passionate."

"Well that explains things. How's your sister?"

"Oh, she's fine now, married with kids." He waved his hand towards the sky.

"Good." It was a relief to hear she had a happy ending. "Thanks again." I got in my car and clicked the locks.

At my apartment complex, I snagged a spot right in front of my unit and fought the urge to run to my door. Ross and Lila were on the couch studying. I let my bag fall to the floor and plunged into the chair.

"Are you exhausted?" Lila asked.

I pulled the sandwich out of my bag. "Yes, and starving."

We sat in silence as I finished my meal. After, they walked around the grounds with Northie and me. Back inside, Lila fidgeted with the zipper on her jacket.

"We may go to the house if you'll be okay alone."

"Sure, I'm exhausted, and I hate waking you guys up."

"Okay." She hugged me.

I went to my room and phoned Doug. We didn't have long to talk, but it was good to hear his voice. After, I showered and dressed for bed. I dreaded sleeping and turned on some music. When that didn't work, I turned on the Japanese audio course I'd started in the summer.

I ran down a path lined with trees on both sides. The branches hung above the lane formed from two ruts, wheel-width apart. Waist-high weeds grew between the ruts and on each side of the path. The smell of smoke and sweat hit me and I stopped, spinning to find the source. Then I heard a laugh, and he jumped from a branch towards me.

I shot up, flinging the covers from atop me. My side zinged, and I froze, trying to slow my breathing. Two twenty, I'd only made it to two twenty.

I got up and flicked on all the lights. Finding my blanket, I wrapped it around me and made my way to the couch. I turned on the TV and started yet another romantic comedy from mom's collection.

Chapter 11

Sleep finally came and I woke a few minutes after six, Northie nudging me from the floor. Since it wasn't quite light out, I grabbed my coat, keys, mace, and a one-foot flashlight I found in the pantry. I walked him through the parking lot to the meadow and retraced my steps back to the apartment. Back inside, I started coffee and got in the shower.

My tutoring session was scheduled for nine, and I talked to Doug and Mom, did some studying, and walked Northie before leaving for campus. I liked the session with my client. She didn't try to hug me, ask about the bruising on my face when I took off my glasses, or look at me with empathetic eyes. If I could fill my days with interactions that were all business, I would be happy.

But the session ended, and I had to walk through the student union and main thoroughfare to class. I scrolled through my messages on my phone's screen to avoid seeing faces in the crowd. Passing a coffee cart, my stomach gurgled. I tried to remember if I'd eaten. Scanning the line for smokers, I took the last spot. At the front, I ordered a bagel with cream cheese and a coffee and made my way to class. At least my lectures were known entities. They didn't come with hugs or empathetic stares. People had moved on.

I wondered how long it would take me to recover. Would I get past the nightmares, the aversion to smoke and sweaty smells, to the orange lights and autumn leaves in a month, a year? Were the sessions with the lawyers helping me move through the trauma or keeping me stuck in it? Thinking about the next week and a half of continued discovery and then depositions, I slid my bagel to the edge of the table.

"That your breakfast?" Justin took the seat beside me.

"Yes." I pulled it back towards me and took another bite, reminding myself that my body was burning extra calories healing. I couldn't skip meals because everything was overwhelming. Dad would surely cart me home in a second if he got any indication I wasn't eating well. I added eating to my list of things to hate. The thought felt crazy stupid, like I was being an angst-ridden teen.

After the meeting with my legal team that afternoon, Chris and I had dinner with Paula and Gary at her condo in the city. Being at her place and having a glass of wine calmed my nerves and helped me relax. But it wasn't just the alcohol. Everything seemed good there. I was warm, I was safe, and I was loved. There was no judgment or threats of carting me away. No triggers lurked around the corner. It was tempting to stay, to create a bubble for myself. They even offered to host Northie. But I had a tutoring client, classes, and legal sessions in Evanston. Promising to visit the next weekend, we took the elevator down to Chris's car in the garage.

That night and the next, after another dinner with Chris and a glass of wine, I made it till four before waking to the sounds of my screams. The only good thing about being up early was it gave me more time to talk to Doug. I told him I was tired and went to bed and got up early to study. I wasn't sure why I felt the need to lie. But he wouldn't be visiting for another three weeks, and by then, I hoped the nightmare phase would pass.

🐦 🐦 🐦

Friday morning I had an appointment with the orthopedic surgeon. The stitches were supposed to come out, and my leg bounced as I waited in the office lobby. The nurse called my name, and I followed her into the exam room where she took my vitals.

"Are you anxious, dearie?" she asked as she stripped the blood pressure cuff off my arm.

"A little. I don't do well with medical stuff."

She patted my thigh, and I fought the urge to back away. "We'll have you in and out of here in a jiffy." She rolled the stool away and retrieved a gown from the cabinet behind her. "Put this on, and the surgeon will be here in a minute."

She left and I took off my top, slid my arms into the gown, and wrapped it around my front. I sat on the exam table waiting, my legs dangling in the air. As I was ready to hop down and start pacing, there was a knock at the door and it opened a crack.

"Are you ready?" a male voice said through a crack in the door.

"Yes." I slid farther back on the exam table. The doctor entered, offering his hand.

"Good to see you again, Ms. Avery." He sat down in front of the computer and typed on the keyboard. "It looks like you had two ribs pinned and some bone fragments of a third removed. How is the incision healing?"

Two pins, a bone fragment? Did I remember this? Suddenly cold, chill bumps formed on my arms. I looked at my lap, trying to stop the room from tilting. I raked my hand through my hair and looked at the ceiling. "Can I? I'm sorry. Things were a bit hurried before. I don't—" I put my hand to my forehead "—remember. Can I see the X-rays?"

"Of course." He spun the screen to face me, pointing out the really thin screws that held the bones together.

Octagonal heads stuck out from the bones. I clenched my jaw and dug my nails into my palms. Fainting would not help. I was not going to have any more medical intervention.

He stood. "Okay, let's take a look at that incision. The nurse reported last week that it was having trouble healing."

I reclined back on the exam table, moving my gown to expose the site. He put on gloves and removed the bandage. "Yes, I see it still looks very red. Usually we like to see more of a normal color. Has it been bleeding?"

"Some, I toss in my sleep."

He turned and opened a drawer behind him. He took out some bandages. "I'm going to replace the bandage you have. We'll keep this on another week and get you in a sling to keep that area still. You need to wear the sling at night if you're moving a lot in your sleep."

A sling? Like a cast sling? It was probably shallow not to want a sling. But it would draw attention, and being noticed was the opposite of what I wanted. I wanted to disappear and come back in a year when life was normal and no one remembered. Tears formed but I swiped them away before he approached me again. The site was tender, and his manipulations with the bandages irritated the skin and made the area ache.

When he finished, he ripped off his gloves and threw them in the trash. "I'll have the nurse bring you a sling. I'd like to see you back in a week. Hopefully we can get those stitches out then." I sat up. He pointed at me. "You take care and keep that side still."

"Okay, thanks." I managed, biting the inside of my cheek.

I dressed and then a nurse brought the sling. It was expensive, fifty dollars, and it was huge. A strap tethered the sling around my chest and kept my arm from swinging away from my body. It was time to break out the sweatshirts again. Hopefully, my legal team believed in dress down Friday.

Lila was at the apartment when I got there.

"Amanda, what happened?"

"It's nothing." I waved my arm in the air, shooing her away as water pooled in my lower lids again. "I've got to get a sweatshirt to cover this thing."

She grabbed my free arm, halting my progress toward my room. I stopped and turned back to face her. Looking to the ceiling, I blinked my eyes, trying to clear the tears. I wasn't normally such an emotional person. I hated crying every other second. Finally facing her, I couldn't look her in the eyes for fear the tears would start again.

"All that flailing around at night isn't helping my incision site. They're trying to keep that side still so it can heal."

"I'm sorry." She wrapped her arms around my back and pulled me to her. It felt nice to be held, and I rested my head on her shoulder.

"No biggie." I lifted my chin before I started to cry. "I have to get to class."

She released me. "Let's eat dinner together tonight and hang out. When are you done with the lawyers?"

"They're ready to get home for the weekend. It won't be late."

"Good." She squeezed my hands.

In my room, I found my softest jeans and the Marquette sweatshirt Michael had given me along with high top sneakers. If I pulled my hood up, no one would recognize me with my sunglasses.

On campus it took a while to find a parking spot. Snagging a spot in a far lot, I tried jogging to class to get to class on time. It jarred my ribs, and had to settle for speed walking.

I slipped into the lecture hall as the professor was coming to the podium. Justin had saved me a seat, and I slid into it. I fiddled with the zipper on my bag, and he opened it for me. Being one-handed annoyed me. I added it to the list of things I hated.

"Thanks." I forced the word out, keeping my eyes facing front. My anger flirted close to producing tears the second I saw the hint of concern in his eyes.

Out of the corner of my eyes, I saw him tapping on his phone, and he held it up so I could read it. WHAT'S UP WITH THE SLING?

I tapped on my tablet. INCISION NOT HEALING AS IT SHOULD.

BUMMER.

When the professor released us, he turned to me. "I can carry your bag."

"Thanks, but I'm good. The other side is fine."

"So you're back to your incognito look."

"That's the plan."

We walked to the physics building and got seats in the lecture hall. Again he unzipped my bag. If he only knew how furious it made me to need help, he probably would've run. It was good to have my huge dark glasses so he couldn't see my eyes glowing red. Where was this coming from? Why was I angry? If I *had* to wear a sling, it was the best possible day because I interacted with few people—Lila, Justin, Dr. Milner, and the lawyers—and I would be done. I couldn't wait to get the darn sling off, buy some boxing gloves, and start hitting something. Yes, kickboxing was going to be my new thing.

Unloading all my pent-up anger and frustration at the counseling appointment was exhausting. After I ran through my what-I-hate list, I told her about my nightmares and the assault training session scheduled for the weekend. She indicated everything I was feeling was normal. Maybe it was supposed to be reassuring, but I felt no less crazy. She gave me her personal number and indicated to call whenever I needed to. Having the option of talking to a professional rather than burdening my friends felt reassuring.

The meeting with the lawyers went well. They'd been prepping me for days and deemed me ready for the depositions with Peter's legal team the next week. We'd set a similar schedule so I could attend classes in the morning and the deposition in the afternoons. Chris and the rest of the team would be present, which helped with my nerves.

When I got home after five, I opened my door to find a huge box beside the doorway and Mark, Bill, Zack, Lila, and Ross huddled around a grill, beers in hand. Seeing the box was from home, I left it and joined the others on the patio.

"Whoa," Zack exclaimed. "What's that?"

"They want me to keep that side still."

Lila wrapped her arms around me. "How was your day?"

"Gross."

"Did you see your package?"

"Yes, I'll get it later. Did anyone walk Northie?"

They all looked at each other. Zack set his bottle on the concrete. "I'll come with you."

He followed me to get Northie's leash and then out the front door. Nudging the box with his foot, he asked, "You really not opening this? Could be good stuff."

"Can't deal with it right now."

"Okay, but I'm thinking cookies, pastries, nuts, good drinking food."

"Does that mean you're condoning me drinking?"

"I didn't mean you. I meant us."

"I'm definitely having a drink or two tonight."

He shook his head as we made our way to the meadow. "Not a good idea."

"You're not my boss."

"You think it'll help with the nightmares?"

"It gets me to four. How did you know about the nightmares?"

"Lila's been at the house all week. She finally fessed up today."

Drat that Lila. "I'm not crazy."

"I don't think you are. You had them last year after your accident too."

He picked up Northie's dog business, threw it in the trash, and pointed towards the trail. "How about a workout? I scouted out a new scene for you."

Following him towards the path, I pointed at my left arm. "Does this look like I can work out. I'm exhausted anyway."

He put a hand on each of my shoulders. "You gotta get rid of this anxiety somehow. Doug's not here. Me and exercise are all you got."

"Ewww!" I backed away from him. "Was that a reference to sex?"

"Sex and exercise *are* the best stress busters."

I covered my right ear with my right hand. "Stop."

"Okay, but they have treadmills and ellipticals in the apartment gym, and it's clean as a whistle. Not a hint of sweaty smell, and tonight it will be vacant. No one works out on Friday night."

"Yeah, except losers like me."

"Well, I'll be there too."

"I'll try anything at this point."

"I knew you'd say that." I ducked away from the hand he threatened to rake down my face.

By the time we got back, they had burgers on the grill. It wasn't my usual fare, but I devoured a sandwich piled with tomatoes, lettuce, cheese, and pickles faster than I ever had before. The guys made me open the box. As I guessed, there were no cookies. Mom had packed it with protein bars and we left them by the door destined for the frat house. She'd also included laundry soap, fabric softener in my favorite scent, and athletic shirts with long sleeves and thumb holes, which were much appreciated.

I sent a text message to Mom, thanking her and promising to get time to talk to her the next day.

Did Tia get a hold of you? She replied.

No.

Check your messages.

I scrolled through my inbox, which was lined with unread messages. Finding Tia's, I opened it. Thought Ed and I would come treat you to dinner tomorrow night. See you at 6?

Ugh, I thought. Could I turn her down? The assault prevention meeting the next day lasted from nine to five. I was already a week behind on my studies.

I replied to Mom's text. Thanks for letting me know. Things piling up here.

No worries sweetie. I love you! Take care.

Love U2.

The crew stayed until nine when they left to go see a band Lila was into. She begged me to come, but I was set on exhausting myself with a workout. A night of studying would've been a good thing, but my mind was mush, so I doubted it would've been beneficial anyway.

Our keys opened the door to the gym in the center of the apartment complex. It wasn't any bigger than our two-bedroom apartment. Zack was right, though. No one was there and it didn't smell at all. The only scent was of bleach and cleaner. It was like music to my nostrils.

I got on the elliptical machine first, hoping the motion wouldn't pull my torso muscles. If I kept the incline slight and the pace slow, I was able to do the exercise.

"I told you." Zack's lips formed a huge gloating smile.

"Thank you."

"Your smile is the only thanks I need."

"Go workout." I batted a hand towards him as he walked away.

I walked on the elliptical for half an hour and then the treadmill for half an hour. Three miles in an hour wasn't half bad, especially since it was the only option I had.

Zack walked me back to my apartment. "Is Lila coming home?" he asked as I found Northie's leash for a walk.

"No, she'll be back in the morning."

"Do you want me to stay?"

"No, that's ridiculous. I've been alone all week. I don't mind."

"Well the offer is out there. Lila said I could put clean sheets on her bed."

"Thanks."

We walked Northie to the meadow and back and said good-night. My leg muscles ached, but it was a good soreness. Finishing a glass of water, I washed my face and brushed my teeth.

I didn't need wine or the imagery of sinking limbs to ease me to sleep, and the next thing I knew my alarm was sounding from my phone. I turned it off and lay back on my pillow. Rested, I felt rested for the first time in two weeks.

Pulling on some leggings, I fitted a sweatshirt over my sling. Northie wagged his tail, and I fitted his leash on his collar. Outside, the sun was coming up. *Small things, Amanda, be happy for the small things*, I told myself. I walked Northie around the deserted grounds. Once I was back to the apartment, I made a pot of coffee and sat at the table with my books.

Lila arrived after eight. She kissed the fabric on my hood and sat down beside me.

"How was the band?"

"Good, I wish you would have come."

"Maybe next time."

She swiped my hood off. "When was the last time you washed your hair?"

I held the pen in my mouth and fitted my hood back on my head. "I don't know, last weekend."

She slid a hand under my arm and pulled me out of the chair. "Shower and hair now." She pointed towards my room. "I'll help you dry it."

The hour of cheer ended as I studied my reflection in the mirror, wondering how I'd missed my hair being almost greasy enough to form dreadlocks. I washed, shaved, and shampooed twice before running conditioner through my hair. Lila was true to her word and had a comb and the hair dryer waiting on my bed.

Remembering to move slowly, I sat beside her. My eyes welled with tears as she ran the comb through my hair. She put a hand around my back. "It's okay."

"It's not, but it's fine."

"It will be." Her voice rose as she spoke.

"Hopefully." I kissed her hand, and she proceeded to comb out my hair and blow it dry.

We drove to campus for the assault prevention course together. When I begged her to come to dinner with Tia and me in the evening, she laughed. "Spend an hour trying not to yell at your sister for giving you a hard time? No way!"

"Do you think I can get Mark to come?"

"He has a date with Holli."

"Maybe I'll ask Kate."

"That is cruel."

"It might not be that bad if she has an audience."

In the meeting room, Stephen greeted us with hugs and questioned the sling. There were pastries out, and I avoided the group hovered around them, opting to find a seat. The chairs were arranged in a circle, and I regretted agreeing to come. Where was my anonymity? My privacy? Gone obviously.

The leader called the group to sit down and explained the purpose of the class and schedule. The goal of the course was to become an assault prevention course instructor. The first day we would learn the material, and the second, how to teach it. I fidgeted in my seat as we introduced ourselves and wondered if Stephen had prepped everyone in the room. There wasn't any reaction when I introduced myself, and I was again grateful for the small reprieve in my sad existence.

The course started with slides. When they got to prevention tips, I chewed my nail. Lila's hand caught my leg as it bounced from side to side. When we broke, I walked outside, but the smokers had gathered near the exit. Back inside, I found the ladies room and washed my hands with hot water until they were red. Peering at my silky hair and perfect makeup, for a second I thought I looked pretty. I wondered how many people walked around hiding pain behind flawless smiles, skin, hair, and clothes. A second glance at the mirror had me inspecting the furrows in my brown, darkness under my eyes, and the lines around my mouth. Would they ever disappear?

In the hall, I sent a text message to Tia, agreeing to meet them at five thirty at my apartment. Back in the room, there were sandwiches, and Lila had heaped a bunch of chips and half of one on a plate for me. I stood near the windows and ate the meat and cheese and some of the fruit.

Thinking the afternoon would be better, I was completely sideswiped by my reaction to the physical training portion. The instructor paired me up with a guy I didn't know, and I stood there frozen in front of him. A warm hand around mine brought me out of my trance, and I realized Stephen inched towards me, holding my shaking hand.

"I got ya." He whispered. I glanced around the room wondering if anyone else had noticed, but other than my prior partner, they all seemed focused on the lesson. "It's cool. No one noticed. Look at me." I looked into his eyes. "You're safe."

"I can't," I whispered, catching the instructor's form approaching out of the corner of my eye.

Stephen turned around before the teacher reached us. "If anyone needs a break, feel free to use the facilities."

"Amanda," Stephen asked. "Do you need a minute?"

Seeing his large hazel eyes, wide with concern, reinforced my resolve. I was not going to be pitied. Peter did *not* get to win. I could work with Stephen. I knew him. He was safe. You had to have extensive background checks to be a resident assistant. Actually all the other kids there, save Lila, were RAs. What was my problem?

As we went through the physical defense training, I began to get cynical. None of the suggested maneuvers would save a girl that was smaller than a guy. The only thing I could've done differently was run. But I hadn't listened to my gut in the beginning. I had passed up my chance to flee.

Stephen caught me mid-thought. "You have to breathe. You're starting to look pale."

I shot him a mean look and refocused on the class. As soon as we were released, I picked up my bag and headed to the door, Lila trailing after me. She finally caught up with me in the parking lot.

I thought she would be mad, rebuke me, but instead, she threw her arms around me. "I'm proud of you."

I gripped her arms. "Thank you. Can I have a drink now?"

"Yes, I have a bottle of wine under my bed."

We drove to the apartment and got out the wine, pouring it in plastic cups so we could walk Northie to the meadow. When we looped back, Tia and Ed were waiting.

Tia took my cup and sniffed at the liquid. "Hard day at the office?"

"They're all hard."

"Well, I'm not buying you alcohol."

"You don't have to."

After dinner, dessert, and window shopping in downtown Evanston with Tia and Ed, I met up with Zack. It was a good thing they didn't like to stay out late as it was after nine.

After my hour-long workout, I slept well again and hoped I had the answer to controlling my dreams.

🦅 🦅 🦅

As we discussed aversion tactics the next day in the assault prevention course, my leg bounced as it had the day before.

"Amanda, do you have anything to add?"

"No?"

"You seem agitated. You seemed anxious when we covered this topic yesterday as well."

Crap, he had noticed. I clutched my chair with my right hand. "You need to put run at the top of the list. The rest of those are useless for stopping an attack. The person needs to run as soon as their gut tells them they're not safe. No matter if they're worried it looks stupid or paranoid. They need to run."

I would've thought it would get more of a reaction, but he was cool as a cucumber. "Thank you for your insight. Let's rearrange that verbiage." He pointed a laser at the graphic on the wall.

Leaving the meeting room, Lila turned to me. "Hey, are we hosting people tonight?"

"Sure, I think I'm working out with Zack later, but that's fine." I texted Zack: MEETING FOR OUR WORKOUT AT NINE?

MAY BE A FEW MINUTES AFTER THAT. HAVE VOLLEYBALL AND NEED TO GRAB DINNER. DO YOU MIND IF I BRING A FRIEND?

NO, GUESS NOT. TEXT ME WHEN YOU'RE READY.

It was only Bill, Mark, Ross, Lila, and me for dinner. Even so, I turned on my auto-pilot, nodding when appropriate. After the class, I really wanted to be alone. As soon as they left, I texted Zack. He and our workouts were my haven from real life. I wondered if having another person there would kill the allure. When I looked through the keyhole, a tall blonde stood beside him. She wasn't the type of friend I expected.

Zack didn't have a warm hug for me. "Hey, this is Leslie. We went to high school together. She just moved here, and I've been showing her around."

"Hi, Leslie." I forced a smile and shook her hand. "I'm going to grab my bag." I held the door open, and they stepped inside. I packed my satchel with books to study if conversation felt weird.

At the gym they paired up for the weight machines, and I took a treadmill. I popped my headphones in to block out their cheery banter. It was really the exercise I was there for anyway. Zack was my bodyguard. After an hour, we were all sweaty. They offered to walk with me back to my apartment, but there was no way I would look like a wimp in front of tall and blonde Leslie.

"Nope, I'm good." I waved and walked away, forcing an extra bounce into each step hoping the swish in my ponytail said the same thing. As soon as I turned the corner I broke into a jog. Being outside alone at night was not somewhere I wanted to be for long.

In the apartment, I showered and talked to Doug. God, I missed him. We only had time for a short conversation before he left for work. Afterwards, I poured a glass of wine and downed it in three huge gulps, wondering why I felt sadder than usual.

❦ ❦ ❦

I woke the next morning from a dreamless sleep to the sound of my phone vibrating on the table next to my bed. I picked it up and the time read five thirty, half an hour before my alarm. Wondering what was so pressing, I looked at the screen.

The text from my Dad read: PROUD OF YOU FOR GETTING OUT THERE. KEEP UP THE GOOD WORK. GETTING ON MY FLIGHT NOW.

Okay, that was random. I sent him a message right back.

?

NORTHWESTERN NEWSPAPER ARTICLE THIS MORNING.

?

HAVE TO GO. JUST READ IT.

I got out of bed and retrieved my tablet from my bag. When the Internet access app opened, I tapped in the search phrase. Opening the link, I found the news article. The headline read:

AMANDA ON ASSAULT PREVENTION: RUN. There was a picture of me kneeing Stephen in the groin.

The last thing I wanted was more press. For the first time, I resented Northie's presence, but fitted the leash on his collar anyway. It was still dark, and I armed myself with my mace, flashlight, and keys. I pitied the person who tried to mess with me that morning. I was a fiery ball of red hot anger waiting for an outlet. At least my target was attainable. I rolled on the balls of my feet as Northie sniffed the grass and forced myself to walk the grounds so he would have enough exercise. The poor dog was horribly neglected. We should've started obedience classes last week. It was a good thing he was easy going and well-behaved.

Once back in the apartment, I didn't even waste time with coffee. I brushed my teeth and grabbed my bag. As I was opening the door to leave, Lila came out of her room.

"Where are you going?"

"To see Stephen."

"At six thirty in the morning? What's going on?"

"Read the Northwestern paper. It's all in there."

I shut and locked the door and hurried to my car, ripping the sling off. I refused to be trapped by bus schedules or bumming rides from friends, so I took it off to drive. On campus, I pulled into the dorm lot and parked in a handicap spot. Fitting the sling on my arm and securing it around my chest, I grabbed my bag and slammed the door.

It was nearly seven so students were already milling around, and it was easy to get in the building. Even at the inner door, no one questioned me as I slid in after some guys returning from the gym. They were sweaty, and I didn't want to get on the elevator with them, but the stairs seemed like a riskier option. I cupped my hand to my nose and crammed into the space. They were silent as we rode up to the seventh floor. When I got out, one guy called after me. "Have a good day." He must've been the brave one of the bunch.

I'd never been to Stephen's room, but I knew the layout of the residence halls. Passing a few surprised towel-wrapped guys, I went straight to his door and pounded on it with my palm. When the door opened, he only had his boxers on.

"Amanda?"

I held up my phone, shaking it in front of his face, surprised I was able to maintain a sizable level of anger for over an hour. "Ever hear of privacy, anonymity? The one thing you knew I wanted... gone!"

"What are you talking about?"

"Nice, dude, didn't know you had it in you," a guy passing commented. I watched him nod as he walked away and thought I would punch that smug smile right off his face.

I held my phone in front of Stephen's face. "Hashtag Amanda, hashtag assault, hashtag run, ring any bells?"

He backed into his room. "Come in."

I stepped around him, and he closed the door behind us. Picking up pants from the floor, he started to lift his leg into the opening.

"Eww." I covered my eyes with my hand.

"You did come to my room at six in the morning."

Hearing a zipper, I looked at my phone. "It's seven."

"What if someone were here?"

"You're a resident assistant. You don't break the rules. Don't try and distract me. Where's your computer?"

He motioned towards the desk, and I stomped to the laptop, touching the screen to turn it on. I tapped on it again, and he slid it away from me, typing in his password and swiveling it back to face me. I brought up the newspaper column and held it up in front of his face.

"This is the opposite of what I need right now."

He took the device and held it out at arm's length. "I had nothing to do with this. How would I know this story would get published?"

"You didn't do anything to prevent it. You're the organizer of this thing. You should've been proactive about stuff like this." I took the computer from him and set it on the desk, my good hand resting on my hip.

"You're angry at me?"

"Yes, very."

"Again, I had nothing to do with this." He turned and walked towards his dresser, opening a drawer and pulling out a shirt. "Find the author."

"I don't have time to hunt people down. This leaked on your watch." I punched my finger into his chest, feeling like I was watching myself in a movie. Had I just hit Stephen? Amazed at my anger's stamina, I stood there frozen.

"Why don't we get some breakfast and coffee? Well, coffee for me, not you." He pulled some socks out of his top drawer and sat on the bed.

"Fine." I slid my glasses off.

"Maybe we could go to Mass."

"You think Mass is going to fix this?"

"Couldn't hurt."

He put on his shoes and held the door open for me. We rode down the elevator to the parking lot in silence. "You parked in a handicap spot?"

"Duh." I pointed to my sling.

"You are having some serious issues, aren't you?"

"No." I flung my door open. God, I hated him right then.

We drove to a café. He ordered a huge breakfast, and I ordered coffee and a bagel.

"You are seriously still mad even though I had nothing to do with the article?" he asked when our food came.

"It's probably not you. I'm angry at everything."

"I guess you're allowed."

"Don't give me an out."

"Now you're mad at me for forgiving you?"

"Yes, see?" We ate the rest of our meal in silence and then went to the Catholic center. Mass was the worst idea ever, as everything about it from the warm smile of the priest to the moments of quiet reflection had me seething about the status of my life.

Afterwards, Stephen and I walked to my car. "Better?"

"No, I think I need to call the counselor. I can't stop being angry. Do you want me to drive you somewhere?"

"Nah, I'll walk."

"Okay, thanks for breakfast and this." I pointed towards the chapel.

"You're not still angry at me?"

"It's not your fault."

"Are you still in for the classes."

"Yes."

"Good." He hit the top of the car and walked away.

I drove to the main student parking lot, sat in the car, and phoned Dr. Milner. She listened to me rant about all the atrocities of my life and suggested we have a session the next morning. I reviewed my organic chemistry in the car and walked to class in time to slip in before the professor.

"Nice story," Justin said, lifting my backpack off my shoulder.

I forced myself to say thank you rather than telling him to shut up.

"Why the long face?"

"More publicity is not my style."

The professor came to the podium and started the lecture. When it was done, we walked towards the physics building. "Do I have a lab partner today?"

"No, I have my deposition. I should be back next week though."

"Good, because those Indian guys reek of curry."

Lab, even in a curry-infused room, sounded better than giving a deposition for hours, but after physics I drove home, walked Northie, and then changed and waited for Chris.

He drove me to the law office where I met the other lawyers. The lead was a woman, and I was sure they'd picked her because she had a soft sweet voice and mellow features. But even her tone felt evil by the end of the afternoon. How many times did I have to tell them the same thing, relive the event again and again? After a day of thinking about Peter, I couldn't get his image out of my head and feared I would end up knees-to-chest rocking in a padded room. My palms sweated and my heart raced non-stop for four hours.

When she left, my head went to the table. Chris's hand rubbed my back. "You did good."

I looked up at him. "Thank you."

"Let's get you some dinner."

We ate at a sushi place in town, and he got me two glasses of wine. He drove me home and walked me to my door. A few more days, and it will be all over."

"Until the trial."

"I guess."

"Thanks."

"You're welcome. See you tomorrow."

Inside, I found Northie in his crate. It was dark out, and I called Kate to come walk with me. With her constant chatter, she was the perfect companion. Being updated on her classes and everyone's dating life was the distraction I needed. I talked to Doug and Mom and messaged Dad, Tia, and Marissa before Zack met me for our workout.

I took my books, as Leslie was meeting up with us. They'd started dating, and it ate into my time with him. It was selfish, but he had such a low-key manner and was one of the few people I relaxed with. With their conversation, I couldn't concentrate on the texts and chose to be entertained by the latest television series. After an hour, I was sweaty and ready to call it a day. Back in my apartment, I showered and snuggled under the covers with my books. Chemistry, physics, and calculus were good distractions, and the perfect prescription for getting to sleep. But even my workout couldn't keep Peter's image out of my dreams.

"Bitch, you better hope you don't remember who did this. And if you do remember, you better not tell anyone. Because if you do, I'll find you, and it'll be way worse than this. For you and your friend Lila."

I shot straight up. "Lila!" Running to her room, I flung the door open. She lay next to Ross, hair strewn on the pillow.

You are *a crazy person,* I told myself as I inched the door closed. I curled up on the couch, arms wound around my legs, trying to slow my breathing. We were safe, he couldn't hurt us.

Chapter 12

My session with Dr. Milner the next day was good. The only exception being she became concerned about my diet when I admitted I was only eating two meals a day. She instructed me to write down what I ate and focus on getting three meals a day. In addition, she wanted me to journal, to get all my thoughts and feelings on paper. I wasn't sure when I was supposed to do the task though. I'd been using my pre-dawn hours to study, and there wasn't any more time.

The rest of the week was a cookie cutter of Monday, and when Friday evening arrived, I was ready to curl up in my bed and not surface for two days. At least I was done with the depositions and could focus on courses and getting back to my tutoring schedule. The doctor had taken my stitches out but wanted me to continue to wear the sling. Anything that would help my side heal faster, get me back to rowing, and into boxing gloves sounded fine. It was annoying, but a means to an end.

My parents, Tia, and Ed descended on my apartment Friday night ahead of the football game. They took Mark, Ross, Lila, and me out to dinner both Friday and Saturday, as well as to brunch on Sunday. Dad hadn't entirely relaxed his stance, but he wasn't as demanding as he had been in previous visits. I hoped he'd decided I could indeed make it on my own.

Mom pulled me aside before they left on Sunday. "I found this." She handed me a package wrapped in tissue paper. "It was your grandmother's. I thought you might like to use it."

I gently unsealed the tissue to uncover a cracked brown leather journal. "This was Bubbe's?" I opened the book and inside was written *Amalie Baar 1945* in a script I hadn't seen in over a year.

"You saved it? Thank you." I hugged her.

❦ ❦ ❦

I wasn't sure whether my post-traumatic stress disorder symptoms were better or I got used to them. My existence consisted of classes, two individual counseling appointments, one support group, study sessions at the athletic building, five tutoring clients, daily updates from the legal team, and nightly workouts with Zack. With Leslie often joining us, the only thing I looked forward to was Doug's visits for Homecoming, Thanksgiving, and Christmas.

The lawyers found three girls who had been paid large sums of money by Peter's family. Two of them wouldn't even talk to them, but one did and agreed to testify. On the night before we received the news, I'd gotten my first full night's sleep since the deposition. Her story was much like mine. She'd been nice to Peter when he was new at her high school, and then he'd turned on her. A complaint was filed, and he was charged with assault and sexual battery, but they had accepted money in return for dropping the case. Her testimony indicated the major reason for not pursuing legal action was her fear of him. Listening to her deposition confirmed my worries, and I became more paranoid than ever. The sensitivity to smells, fear of new people, crowds, and enclosed spaces increased. The glasses of wine and workouts ceased to keep away the nightmares.

It didn't help that I was ridden with guilt. All of my friends, even some from high school, and all of the fraternity brothers and potentials that were present the night of my attack were deposed by both legal teams. Lila, Mark, Ross, Bill, and Zack's depositions each lasted half a day. Even though they assured me they didn't mind, I couldn't help but feel responsible for the disruption. If I'd let it go, not pursued charges, perhaps we would've moved on sooner.

When I voiced my concerns to Lila, she was adamant. "What is the slogan?"

"He doesn't get to win."

"Right."

❦ ❦ ❦

As long as I kept doing all the right things, I figured I'd be okay. The assault classes boosted my confidence. They were small, about twenty girls in each, and Stephen and I were paired up to teach. Midterm week came, and I studied every free second. Lila complained that it fell on Homecoming week, but I didn't care.

I had no life outside my responsibilities. Going into my tests, I felt certain about my grasp on the material.

"Okay, Avery, what'd you think?" Justin asked after we finished our third test in two days.

"Good, I feel good. How about you?"

"Yep, aced it. We should go out and celebrate tonight."

"It's Tuesday, and I don't go out."

"Ever?"

"Ever."

"That is seriously messed up. You went out all the time last year."

"Can we not talk about it?"

🕊 🕊 🕊

I got through all my other tests feeling confident. The organic chemistry and physics grades were to post Wednesday morning by ten, and I checked them before the chemistry lecture. When I pulled up the marks, I couldn't believe my eyes. I'd made a seventy-two in chemistry and seventy-four in physics. How could that be? I knew the information. I'd studied hard and felt good about the tests.

Justin sat down beside me, and I wiped away the tear that had formed.

"What's up Avery?"

"Not much. Did you check your grade?"

"Yes, I didn't do as well as I wanted though. I only got an eighty-two. This prof must be a stickler."

"At least you go that."

"Your grade was worse? No way. We studied together. You knew everything."

"I know. I don't know what happened."

The professor started the lecture and handing back the tests. I had to work hard at not crying on the sheet. I couldn't make Cs in two subjects. It was only mid-term, but it would be hard to bring it up. It would ruin my GPA. Dad was going to flip. The only solution was to drop the classes. I'd still have enough hours to make the minimum if I'd done well on my other midterms. No one would slight me, right? I'd been doing everything right, but it wasn't good enough.

As class finished, I spun out of my seat and brushed past Justin before he could say anything. I'd seen Dr. Milner the day before, but I headed straight for her office. She had a few minutes to spend with me, but in the end I had to the decision for myself. I waited until the deadline on Friday and dropped the classes. Doug and my friends supported my decision, but I still had to tell my parents.

That evening, Doug arrived from Japan. It was nice of him to fly twenty-four hours each way for a four-day weekend. His presence felt like finding an oasis in the middle of the desert. I felt warm, safe, and happy with him there. I knew he was a horrible mental crutch but convinced myself it was like vacation. Everyone needed a vacation, a break from their normal drone of life. With the night terrors, arrhythmia, and anxiety from triggers, my existence was far worse than the normal drone, and he was my break.

For the first time in weeks, I didn't wake up screaming. On Homecoming day, we went to the fraternity house and walked to the football game with Bill, Mark, Zack, Ross, and Lila. It was good to be out doing something normal even if I did keep scanning my surroundings, scouting for danger.

My family was in town for the game too, and on Sunday we had brunch with them. When I admitted to dropping the classes, Dad slammed his fist on the table. "See, I knew you were taking on too much. You should've listened to us."

My eyes started to water, but I dug my nails into my palms and looked him right in the eyes. "I still have four courses that I'm doing well in and can pick up more clients to pay off the medical bills quicker. I was a quarter ahead anyway, and I'll be more prepared to take them next quarter."

He pointed a finger at me. "That's right, missy, you will take them next quarter. Don't you think for a minute that you can get out of this chemistry major."

The tears ran down my cheek. I hated crying in front of Doug. "I'm not trying to get out of anything. I'm doing everything you guys required."

Mom put her hand on Dad's arm and pulled it from the table. "Charlie, we wanted her to take a break. She is giving herself a break. Don't chastise her."

We rarely witnessed Mom criticize Dad and when I glanced at Tia, her eyes bulged. Mom wrapped her arm around my shoulders and kissed my temple. "I'm proud of you, sweetie. That must have been hard to do."

Her words made it clear why I'd had such a problem with the decision. It was admitting weakness and defeat. In my family, we didn't fail. I justified it by telling myself I needed a break. But in my mind, I had failed. It would've been better not to have started in the first place than to quit mid-way.

Dad cleared his throat. "It seems like you could've at least stuck with the courses in your major and dropped the Chinese lit or Japanese. You should've called me before you made that decision."

I opened my mouth to defend myself, but it seemed useless. As it had been for the past year, little I did was right in his eyes. I hated Doug had to be there to witness the conversation. When my family left, Doug and I drove into the city to spend the evening with Paula and Gary. We went to Mass, and Paula made ham and black beans for dinner.

The next two days, Doug came to campus with me, and we met between classes and then had dinner in the city with his mom. On Wednesday morning, I hated to see him go. Tears streamed down my face as I pulled away from the drop-off area, and I stopped in the cell phone lot to talk to him until he boarded.

After the weekend with them, Mom sent me care packages every week. They included cookies after the guys made the request. Most of the stuff I gave away, but I was grateful for the coffee and laundry soap she sent. The dreams were intermittent. Journaling my activities as Dr. Milner instructed didn't reveal any patterns, and Lila continued to sleep at the house.

But things did get better. Little by little I could tolerate more smoke and body odor scents. The orange streetlights still made my stomach turn, but as the depositions wrapped up, I felt more balanced. In mid-November, they took an X-ray of my ribs. They were healing nicely, and I was able to stop wearing the sling. The doctor wanted me to take it easy a month more, but

I was able to increase the incline on the treadmill and speed on the elliptical.

The girls in the support group, save Misty, started to warm up to me. Dr. Milner dropped my counseling sessions down to one a week. I still didn't eat as well as I should, with only two complete meals a day. There was something about eating on campus that I couldn't handle. I always had good intentions but then ended up with coffee. I made a point to order a latte or something with a few calories, so I didn't lose weight, or appear to. I didn't really care if I lost weight, but Dad would tote me home in a second if he thought I looked thinner. In my food log, I wrote that I ate a sandwich for lunch. It was lying. I was lying to Dr. Milner, but I rationalized it by thinking my coffee drink equaled the same amount of calories.

I was able to pick up extra tutoring clients, and my debt started to decrease. At the rate I was going, I'd be able to pay off all the medial bills by December and planned on taking a real vacation during winter break. The first two weeks of the break would be taken up with trial prep, but afterwards I'd have two weeks of free time.

There was no time for social activities, but it didn't bother me. For the first time in our ten-year friendship, Lila didn't bug me about it. We had dinners at our apartment or Kate's every week, and I met up with Paula in the city most Sundays. It was enough for me.

❦ ❦ ❦

Time was measured by Doug's visits. He came for the Thanksgiving break and then again Christmas Eve. I picked him up at the airport, and after dinner, mass, and a midnight snack with Paula and Gary, we walked towards Doug's room.

"You must be exhausted." I wrapped my arms around him.

"Not too exhausted to stay up with my girlfriend." He kissed me and tugged at my shirt. Inside, he backed me into the closed door, and I let him lift the shirt over my head. He pulled his off and spun me towards the bed. It felt wonderful to be with him, and I would have been happy to never sleep again. He drifted off and I lay awake with my head resting on his chest. The nightmares had subsided in November, but with the pre-trial prep during the weeks leading up to Christmas, the dreams had resumed and I didn't want to wake him with my screams.

I got up and slipped on some pants and a jacket. When I turned the door handle and heard him stir. "Hey, where are you going?"

"I was going to sleep in the other room. I didn't want to wake you in the morning."

"What are you talking about? It won't bother me."

"I toss a lot at night."

"How do you know if you're sleeping?"

"My hair is always a mess." I hedged.

"I don't care, come back to bed. We only have a week together."

I closed the door and leaned my back against the wood. "I'll wake you. You need a good night's sleep."

He got up and slid some pants on. "And I'm telling you, you won't." Standing in front of me, he kissed my forehead. "What's going on?"

"I'm having nightmares again. I wake up screaming."

"Again?" He tucked a strand of hair behind my ear. "You never said anything about nightmares."

"They're not a big deal."

"Waking up screaming sounds like a big deal."

"Well, they were better, but with the trial prep, they came back."

"How did you deal with them before?" He took my hands and pulled me toward the bed.

I sat beside him. "Exercise and alcohol help."

"It's nearly two. I can't believe you're not exhausted. Sleep with me tonight. We'll deal with it as it comes."

"Okay, but I'm warning you, it's bad. Lila couldn't stay at the apartment."

"I can't believe you didn't tell me."

"I didn't want you to worry." I snuggled into him, praying he would keep the dreams at bay.

It was nearly nine when I woke to him snoring beside me. Content after my dreamless sleep, I tiptoed to the kitchen for coffee. After a light breakfast with Paula and Gary, we drove to Champaign. With the pre-trial meetings, I hadn't been home since August, and it felt strange. Mom was disappointed I wasn't coming to the Caribbean with them, but Doug was in Chris's wedding on New Year's Eve. They'd already lectured me on putting family first, and complained more when I announced my travel plans for spring break. Sticking true to their inability to approve of anything important to me, they criticized my spring trip to Japan and course choices.

"Psychology?" My dad threw his arms toward the ceiling. "What are you thinking? Don't you get enough psychology seeing that shrink?"

"Dad, it's a humanities course, and I need credits in that area. I thought it might be useful to have. I mean CIA, FBI, diplomatic protocol. You have to know how to read people, interpret more than what they say, and understand what motives they may have."

"I guess when you put it that way it makes sense." Dad didn't argue against my reasoning but continued to be critical of me the rest of the visit.

❧ ❧ ❧

We had an amazing time at Chris's wedding in New York. I felt bad they had to cut their honeymoon short because of the trial, but Nicole stopped me from apologizing mid-sentence. "It's his job. If it wasn't your case, it might have been another one." I guessed it was a good thing she was an attorney too.

At the service, Paula made sure I sat in the front row with her, Gary, his daughters, and their dates. It was a huge affair with six groomsmen and bridesmaids. At the reception after, the families and wedding party alone took up ten tables, and there were over two hundred guests. We rang in the New Year on the dance floor, and it was two when we went outside to see Chris and Nicole off.

On New Year's Day, Doug and I flew back to Chicago, and then he had a connecting flight to Tokyo. Our only disagreement the whole week was on the topic of whether he would come for the trial. He wanted to be there, but I didn't want him to. First, he'd already taken a week off for Christmas and Chris's wedding. Second, the trial was expected to last for two weeks. But I could see what witnessing trauma firsthand did to people, and I didn't want him to have the same experience. It was one thing to hear about it, but to have a front row seat was different. I saw it in Lila, Mark, Bill, and Zack, and I didn't want Doug to look at me the way they did. Finally, he caved and agreed to stay in Japan.

❦ ❦ ❦

When he left, there were a few days before the trial started, and I stayed busy with tutoring clients. Even with full work days and work outs, I couldn't sleep. The day before the hearing we had the last prep session and the lawyers felt everyone was ready. The first day of trial coincided with the first day of the new quarter, but I was able to get excused from classes and all my assignments until after the hearing.

What I dreaded most was seeing Peter's face. The day of the hearing, I was in my seat in the courtroom half an hour early. Chris sat between the DA and two of the senator's lawyers at the prosecution's table. Mr. Taylor and two of the other lawyers sat with me in the front row. Our group quieted each time the doors opened, but I didn't look back. The room filled, and although Peter's lawyers were in their places, he wasn't there. It was almost eight when the doors opened again. Mr. Taylor turned towards the back of the room and then squeezed my hand. I kept my eyes trained on Chris, only seeing Peter after he passed our row. In the dark suit his skin looked ghostly pale and a shiver ran down my spine.

His parents hugged him and filed into the row across from us. As soon as his mother was seated, she craned her neck and looked directly at me. I couldn't help but meet her stare. Her lips formed the same thin-lined expression I remembered as his, and I fought another shiver. Turning away, I caught Peter's glare and froze. He smiled—the thin-lipped smile I saw in my nightmares—nodded his head, and then turned towards the front of the room.

"All rise for Judge Akins."

As if pulled by some mystical force, I stood, gripping the railing in front of me. I was safe I repeated in my head. Everyone in the courtroom was instructed to sit, and the jury members filed into the room. The DA made his opening statement and the defense followed. I wasn't prepared for their attack. The attorney pointed at me, alleging I lead the victim on and initiated our encounter, kissed him, and faked my injuries.

After the initial statements, my testimony came next. I stood when my name was called, positioned my hands at my side, and walked to the witness box, trembling. Focusing on my steps, I didn't look at Peter until I was seated. When the questions from the prosecution were answered, the defense cross-examined.

"Do you believe the defendant to be a good-looking young man?"

"He is a nice-looking person," I heard myself say. It was what I believed before the accident.

"Were you attracted to Mr. Scalini?"

"No."

"But you just said…" All of her questions went like that. She asked me to review again the sequence of events the prior night as well as the evening of the attack. It was grueling sitting in front of him and reliving the attack time after time, and I wondered if I'd ever have a restful night again. My attorneys could tell when I was about to slip into auto-pilot, and we had a system worked out to prevent it. We'd practiced so many times they knew my body language. I'd get to a point when I wanted to shut it off, disconnect, and relate the story as if it were a sad movie. Chris would strum his fingers on the table, and I would know I had to reset and stay engaged. It wouldn't do to have the jury see me as a robot. I had to be the real victim, not my anti-self that I liked to show the world.

The prosecution presented the physical evidence next. They showed video footage of him entering and leaving the dorm, withdrawing cash from an ATM, hailing a cab after the incident, and buying a bus ticket. There were samples of his hair on my clothes, pictures of the crime scene, with me sprawled unconscious on the ground, and my wounds. I hadn't seen those before, and I dug my fingers into my palm, trying to control my breathing. My arrhythmia kicked in, and I thought I might hyperventilate.

Mr. Taylor wrapped an arm around me and whispered in my ear, "You were right not to have Doug here. He would have charged across the aisle and killed that guy."

The next two days included testimony from Lila, Bill, Mark, Zack, a few other fraternity brothers, and Peter's roommate. On Friday, the prosecution had the other victim testify. Her cross-examination was even harder than mine, but she did a good job, and our team was happy with how the week had gone.

When I got home, I was on auto-pilot cramming in all my coursework until the dreams came in the middle of the night. They got worse and worse, and Peter came closer and closer to touching me in each one, eventually grabbing me and holding me under the surface of a river, drowning me.

On Monday, the defense started its testimonies, including bringing Law to the stand. I couldn't believe they had dug him up, a guy I'd been on one horrible date with. He testified that he'd taken me to a picnic spot and I had freaked out, running out into a field and calling 911. In truth, he'd wanted me to have sex with him and refused to drive me home. After the defense rested, the prosecution team was able to rebut Law's testimony. Mark, and the manager from the gym where Law and Mark worked, testified and corroborated my story. There had been other complaints from women clients about Law's behavior, and he'd been fired not long after my date with him.

Closing arguments were heard on Friday morning. The jurors were reminded of the rules for deciding a judgment and sent to deliberate. We sat in a café across the street waiting for a verdict. How people could eat like it was a normal day I couldn't fathom, but I sat there smiling, nodding my head, and replying with an appropriate answer when engaged. Not an hour in, Chris got a call that the jury had the verdict. We waited in the lobby for the defense team and Peter to enter the courtroom first. Then we filed in and took our seats, standing again when the judge entered.

"What does the jury find?" Judge Akins asked.

The head juror stood and opened a paper. He looked straight at me. "The jury unanimously finds the defendant guilty of the felony of aggravated assault and sexual battery."

"Noooo!" Peter's mother stood and cried out. His father wrapped an arm around her shoulders and urged her back onto the bench. I looked to Peter who stood chin up with his hands locked behind his back.

The judge struck the gavel to the desk. "I would usually wait to do the sentencing phase another day, but I believe this case is fairly straight forward. I will hear sentencing arguments in an hour." She rose along with the rest of us.

We retired to the coffee shop across the street again. I was glad my friends and family were able to make it to the hearing the final day. I felt better with my people there as the rest of the chamber had been filled with reporters who took their stories back to the TV stations and papers each break. Outside the media people stood shoulder to shoulder onto the steps of the courthouse.

Mr. Taylor pulled me aside. "You need to think about what you want to say." They'd whisked me past the crowd once, but after sentencing, there would be more pressure to make a statement.

At one, we squeezed our way through the crowd back into the courtroom for the sentencing hearing. The prosecution argued for the maximum penalty of three years with registration as a sexual offender upon his release. The defense argued for the minimum sentence of parole and therapy. The judge seemed to listen politely, nodding with each comment.

When the defense was done, she didn't hesitate. "Please stand for sentencing."

Peter stood, chin to chest for the first time. "Mr. Scalini."

Peter raised his chin. "Yes ma'am."

"Normally in a first offense case," Judge Akins began, "I would be swayed towards a lighter sentence. In this case, however—"

she looked at me "—due to the brutality of the attack, and the evidence of repeated behavior, I sentence you to the maximum sentence of three years in Illinois State prison. You will be registered as a sex offender and will be required to follow the guidelines as such."

Motion from my right side caught my eye. Her finger was pointed at my face. "You, you did this. He's just a boy. You've signed his death warrant. You might as well have killed my son yourself."

I looked to Peter, but his expression held no insight to his emotion. His eyes were blank, his lips stoic for the first time. I was right, wasn't I? He'd forced his tongue into my mouth. He'd beat me, threatened to kill me and Lila. He didn't get to walk the streets after doing those things to me and the other girls. He got what he deserved. He would be somewhere he couldn't hurt anyone. Hopefully, he would be reformed, learn he couldn't hurt people. Justice was served. He didn't get to win.

Chapter 13

In the evening, Senator Russell hosted a party for the legal team, my friends and family, and a host of politicians. I walked through the night in a haze. Maybe everyone else thought it a foregone conclusion that he would be found guilty, but I had prepared for the worst. In my mind, I planned for a reality that included him walking free and all the hours spent prepping for the case to have been wasted. But the attack, the trial, all of it was behind me like a bad dream.

I could see the relief, the absence of tense shoulders and focused stares in everyone's eyes. It made me happy they felt good, but the image that played in my thoughts was of Peter's mom pointing at me from the other side of the aisle. Her words, *"You did this. He's just a boy. You've signed his death warrant. You might as well have killed my son yourself,"* played in my memory again and again.

A hand on my bicep brought me out of the script. I snatched my arm away from Zack's grip.

"She got a little soft. But she'll be ready for spring season, right Amanda?"

My cheeks burned with embarrassment. I scanned the faces around me. There was no way I would be seen as soft. "Coach says I can start training tomorrow. With rowing, kick boxing, and swimming, I'll be in shape in no time."

"You should take it easy, start slow," Dad commented.

I was done being coddled, finished with thinking of myself as needing special treatment. Peter did not get to win, and neither did his mother. "I've been ramping up. I'm ready."

That night Peter did not star in my dreams. His mom's face, eyes large, mouth agape, distorted by terror, floated above me as I slept on a bed of flowers under a sunny sky.

You did this. He's just a boy. You've signed his death warrant. You might as well have killed my son yourself.

She repeated the words over and over.

I sat straight up in my bed, but there were no screams as my breath stuck in my throat. Swallowing a whole glass of water I hooked an arm around Northie, but sleep didn't come. Finally at six, I snuck grabbed my sneakers to take the puppy for a walk. As I walked out the door, I saw Zack approaching.

"Hey, you're up early."

"I'm getting an early start."

"Sweet. Hey, I have a new smoothie recipe. I'll come by after my workout."

"Cool, I'll see you in an hour then."

I walked Northie to the dog area and then around the grounds. Back at the apartment it wasn't ten minute before I heard a knock at the door.

Zack shook a can in my face. I took the can from him, my nose wriggling up. The ingredients read whey, soy, and casein protein.

He snatched it away from me. "I won't put it in yours if you don't want."

"Yeah, I don't want."

He mixed strawberries, bananas, and ice in the blender and poured half of it in a glass for me, adding a spoon full of the powder to the rest for himself. We sat at the bar, drinking our shakes. When we finished, I took the glasses and filled the dishwasher. I packed my bag and we headed to the parking lot.

In athletic lot, I grew anxious about my smell triggers. But my jacket was freshly washed and the sleeves smelled of my fabric softener. The workout was good, and by the end, I'd gotten my groove back. I wasn't as strong or fast as the previous season but felt confident I could get there. We weighed in at the end of the workout.

Coach lever until the bar was balanced and checked his electronic tablet. "Down from last year Avery, two pounds, let's not make that a trend. We need light, but I want everyone healthy."

"Yes, sir," I said as I jumped off the scale. Two down from last year meant I was below ninety. Dad wouldn't be happy about that. I liked that I was lean, now I needed my muscle tone back. Increasing muscle would add some weight anyway.

Bill and Zack waited outside for me. "You coming to brunch, softie?" Zack asked.

"Don't call me that. But no, I'm meeting my parents."

"Okay, catch you later," Zack said, walking towards Bill's car.

At my apartment, I showered and washed my hair. My family scheduled our brunch for noon, but I was starving and shaky after the workout. Frustrated but figuring I'd never make it till brunch, I made a large latte with skim milk to get some protein. Routine, getting back in a routine was good, I thought. Breakfast, workout, and my coffee lunch felt like a good habit for Saturday. I walked Northie around the complex before I drove into downtown Evanston to meet my parents.

I ordered a mug of hot water and added a tea bag. "You aren't eating?" Mom asked.

"I was hungry after my workout, so I ate before. Sorry."

"It's okay, sweetie, the point is to see you."

We chatted about my classes and the rest of the quarter. Mom's birthday fell in mid-February, and I committed to visiting for the weekend.

They left for home from the restaurant, and I did some food shopping before returning to my apartment. Lila was there, and we cleaned and did laundry the rest of the afternoon. She had a date planned with Ross, and I settled in with a grilled chicken salad for a night of studying.

On Sunday, I attended Mass with Stephen and we got coffee afterwards. In the afternoon, I had study sessions with Kate and

Justin. Kate and I had organic chemistry and physics together, and Justin and I were in the same calculus section again.

Addie and I met up in the evening to start my kickboxing endeavor. The apartment complex gym had a punching and speed bag, which was perfect because I wasn't ready to go to any other gym. She'd invited me to come to her classes, but the building was near Peter's apartment. I didn't need one more thing to trigger me. Plus, I wasn't ready to be in a room with a bunch of people I didn't know.

My days and weeks took on a definite pattern. On Monday, Wednesday, and Friday, I'd scheduled earlier classes, and Kate rode with me to campus for chemistry and physics. Tuesdays and Thursdays were rowing practice. On off days, I worked out with Addie, Zack, or went running. I had tutoring clients most afternoons.

Support group was on Tuesdays, and Misty still hated me. It was okay because her and her band of let's-stuff-our-faces-every-Tuesday people kind of made me sick anyway. None of them were slim. Didn't they want to look nice? It was horrible that I'd begun to think of how much a person ate or weighed as a judgment on what type of person they were. I wasn't sure how it'd crept into my psyche. It was wrong and senseless, but it was all I had. A miniscule part of me could acknowledge the error in my thinking, but I had nothing else to define myself by. I wasn't achieving anything else except looking good. So my goals had morphed into becoming as trim and chiseled as possible when I saw Doug in March. Then I would be in top shape for spring rowing with no hint of softness anywhere. There would be no room for Zack to call me mushy.

Every night since the trial, I woke unable to catch my breath, hearing Peter's mother's words repeated again and again. How could I sleep in a warm bed when Peter was in prison? Why did I feel guilty? It made no sense. He had made his choices. Dr. Milner asked what the worst part of the trial was, and I'd been honest. She'd assured me that victim guilt was normal, but Peter was responsible for his actions. After a while, I kept the feelings and dreams to myself.

My days ticked off. I still hated chemistry and campus. The college grounds reminded me of Peter. With the cold weather, no one was out at the coffee cart but the smokers, and I started taking a coffee in an insulated tumbler to drink between classes.

Two weeks later, Zack stood me in front of the mirror and held up each arm. "Look, they're the same. That's awesome! You are getting super cut."

"Darn straight."

"You keeping up your cardio?"

"Swimming freaked me out, so I started running."

"You still have to take the swim test again."

"I know, but I'll be in shape for it."

"I don't doubt it."

I got a lot of praise on my super muscular, chiseled physique. Doug even noticed in our video chats. My workouts and planning for Japan kept me sane. It occurred to me I hated most everything about Northwestern. The only reason I was staying was my scholarship. Mom and Dad might not have been wrong when they suggested a different environment. They only had the choice of location wrong. I craved to be in a different setting, taking classes in linguistics, language development, and speech pathology.

Research into Japanese schools indicated I had several options around Tokyo. I contacted the schools and set up interviews for spring break. It was exciting to think about moving beyond Evanston, and I used my workouts to fantasize about what it would be like to live in Tokyo with Doug.

☙ ☙ ☙

The first of February, I stepped onto the scale to weigh-in for rowing. The coach slid the level to the right and balanced it at eight-six pounds. I swallowed hard and looked at the coach.

"See me in my office after this, Avery," he told me.

I waited outside his office, and he motioned me in. "Strength wise, I see you're making progress, but I'm not sure what is going on with your weight. Do you need to talk to someone?"

"I'm already see Dr. Milner."

"Okay, well, I am going to give her a call. If your weight doesn't move in the correct direction, then we'll have to think about making different decisions."

He wasn't my dad. I couldn't stomp out and pretend it didn't matter. He was my coach and he stood between me and a season of rowing. Outside the gym, Zack and Bill waited for me.

"Everything okay?" Zack asked.

"Yeah, sure."

"You coming to brunch with us?"

"No, I'm studying."

"Had to ask."

"Thanks, maybe next week," I told him, although I had no intention of putting greasy breakfast food in my mouth.

Then, I was left alone to think about dealing with the vague threat of different decisions. I'd stopped journaling my food for the counselor in December when it seemed there was no need to monitor my weight. I'd have to go back to putting down what I ate. I'd have to admit I ate the same thing every day. Would I lie about lunches again? I liked my routine. It worked for me. And what would I do about my weight? I'd have to add in some calories if I wanted to stay on the team.

I went home and started the coffee maker and went to the fridge to get milk. We had skim as well as two-percent. I could use two-percent to help with my calorie intake. But I really liked how I looked. What if the extra calories made me soft again? *No*, I told myself, *you should stick to your routine*. I filled half the cup with espresso and filled the rest with skim milk like always. It wasn't as good as the baristas' at the café, but it was warm. I sat at the table and sipped my latte and studied. Afterwards, I showered, cleaned my bathroom, started laundry, and settled in to read coursework again.

Sunday came and I opted out of Mass with Stephen and Paula. I couldn't sit in a chapel for an hour with my guilt loop playing in my head. Even knowing Peter had made his own decision, broken the law, and had been given fair consequences, I couldn't get the thoughts out of my mind. His mom's words haunted me. Maybe he only needed counseling. I didn't buy for a second that he was insane but maybe damaged to the point of insanity.

On Monday morning, I got an email from Dr. Milner about the weight issue, and we moved my appointment up to the next day. I agreed to journal my food again. What did it hurt? I could lie again. Really I wasn't doing anything wrong. I would get into shape, and then I could moderate my food choices. My habits were working—how I looked proved it. I got compliments all the time. Standing in line at the coffee shop a group of girls would order huge drinks containing six hundred calories a piece. I'd order a black coffee, and they'd be surprised at how I could drink it when the tall whipped cream topped drinks were right in front of me. Then they'd proceed to complain about their weight and cravings. Well, I had that kicked. It wasn't hard. I could tell them how to do it. All they had to do was ask. Forming habits was easy, a matter of doing the same thing every day.

Kickboxing was amazing. I could kick the bag or punch the speed bag till my muscles screamed in protest. All I had to do was imagine Peter's face, his thin-lipped smirk, or his mother's voice reprimanding me. I'd scoured my psychology book, reading it cover to cover. Victim guilt was common, and I had tons of it. I should've had my mace out. I should've run. These regrets piled on top of remorse I felt from putting an eighteen-year-old boy in prison.

My perception of the world had changed, and the shame filled my psyche. I no longer believed in the innate goodness of people, no longer trusted people. I hadn't made a single new friend since the attack. Every time I'd been paired up in class, I'd gone to the professor to ask to do the project alone. Was I letting Peter win? The answer was probably, but I was doing all I could. I was staying in school, making good grades, paying my bills, and getting stronger every day.

Reading the chapter on eating disorders, I found a picture of Karen Carpenter. She was a musician from the seventies who died of heart failure due to anorexia nervosa in the nineteen eighties. Studying her picture freaked me out, as the image of Peter's face transforming to a skull flashed through my consciousness. At least my diet was healthy.

The days ticked on, and I stuck to my routine. My grades were good, and I looked forward to the interviews with three colleges near Tokyo. Doug had a sight-seeing plan mapped out for my visit, only six weeks from then. Before I realized it, we were already halfway through February. Doug sent me a dozen roses along with a silver chain and heart locket for Valentine's Day.

Saturday came, and after our rowing workout, we lined up to get on the scale. I never weighed myself, didn't even own a scale, although Lila did. I was anxious. Maybe I should've been checking to make sure I stayed heavy enough. But then it was too late, there was nothing to be done about it. I stepped onto the scale, and Coach set the bar to the previous number. It tipped to the right, and my heart skipped a beat.

He didn't try to balance the scale. "Okay, Avery, we'll talk after."

My heart raced as I went to the locker room to retrieve my bag. I made my way to his office and leaned against the wall outside. He approached and unlocked the door, holding it open for me. Switching on the light, he motioned for me to sit down.

Hands shaking, I slid into the seat in front of his desk. He sat down, leaning way back and stretching his arms into the air. "I hate this Avery. You're a good coxswain and were getting back in shape to be a great rower. What's going on? Can I help in some way?"

My brain reeled. Was he kicking me off the team? "I had a cold last weekend and wasn't hungry. That must've been it."

"Well, I can't let you continue here. We need healthy people. I wish you the best with figuring this out. I hope you can."

"Can't I have another two weeks? I was sick."

"I already gave you two weeks. I'm sorry."

There was a thud in my chest, and I steeled my jaw to keep the tears from forming. "I'll pay attention to my calories better, keep tabs on my weight. I don't have a scale, so..."

He placed his palms on the desk. "Avery, come back when you're at ninety again."

I nodded my head, fighting the water threatening to pool in my eyes. "Okay, I can do that."

"Good, we'll see you in a month."

I picked up my bag and walked out of the room. No rowing, he was taking rowing away from me? Tears filled my eyelids and spilled onto my cheeks. I had to get out of the gym without seeing anyone. Wiping my face with my sleeve, I found the stairwell and jogged down the stairs and outside. At my car, I slid into the driver's seat, trying to figure out what to do. I was supposed to ride home to Champaign with Tia and Ed for Mom's birthday. I was in no shape for that. I couldn't face them. Taking a deep breath, I dialed Tia's number.

She answered right away.

"Hi, Tia."

"Is everything okay? You sound horrible."

"I was up all night with a stomach flu. I don't think I can make it today."

"Mom will be disappointed."

"I know, but I don't think I can sit three hours in the car and don't want to get everyone else sick."

"Totally get you there. I hope you're feeling better soon."

"Thanks. I'll call mom."

"Okay, love you."

"Love you too."

I backed out of the lot and drove to my apartment. It was empty, as it usually was on the weekends. Heading straight for Lila's bath, I pulled the scale out from under her sink. Eighty-four, the screen read eighty-four. I certainly hadn't wanted my weight to skyrocket, but I guessed this was a little low. I'd have to shore up my diet a bit.

Dialing mom, I apologized for not seeing her on her birthday. Next, I went to the bathroom to shower. For a split second, I could see the thin girl in the mirror, but I blinked and she was gone. Instead, I saw the same image as always, a muscular strong, normal size girl. I showered and walked Northie.

Back in the apartment, my stomach growled. *Remember, calories*, I told myself. When I made the latte, I talked myself out of the two-percent milk version though. I'd had a yogurt shake for breakfast. Surely I only needed my regular coffee for lunch. I'd have chicken salad for dinner anyway.

I cleaned, studied, and talked to Doug until Lila came in. We had an early dinner and watched a movie before the crowd arrived. They were all going to see a band at a club, and they filed out quickly, leaving me to curl up in bed with Northie. I dreaded sleep almost as much as I did chemistry. Even my workouts didn't keep the dreams away. I wondered what I'd do to replace rowing. Running sounded like a good option, and I checked to make sure my running gear was clean. Passing through the apartment, it was too quiet and chill bumps rose on my arms. *You're being paranoid*, I told myself as I slipped into my room. But sleep didn't come.

I sat up and flipped on the light. I needed a drink. In the kitchen, I found the vodka in the back of the cabinet where Lila stashed it. Mixing it with a no-calorie raspberry vitamin drink, I sat on the sofa and turned on a movie. Before I knew it, Northie was nudging me with his nose. I opened my eyes to see sun pouring in the window. Perhaps exhaustion and vodka worked for keeping the night terrors at bay, but I couldn't make it a routine, could I?

It was exactly five weeks till spring break when I would fly to Japan. I could make it five weeks until the hellish winter was done. I changed into my running clothes and took Northie for a walk. Afterwards, I downed the rest of the vitamin drink from the night before and headed out. It was cold and the wind stung my face, but it felt good to be pounding the pavement, driving air in and out of my lungs. I'd forgotten how much I liked running and it gave me an hour's time to think about being with Doug.

The days ticked by. Mondays, Wednesdays, and Fridays, I ran in the evenings. Tuesdays and Thursdays, I ran in the morning before going to campus. On the days when Kate didn't join me for a smoothie breakfast, I left out the yogurt and mixed a vitamin drink with some fruit in the blender for extra energy. My energy level had been waning, and I was tired more and more of the time, so I dropped the kickboxing sessions. The runs were getting longer with my increasing endurance anyway. I used weights in my apartment to work my arms. By the time I saw Doug, I would be an absolute powerhouse.

Monday, the last week in February, I chose a route than ran me to campus and back. I started at four to have enough time to get back before it was too dark. It had started to snow, but it was only thirty two. Nothing was going to come between me and my hour of adrenaline. I put on my rain jacket and warmest gear and headed out. By the time I got to campus, the snow was coming down hard. It made it hard to see, and the pavement was slippery. Jogging through the dorm area, I stopped at an intersection. A car pulled up beside me, and I almost bolted in front of it but heard Stephen's voice.

"Amanda?"

I ducked down to look in the window. "Hi."

"What are you doing?"

"Running."

"It's nearly a blizzard, and you're more than two miles from home. Get in the car."

Looking at the sky and the snow piling up on the sidewalk, I decided it might be wise to grab a ride. I wound around to the passenger's side and got in, warming my hands with the air from the heater.

"Aren't you frozen?"

"It's not too bad. I do it all the time."

"I was concerned about you before, but I think we should commit you right now."

"Why are you worried about me?"

"Have you looked in the mirror?"

"Yes, why?"

"You're skin and bones."

"I had the stomach flu last week and a cold the week before." I repeated the same lie I used when anyone mentioned how thin I looked, which seemed to be almost every day the past week.

"Are you better now?"

"Yeah, good as new."

He pulled into a parking space at his residence hall. "Do you want to grab a hot meal? We could go into Evanston."

"Oh, that sounds nice, but I am watching my budget. I usually make a salad at my apartment. I can take a bus if you don't have time to drive me."

He looked at me. "That's not the point. I don't think you're eating well, and I can't figure out why. I want to help."

My hands were shaky, and I shoved them under my thighs. He was too close to my secret, to my key to control. I hadn't admitted it to myself, let alone anyone else until that moment. "I don't think you can help me. I've tried to eat differently. But I can't." Tears started to stream down my cheeks. "I can't make myself. I tell myself I will, and then I can't do it. When I look in the mirror, for a second I see a thin person, but—" I patted my cheeks with my hands "—then she's gone, and all I know is that I can't gain weight."

He looked out the windshield and then back at me. "We should go see Father."

I doubted it would help, but I agreed. Part of me wanted help, but another resisted. It felt like I had multiple personalities. One side of me craved a solution, and the other needed to protect the behavior as if my life depended on it. He phoned Father and drove me to the Catholic center. Inside, Stephen waited in the chapel while I sat with Father in his office.

The answer the church offered was confession and forgiveness. If I bore my sins, I would be forgiven and healed. I knew it wouldn't work, was one hundred percent sure that telling my secrets wouldn't help me put food in my mouth, but I played along. I confessed that I lied about what I ate, that I lied about being sick. I asked forgiveness for having sex outside of marriage and underage drinking. When I told Father I was seeing Dr. Milner, he asked me to say a prayer of repentance each day for a week and to renew my vow of taking communion. He offered me the wafer and wine, but I didn't feel any different.

I thanked him for his time and joined Stephen in the chapel. "Better?" he asked.

"Thanks for helping me. It was good to talk to someone."

"Anytime." He wrapped his hand around mine.

"Do you want to get some dinner now?"

My head screamed no, and my heart thudded in my chest. "Sure," I heard myself say. *You have to play along,* my thoughts told me. *You have to pretend you're better. Then he'll leave you alone.*

He chose a pub in downtown Evanston, and I ordered a burger and fries. *See,* my psyche told me, *this'll show him you're okay.* Finishing half the burger and fries, I boxed the rest for later.

"What now?" he asked as we walked to the car.

"Studying."

"Everything else is good, your courses, your family, Doug?"

"Yes, all good, I have an A in every class, and it's four weeks till I go see Doug."

"Wow Japan, that's great."

"How about you?" I asked as we drove.

"Actually staying here for break, doing some training. Dad finally hired someone for the farm, so I'm off the hook there."

"That's awesome. I'm happy for you."

"How about your parents, they ease up at all?"

"Dad pretended to because of the, you know, thing this fall, but every time I mention anything about speech development, he freaks."

"That's too bad. What's the plan then?" he asked as he pulled into my apartment parking lot.

"Nothing, I don't have one. I'm sticking it out till I finish chemistry."

"Kate mentioned something about schools in Japan."

"Yes, I have interviews. I just need to choose one and take the plunge."

"That's a pretty big ocean."

"I know." I put my hand on the door latch. "Thank you for tonight."

"I am here to talk any time."

"Thanks." I pulled the handle and opened the door. "Bye."

"Don't be a stranger."

"Okay." I closed the door and waved at him through the window.

In my apartment, I stowed the food in the fridge and went straight to my mirror. I didn't dare get on the scale. It was weeks since I'd weighed anyway, so I had no point of reference anyway. *It's okay*, I told myself, *you needed the calories*. The beef will be good iron, the fats will soften your skin, help your nervous system. Your body needed those nutrients today, I thought.

The next morning I couldn't use yogurt in my smoothie. I mixed a no-calorie vitamin drink with frozen strawberries. The snow was thick on the ground, and I went to the apartment gym to run on the treadmill. The exercise room so it was the perfect hiding place.

And so my days went. I ran in the morning, mixed a fruit smoothie for breakfast, had a black coffee for lunch, and ate salad made from lettuce and dressing for dinner. In between, I hid from most everyone except Kate, who I could only avoid for short periods.

Chapter 14

March 21

I heard my voice. *"He's dead. It's my fault."*

Then I heard a woman's. *"You did this to yourself."*

I heard the words in my dream and opened my eyes to a dark hospital room. I wasn't dead. The door opened and light streamed in. A team of doctors entered and one of them approached me.

"Amanda, how are you feeling?"

"Tired."

"That's normal for having experienced a heart attack. Can you tell me what you think led to your condition?"

Tears pooled in my eyes. "I couldn't eat anymore."

He asked me to describe my reasoning, and I even thought I sounded crazy. Funny how it'd made sense at the time. How I'd convinced myself I had to eat light and work out every day. When I'd wanted to change, be healthier, the disease had taken over and wouldn't let me.

"Okay, well, I am going to have a psychiatrist come by and talk to you. You take care."

I wondered what could be done to fix me but was too tired and fell asleep, waking again at the sound of noise from the hall. A woman carrying a food tray walked in. She crossed to the window and opened the shade.

"Good morning, dearie. I have a special breakfast for you. They ordered you one of everything." She placed the meal on a table and rolled it towards my bed. "You know, sweetie, all you need is a good hot meal and your momma."

I turned away from her, tears forming in my eyes. All the food in the world, or my mother, couldn't help me.

"You get some good meals in you and you'll be as good as new." The door closed behind her.

Despite my aversion to all foods, I forced as much into my stomach as I could. When I surveyed my plate, I realized it was only a few bites. I had barely consumed a normal snack. I shivered, freezing. Rolling the table away, I huddled under my covers.

My phone was on the table, and I picked it up. Overwhelmed by the number of messages on the screen, I set it down. So tired, I was so tired. I heard someone enter and opened my eyes again. A nurse slid a pole with a blood pressure monitor towards my bed. I used my hands to push up to a sitting position and rolled my sleeve up. She tried to fit the cuff around my arm, but it was too big.

"I'll be right back." After a few minutes, she re-entered my room with a child's cuff. "This is better." She tapped on the screen of an electronic tablet. She measured my heart rate, took my temperature, entered the data in her device, and then left the room.

I was alone again, and tears formed in my eyes. How in the world was I going to get myself out of such an awful situation? What was I going to tell my parents, Doug, my friends? As I wiped the tears away, the door opened again and Dr. Milner walked in.

"Good morning. I see you got breakfast. That's good." She moved the table and pulled a chair up beside my bed.

"How did you know I was here?"

"Det. Gardner called the University. You don't remember me being here last night?"

"No, did someone call my parents?"

"Yes, you talked to them last night."

"I don't remember talking to my parents."

"You were a little out of it, but they say your electrolytes have stabilized for now."

I looked at the tubes strapped to my arm and up to the bag of saline hanging on the pole. Did I remember them putting in an IV line? Squinting hard, I refocused on Dr. Milner.

"What now? How long will I be here?"

"Are you ready to be honest?"

I tucked my knees into my chest. "Yes."

"Can you tell me what's been going on?"

Leaning forward, I propelled back again with my toes and started to rock. "I couldn't stop. I couldn't make myself eat no matter how hard I tried. I thought I was controlling it. But it turned on me, and it was controlling me." Tears poured out of my eyes and down my cheeks, and she handed me a tissue. Wiping the water from my face and neck, I continued. "That's what happened yesterday. I had a latte, and it backfired on me."

"Well, a lot more than that happened yesterday, but we can leave that for another day."

"Do my parents know that I was at the police station?"

"Yes."

Relaxing my shoulders, I forced the breath out of my lungs. "Do you know what I can do to get help?"

"Yes, and your parents have some ideas too." She pulled an electronic tablet from her bag and held it towards me. "They consulted with the psychiatrist you saw this summer and did some research. Your dad is willing to pay for your stay at this facility." She pointed to the screen. "It's very highly rated."

I scanned the website. Utah? They wanted me to go to an eating disorder recovery center in Utah? With horses? I hated horses, always had. "I'm not going to Utah. Do I really need an inpatient facility? Can't I see you a few more times a week? I have finals next week."

"No, you're past that point, and I think you know it. Look around. Your way isn't working." She tapped on another tab in the Internet browser on her device. "There is a facility in Chicago I recommend. I know the staff. They are reputable and very good."

"That's where I want to go. I'm not going to Utah." It wasn't just Utah. It was that my parents had picked it. They were still controlling what happened to me. I'd been letting them control my decisions for too long. If the recovery was going to work, it had to be mine.

"Okay, I'll make some phone calls. Why don't you call your parents?" She stepped back, turned, and put her phone to her ear.

I took in a deep breath. It wasn't going to be an easy conversation. Dialing Dad's number, I waited for him to answer. After the fourth ring, he picked up.

"Amanda?"

"Yes, Dad."

"Are you okay?"

The tears started again. Looking to the ceiling, I answered. "Yes, Dad."

"Well."

"I'm going to a facility here in Chicago."

"I won't pay for that. I told Dr. Milner I would pay for the Utah facility."

"I'm not going to Utah. I can use the insurance and my savings."

"That's a stupid decision."

I couldn't stop rocking. "I'm sorry you think so Dad, but I have to do this my way."

"Your way? Look where your way has gotten you."

"Dad, this is a treatment facility, the same as in Utah. Dr. Milner says it's one of the best."

"You just don't want to leave Chicago."

"No, I don't."

"You're nineteen. I can't tell you what to do."

"No, you can't."

"Okay then, well, let me know if you change your mind." He ended the call.

Whatever! I tossed the phone on the blanket.

Dr. Milner turned back to me. "Doesn't sound like that went well."

"No. That's okay. What else do I need to do? What about school?"

She had the medical leave documents with her. I would be able to take my finals and have the grades count if I completed the exams before the end of the spring quarter. With a shaking hand, I signed the papers. *What was I doing? Withdrawing from school? Going to a psych hospital?* My mind yelled at me. But what choice did I have. I had almost died.

I could not die. I had to do everything in my power to live, no matter what my life looked like. Funny how I hadn't really wanted to live anymore, even for Doug. It was hard for me to admit, but it was true until the previous night, when it looked like I may not. Then, I decided I would do anything to keep myself alive. I steeled my resolve. I'd leave school and get help at the treatment facility. I would let someone help me, starting with Dr. Milner.

"The facility can take you tonight. I will drive you."

"I need to go back to my apartment and get some clothes."

"I can't let you go alone. I'll take you, you can pack a bag, and then we'll drive to the facility."

"You don't have to do that. I can go myself."

She put her hand on my arm. "What if you change your mind, start thinking you can make it on your own again?"

"Okay, I guess I'll go with you."

"Good, you're making a good decision."

"It doesn't feel like it." It felt as if my chest were going to split open and my grief, shame, and guilt would swallow me like a black hole.

"I'm here for you." She squeezed both my hands. "I'll be back around four. The doctors will hold you till then. Detective Gardner said she would come by today too."

Again I drove the image of Peter's face out of my brain, choosing a vision of sandy beaches. "Thanks."

I sat curled up for a while but finally needed to get up to go to the restroom. Finding my clothes in a bag, I put them on and slid back under the covers. Next, I phoned Lila.

"Oh my goodness, I was so worried about you. When can we come see you? Your parents said you didn't want visitors."

"What? No. I don't know. I was kind of out of it last night."

"What happened? I mean your parents told me about the heart attack and the police station. But how did you get there?"

"I saw Peter's picture in the paper and lost it."

"I'm sorry. I didn't know what to do. I was trying to figure out how to tell you."

"I know. It's not your fault." I didn't want to talk about Peter anymore. I couldn't think about him hanging by his sheets in a jail cell.

"I feel like the worst friend in the world. How did I miss you getting so thin?"

"You're not a horrible friend. I worked hard at hiding things, and I lied to you a lot. I'm sorry."

"None of that matters. I want you to be healthy."

"Thanks, I love you." Fresh tears formed in my eyes. "I have to go. I'm coming by the apartment to get some things this afternoon. Can you be there?"

"I'll be here. Have you talked to Doug? I know Zack called him. He told him you were in the hospital but okay."

"It's night there. I was going to call in a few hours. I think he'll pretty much break up with me, so—"

"Why would he do that?"

"Crazy girlfriend number two?"

"This is different than Zoey."

"I hope he sees it that way."

"He loves you. Everything will be fine. I have to get to class. I'll see you this afternoon."

"Okay. I love you." I ended the call and leaned back on my pillow.

Next, I repeated the call with Mom, Tia, and then Marissa. By the time the doctor came in for rounds just after noon, I was cried out. But my vitals were stable, and they were releasing me to Dr. Milner.

Detective Gardner came in as the doctor was leaving. "You're looking better."

"I feel better. I'm sorry about yesterday. I really didn't mean to scare anyone, and I wouldn't have hurt those people in the coffee shop."

"Those charges are being dropped. Amanda, I am a detective, but I work with lots of victims too. We should talk about Peter."

I didn't want to cry in front of her, but new tears welled up in my eyes. "I feel so guilty. Do you know what his mom said to me at the trial? And now—"

"I read through the court documents. This is not your fault."

"He hung himself in prison. Him being there was my fault."

She sat on the bed and took both of my hands. "No, it's not. He chose to attack you. He chose to attack those other girls. He broke the law, and he was punished appropriately. He chose to take his life. I talked to Dr. Milner. She told me you were getting help. I hope that you can move past all this."

"Thanks." I patted my face with a tissue. "And thanks for coming today. It was nice of you."

"You were a little out of it last night. I wanted you to know that you were clear, legally."

"Thanks."

There was a knock on the door, and Mark poked his head in.

"You have visitors. Take care." Det. Gardner squeezed my hands and walked from the room.

Ross, Bill, and Zack followed Mark in. I would've preferred to curl up under a rock than face them. I dried my face and put on my best smile.

Mark looked back at the other three. "Do you guys mind giving us a minute?"

Ross, Bill, and Zack cocked their heads towards the door. "Sure," Zack said.

As soon as the door shut, Mark rushed towards me.

"Oh my God?" His hands went to his head as he paced the room. He stopped and looked at me. "How did this happen? I mean, we knew you were being all anti-social. But this? I feel sick." He put a hand to his stomach and leaned down.

"Sit." I pointed to the chair. He pulled it up to the bed and sat down. "I'm sorry. I couldn't handle all the anger and guilt. I tried to numb it, but that backfired."

"You're getting help, right?"

I nodded and told him about the treatment center. He stood and gave me a big hug. "Get well, okay? We're all worried about you."

"Thanks." I started to cry again.

Mark left and Zack and Bill filed in. Zack crossed the room in two longs strides, taking the chair next to me. "Girl, what happened? You scared us to death."

"I'm sorry." I covered my face with my hands.

"We feel horrible." He motioned towards Bill. "How didn't we see this?"

"I lied a lot. I'm sorry."

He looked at the floor and then back at me. "Well, you get better and come back to do kickboxing with me, okay? Promise?"

"I promise."

Bill pointed at me. "The rowing team always needs a good coxswain."

"Thanks, guys."

"Okay, hmm, you need anything?" Zack rubbed his hands down his pants.

"Do you mind helping with Northie?"

"Got it." They backed away and out the door. Mark and Ross entered the room again, each giving me a hug.

"Lila said she'd see you this afternoon. You know how she gets about hospitals," Ross said as he backed away.

"Yeah, I know."

"Okay." Mark patted the mattress. "Get better."

"I will. Thanks." I waved a hand at them as they walked out.

My chest swelled with love for the people I'd pushed away. Why hadn't I reached out, been open? It was dark inside my mind. I was broken, and no one should have to bear those feelings with me. Shame, guilt, remorse, and regret descended like a thick fog, and I clung to my knees, tears spilling down my neck, soaking my shirt.

I heard the door open and rubbed my cheeks with my sleeves. "Oh, honey." It was the cafeteria lady from earlier. "You don't need to fret. Those boys your friends? If I were you, I'd be all over that tall blonde one." She handed me a tissue. "With men like that looking out for you, you got nothing to worry about."

"My boyfriend's in Japan."

"Well, he better watch out is what I'm thinking." She put a hand to her hip. "You know what I mean." She waved her index finger in the air. "You like chicken or beef better, sweetie?"

"Chicken."

"Okay, I'll be right back."

She left and returned with a tray covered with a metal top. "I came to your room first so it would be hot. The sandwich and fries are real good. And there's some lettuce salad and fruit for you."

"Thank you," I told her as water pooled in my eyelids again. Would every emotion lead to tears? Dabbing my cheeks, I piled the lettuce on the bun and made it halfway through the sandwich before I couldn't eat more.

It was only one in the afternoon, and I had an hour before I could call Doug. Not that I was really looking forward to the call, but I wanted it over with. Finding a pad of paper and pen beside the Gideon's Bible in the drawer, I tried to write out what I would tell him. There weren't words, and I laid the paper down beside me and closed the drawer on the Bible. It only reminded me what other help I hadn't accepted.

My phone buzzed with receipt of a text message, and I read the screen. Kate wrote: LILA TOLD ME WHAT HAPPENED. I DON'T UNDERSTAND HOW I MISSED IT. I FEEL HORRIBLE. JEREMY SAYS GET BETTER SOON. STEPHEN SAYS HE'LL TEXT YOU.

Drops of tears littered my screen. I wiped them on the blanket and tapped my reply. PLEASE DON'T FEEL BAD. I HID IT FROM EVERYONE. YOU'RE A GOOD FRIEND.

Next, I sent Stephen a message. I HEARD LILA TOLD YOU WHAT HAPPENED. I AM SORRY I COULDN'T ACCEPT YOUR HELP BEFORE. THANK YOU FOR TRYING. TAKE CARE.

JUST GET HEALTHY, he replied immediately.

I checked the time and flipped on the TV, dreading my conversation with Doug. What an idiot I was. I ruined everything. Our vacation in Japan, my opportunity to attend school in Tokyo, and our chance to be together were all gone. Instead, I was psycho girlfriend number two right behind Zoey.

I understood her or what I guessed she went through. Realized how something could hurt so bad it wouldn't go away. How pain led you to do insane things. My sobbing started again. Peter Scalini and I had done a pretty good job of ruining each other's lives. But if there was one thing I knew after staring up at that white light and having the doctor tell me there was nothing they could do, it was I was going to fight. I would not let myself die, and the hole in my chest would be filled somehow.

By the time I recovered from the bout of weeping, my phone read after two. I dabbed my cheeks and picked up the phone with trembling hands. Blowing my nose, I dialed his number.

He picked up immediately. "Amanda. I was so worried. Zack said there was an incident. That you were okay, but in the hospital? I couldn't get information from anyone. What's going on?"

I blinked to stop the tears from starting again, took a deep breath, and repeated my story. He didn't speak for a long time.

"Doug, are you there?"

"Yes."

"Lila and I decided to wait until she was with you to tell you about Peter. We thought it best if you weren't alone when you found out."

"Well, I was alone. I'm sorry. I love you, and I messed everything up. I won't blame you if you want to be done with me."

"What? No. I am the one who's sorry. I should have come. Three months was too long to be apart."

"This is not your fault." I tried to wipe my face with my sleeve and sniffed to stop my nose from running.

"Well, I'm definitely coming to see you."

"Thank you. I miss you." There was a knock on the door, and Stephen's head appeared in the opening. I held my finger up to him. He nodded and retreated out into the hall.

"Stephen's here."

"Okay, well, I have to get to work. I'll let you know when I get my flight. I love you."

I went to the bathroom to toss the tissues in the trash and splashed water on my face. Then I opened the door for Stephen. I really didn't want to see him. My guilt was gnawing away at me, and the sight of him made it worse. I'd been trying to avoid the hole of regret in the middle of my soul, and I'd only created a bigger one.

"I had to see you. I hope it's okay that I came." He sat down in the chair.

"Of course."

"I don't know what to say. I feel scared for you."

"I'm going to be okay."

"I hope so. Everyone really cares about you."

"Thanks, and thanks for trying to help before. I'm sorry I just wasn't ready."

"Okay." He stood. "Take care and don't be a stranger."

"Thanks, I won't."

After he left, it wasn't long before Dr. Milner arrived, which was good because the fear, shame, and guilt had started to engulf me again.

We got my discharge papers, and she drove me to my apartment. A fresh set of tears welled up seeing Lila and Northie. Dr. Milner, Lila, and I walked him to the meadow and back to the apartment. Lila helped me pack a bag with leggings, tanks, sweatshirts, and Bubbe's journal. Saying goodbye to Lila was maybe the hardest thing I'd ever done, and the impression of her hug clung to my skin as I walked away.

The drive to the facility took more than an hour with traffic. It was a big property, lined with a tall iron fence and iron gates. The grounds were lit with the same orange lights I hated. After the guard opened the gate, we made our way down a long tree-lined street. The facility was positioned beyond a circular drive. The cinder block building looked exactly like a mental institution should, old, dark, and sterile.

As if reading my mind, Dr. Milner put her hand on my leg. "It's been updated inside."

I expected to see white tile floors and white cinder block walls, but the foyer was nicely carpeted and plants grew in the windows. It almost looked like a hotel. A woman in a suit sat behind a desk near the far wall, and I followed Dr. Milner towards her.

She opened a file and handed it the woman, who studied the paperwork and then looked up at me. "Hi, Amanda, I'm Mindy. I'll get you checked in. We have some paperwork for you to sign. Why don't we use this office?" She motioned towards a door on her left.

Dr. Milner didn't follow. "This is where I say goodbye."

I was beyond afraid. Was I doing the right thing? Maybe I could go back to my apartment, finish the rest of the quarter. She put her hands on my shoulders. "You're doing the right thing. They can help you."

I pressed my nails into my palms and straightened my shoulders. "Thank you."

"You're welcome." She backed away, then spun and walked out the door.

Frozen, I watched her leave. "Ms. Avery, you ready?"

I followed Mindy into the office and sat opposite her at a table.

"I need you to sign the power of attorney, and then I'll take you back to your area where the nurse will check you in." She slid some papers towards me.

Tears dripping down my face, I read the document. My heart pounded in my chest. Part of me wanted to scream that I would be fine. I could fix this myself.

No, you've tried your way. You need to let someone else help.

I scribbled my name as quickly as I could.

THE END

About the Author

Tricia Copeland grew up in Georgia and now lives in Colorado with her husband, three kids, and multiple four-legged and finned friends. This work is the third in the *Being Me* series. The first, *Is This Me?*, released in May 2015, and the second, *If I Could Fly*, published November 2015. Her first paranormal work entitled *Drops of Sunshine* will be available May 2016 in *Spellbound*, a YA paranormal novella collection. If not on the trail, you can find Tricia at triciacopeland.com or on most social media channels.

Goodreads: goodreads.com/author/show/14055439

Amazon: amazon.com/Tricia-Copeland/e/B00YHN5Q4G

Facebook: TriciaCopelandAuthor

Instagram: AuthorTriciaCopeland

Twitter: @TCBrzostowicz

Pinterest: Triciacopelanda

Youtube:
youtube.com/channel/UCVMf9vfDLk-cIDV3NnX2DpQ

Google+: plus.google.com/u/0/collection/8wque

Blog: triciacopeland.com/blog--e-newsletter.html

Web: TriciaCopeland.com

Is This Me?
(Book I of the Being Me Series)

Have you ever chosen a path that led you astray?

Amanda has no trouble choosing a college or picking a major. What she does have a problem with is what she would have least expected, a guy. Smart and sexy, Doug is focused on school responsibilities and post-graduation plans. Their paths intersect and Amanda must accept his help or risk losing her scholarship. Determined to maintain appearances, Amanda begins to lie to family and friends. The ease at which she repeatedly deceives those closest becomes disturbing and leaves her questioning: "Is this me?"

Can Amanda find her way out of her contrived world?

Is This Me?
amazon.com/dp/B00YIABVKG

If I Ccould Fly
(Book 2 of the Being Me Series)

After the happily ever after...

Did you ever wonder what the family thinks when the girl rides away with her prince? Amanda's parents think she's abandoned her friends, goals, even morals to be with Doug. The assessment is ludicrous, but Amanda can't convince them otherwise. Their disapproval undermines her self-confidence and she is determined to prove them wrong. To make things worse, Doug has a huge roadblock thrown in his path. Amanda isn't able to talk about the situation with anyone except Zack, her ex-boyfriend. Can she endure the strain of keeping Doug's secret? Can her already fragile psyche survive a whole summer with parents who condemn everything she does? Amanda begins to doubt she can, and there's no castle, no fairy godmother, no magic wand to rescue her.

If I Could Fly
amazon.com/dp/B017KT3BXG/

Drops of Sunshine
A Spellbound Story

"Three things cannot be long hidden: the sun, the moon, and the truth." ~Buddha

Working as lifeguard at a camp for the blind seems like the perfect escape for Nina. But a few perceptive kids can hear her thoughts. Can embracing her truth help her heal and reveal possibilities she never imagined?

www.brixbaxter.com/index.php/coming-soon-menu

www.ingramcontent.com/pod-product-compliance
Lightning Source LLC
Chambersburg PA
CBHW050545260626
47157CB00002B/451